the claiming

BOOK TWO

DEFENDERS OF THE REALMS

the claiming

by

Nathan D. Thomas

Also By Nathan D. Thomas

The Calling

Be Confident in Your Creation

Be Confident in Your Calling

What's Stopping You?

Copyright

First Edition February 2016

Editing by Nathan D. Thomas

Published in the United States of America 2016 by Nathan D. Thomas

Paperback ISBN: 1530029007 9781530029006

Young Adult Christian Fiction/Fantasy

This book is dedicated to
the many friends and loved ones who encouraged
us to stand for truth, no matter the consequences,
as we faced a time of claiming in our own lives
and ministry. Thank you. You will never know
how much your love means to us.

table of contents

(table of contents continued)

the slave and the signet ring

The story is told of a glorious kingdom of life. This kingdom was founded by the one true King and within the walls of this kingdom love reigned and joy was shared by all.

But even here, within the walls of life, death was brewing, for one of the King's captains was not satisfied with the life the King had given him nor the position of honor he had been granted. This captain had a single desire: to reign in place of the King.

This captain planned and plotted with his fellow soldiers to overthrow the Great King, but all their planning was in vain. Knowing the hearts and minds of His subjects, the King called this wicked captain into account for his actions. At that time the captain and all his cohorts were exiled from the kingdom of life and doomed to await their judgment elsewhere.

Full of wrath and bitterness against the Great King, the captain and his men invaded the King's land and laid siege to the King's precious city of Man. But try and try as they might, the captain and his men could not break through the fortifications put in place by the King. Frustrated, the captain realized he had to change his approach. Instead of charging the gates of Man, the captain brought forth his ambassadors of peace; Lust, Greed, and Pride. These three ambassadors promised the people of Man that if they would allow the captain and his army entrance, the people of Man would see all their true desires come to fruition. The leaders of Man were deceived and opened the gates. The captain and his army invaded the city and installed their cruel dictatorship over the people enslaving them all.

Years passed and the people of Man grew accustomed to their new slavery. Though rumors swirled concerning the Great King's plan to overthrow the captain and reclaim possession of His beloved city, no such salvation occured.

One day, a child was born to the last remaining descendants of the original leaders of the City of Man. The parents of this child named him Hope, and Hope became a reminder to the people of Man of the King's plan to free them. As a result, Hope drew the hatred of the captain and his ambassadors of peace, who had now taken their place as nobles in the captain's kingdom.

The Captain and his nobles ripped Hope away from his family, labeled him a child of disobedience and a child of wrath, and renamed him Condemned. Condemned was placed under the penalty of death, yet was sentenced to a life-time of slavery to the nobles and the Captain.

The nobles Lust, Greed, and Pride would all promise Condemned freedom for doing their bidding only to further enslave Condemned for his actions they pushed him to commit. If Condemned ever refused, the nobles would whip and torture Condemned until he carried out their orders.

At the end of every day, the Captain would call Condemned before him and tally the daily wages of Condemner's actions. At the end of every day, the Captain would pass the penalty of death and remind Condemned that one day he would be put to death for his sins.

One day, a stranger appeared in the City of Man who proclaimed to the people that their freedom was nigh. This man reminded the people that Man was the property of the Great King and that it was not the King who abandoned Man, it was Man that had abandoned the King. This man claimed that the King's plan to redeem the City of Man had come and that this freedom would be known to all who would believe. This man spoke words that lifted the spirits of the people and gave Condemned hope that he might yet be free of the Captain.

But the Captain and his men arrested this stranger and put him to death publicly as a means to squelch any thought of freedom from the people. Three days later, the people of man ran to Condemned and brought him to the gates of the city. Outside of the gates was the stranger that had been put to death, only now he wore the robes of the King and was standing outside the city gates.

When Condemned climbed the walls of the city and stood atop the gates, the man called out to him.

"Brother, I have returned to free you and this city from the power of the Captain. I am the Great King, and I have brought you the freedom I spoke to you about while I walked among you in the city. I can free you, but you must open the gate. Only the leaders of the City of Man can open the gates of Man. You, my beloved Condemned are the only one who can allow me entrance to grant you a new life."

"But, you are dead! I watched the Captain and his men kill you and bury you!"

"Yes, I was put to death, for you were under the penalty of death, a sentence that could not be ignored."

"Get away from that wall!" demanded the Captain as he and his host of men ran down the streets of the city toward the gates, "I said get away or you will feel my wrath as never before!"

Condemned, fearing the wrath of the Captain, looked again to the King.

"But there are so many of them and you stand alone, how could you free us?"

"I have conquered the Captain and taken all of his power. If you will put your faith in Me, I will free you."

The Captain and his host reached the wall, shoving all the spectators aside storming up the stairs to capture Condemned. Knowing he had but moments to decide, Condemned called out to the gates, "Open and allow entrance to the Great King!"

The gates flew open and light flooded the city. Instantly, the King was standing next to Condemned and holding the Captain by the throat. The King spoke to the Captain in a voice too powerful for Condemned to understand and then threw the Captain over the walls and out of sight. The Captain's host was fleeing from the King and begging for mercy. In a short time, the Great King had cleansed the City of Man from the presence of the Captain and his host. The King walked up to Condemned and held out a beautiful red box.

"My beloved child," said the King, "I have loved you with an everlasting love from before your birth. I have seen your travail and I have heard your heart's cry for deliverance. I have come to free you from the kingdom of darkness and translate you into the kingdom of My dear Son. You will no longer be called Condemned for your name shall be Redeemed."

"I go now to prepare your place in my kingdom, but though I leave you here, I give you a gift that will grant you the power and authority you need to never be a slave to the former rulers of this city again."

Redeemed opened the box and took out a large golden ring with a diamond cross in the center.

"That, my child, is my personal signet ring. The wearer of that ring receives all the privileges, honor, and authority of one who bears my name. With this power, I charge you to prepare this city for My return. Upon My return, I will take you to your new place I will personally prepare for you in My kingdom. I leave you with all the power you need to fulfill My desires, and I promise you that I will be with you always. Farewell My beloved Redeemed!"

The King returned to His kingdom and the next day Redeemed ventured out into the streets seeking to prepare the City of Man for the King's return. Not long after Redeemed walked the streets, he ran into a familiar foe: Lust.

Lust belittled Redeemed and his new found position and demanded that he submit to Lust's authority and do as Lust commanded. When Redeemed refused, Lust raised his hand in order to punish Redeemed with the whips.

"Stop!" Redeemed commanded, "You no longer bear rule in this city."

Lust's whip disappeared and he was thrown to the ground. Furious, Lust demanded that Redeemed do as he commanded, but Redeemed refused.

Now that Redeemed possessed the signet ring of the Great King, he had the authority to overcome the desires of the nobles.

One by one, Redeemed confronted the powerless nobles that had bound and whipped him into submission in the past. From that day on, Redeemed never again submitted to the former authority of the nobles but through the claiming of the King's gift and authority, he conquered his foes and prepared the City of Man for the return of the King.

Romans 8:1; 14-15; 31-32; 35,37

[1] *There is* therefore now no condemnation to them which are in Christ Jesus, who walk not after the flesh, but after the Spirit...

[14] For as many as are led by the Spirit of God, they are the sons of God.

[15] For ye have not received the spirit of bondage again to fear; but ye have received the Spirit of adoption, whereby we cry, Abba, Father...

[35] Who shall separate us from the love of Christ? *shall* tribulation, or distress, or persecution, or famine, or nakedness, or peril, or sword...

[37] Nay, in all these things we are more than conquerors through him that loved us.

chapter 1

an urgent message

So you want to play hide and seek, thought Eli, *have it your way. Ready or not, here I come.*

The sky was a light shade of purple, the light of the King shined brightly covering the land in a glorious warmth, and a sweet fall-feeling breeze gently flowed over the grass. Even though Eli was on a dangerous mission for the King, he could not help relishing in the beauty of this land.

Eli stood on top of a tall round hill covered in lush green grass overlooking a rolling prairie occupied by a large band of sheep. The band of sheep was exactly what Eli was looking for, but he was not here for sheep; he had followed the tracks, the blood trail, and the discarded bones of a vicious pack of ravenous wolves currently terrorizing the creatures of this region. Eli knew that within that large band of sheep lurked the deadly predators he had come to destroy.

Ravenous wolves are unique among many of the Enemy's servants that roam the spirit realm because they have the ability to disguise themselves as sheep. A ravenous wolf can look identical to a sheep and in some cases, an under-shepherd in order to prey on the King's sheep. After seeing the destruction and death a pack of ravenous wolves can cause, Eli better understood why the King's Spirit took the time to warn the early church about the wolves through the Apostle Paul.

Eli's appearance atop the hill had not gone unnoticed by the band of sheep as many of the sheep walked in his direction bleating happily. Ever since his commissioning as a defender of the realms, Eli had become well-known among the inhabitants of the spirit realm for better or for worse. The peaceful creatures of the King wanted to be around him, whereas the Enemy's followers wanted to destroy him. Either way, it seemed to Eli that wherever he went, he garnered more attention than he wanted.

Continually scanning the band of sheep for any sign of the wolves, Eli slowly walked down the hill. Not knowing if the ravenous wolves knew he was tracking them, Eli kept his sword sheaved hoping the wolves would think him to be ignorant of their presence. Eli knew that if he could give the wolves a false sense of security that they would be the ones surprised if they chose to launch a surprise attack.

The band of sheep reached Eli pushing and pulling each other in hopes of getting the defender's attention. Thronged by sheep on every side, Eli realized that he had walked into a precarious situation. Surrounded by a large number of sheep, Eli realized the wolves now had the ability to approach him unnoticed. This realization pushed Eli to scan the sheep for the wolves more vigorously. As the sheep swirled around him, Eli caught sight of the first wolf. Standing just to Eli's left, outside the band of sheep swirling around him, the wolf, which looked identical to the other sheep, stood still examining him. When Eli turned to see the wolf, the King's light reflected off of his helmet and shined on the wolf's eyes. When the light hit the eyes of the wolf, they glowed red, giving the wolf's identity away. Knowing it had been identified, the wolf snarled revealing a mouth full of sharp teeth, then dashed into the swirling cloud of sheep.

Eli tried to follow the wolf, but lost track of it. Spinning around, he noticed another sheep, standing still, directly behind him about ten feet back. Then another sheep, to his right, also just standing looking at him. Eli continued to scan the band of sheep, and to his chagrin, he realized that the pack of ravenous wolves he had tracked was larger than he thought.

Pain shot through his body as something bit his left calf. Eli looked down to see bite marks on his boot, but he could not identify the assailant because the sheep kept jockeying for position trying to get his attention. Another painful attack, this time it felt like a massive paw, struck across Eli's back. Turning around to see his attacker, he was again too late to identify the assailant.

"If that is how you want to play," shouted Eli, "then let's play."

Eli drew his sword and concentrated to connect with the Illuminator the way Michael had taught him to do in training. Eli's sword, which was actually a Bible his grandfather left for him after his grandfather's death, had become his most valuable asset in the spirit realm. It was his Bible that allowed Eli to overcome his flesh in the Cemetery of the Old Man and grasp the helmet of salvation which he now wore. After he gained the victory over his flesh, the King commissioned him as a defender and transformed the Bible into the sword that he now held ready to do battle with the pack of ravenous wolves.

Eli heard the rumbling growls of the wolves all around him communicating their anger at the appearance of his sword, but his concentration could not be broken. Eli had learned the hard way that the power of the King's Word could only be unlocked through a connection with the Illuminator.

"The Illuminator," Michael's voice echoed in his mind from one of his training sessions, "is the Key that unlocks the power of the King's Word for it is the living Spirit of God that breathed the King's Word into existence. The King's Word is living and active and more powerful than any other weapon in all creation but for you to unlock the great power of the King's Word and wield the great weapon of defenders, you must learn how to submit your spirit to the King's Spirit and allow Him to illumine the truths of the King's Word."

A surge of power flowed through Eli as his spirit connected with the Illuminator. Eli opened his eyes and scanned the band of sheep as he spoke the King's Word the Illuminator placed into his mind.

"Beware of false prophets, which come to you in sheep's clothing, but inwardly they are ravening wolves. You will know them by their fruits."

A powerful blue ring of fire exploded from Eli and spread across the plain like a growing ripple of water after a stone is thrown into a lake. The ring of fire spread harmlessly over the band of genuine sheep, but caught the wolves' disguises on fire.

Eli watched as five ravenous wolves morphed from sheep into large, werewolf-like creatures growling in pain as smoke sizzled off their now dark grey fur. The wolves were tall, roughly seven feet tall, had a powerful build with large rippling muscles, and stood on their hind legs. The wolves' paws sported long sharp claws and their mouths were lined with long canine teeth. The wolves stood in a star formation surrounding Eli with one wolf in front of Eli and two wolves on either side. The appearance of the wolves sent the sheep scattering until Eli was left alone with the predators.

"You'll pay for that Defender," growled the wolf standing directly in front of Eli, "we're going to rip you to shreds!"

"I'll be honest," said Eli in a tone of relief, "I'm happy to hear you say that. I was afraid you were going to try and talk me out of a battle. But seeing we both understand each other, let's dance!"

Eli rushed at the wolf in front of him ducking under the wolf's right paw as the wolf swung at his head. Eli sliced his sword across the wolf's abdomen and circled behind. The wolf howled in pain and doubled over. Eli plunged his sword into the wolf's back and the wolf disappeared in an explosion of blue light.

Eli quickly rolled to his left to keep the oncoming wolves on his right side. After defending several paw swipes with his sword, Eli summersaulted forward through the legs of the closest wolf, exploiting his tall adversaries' weakness. Coming up from his summersault, Eli sank his sword into the stomach of a surprised looking wolf which stood behind the attacking wolf. The surprised wolf did not even get a howl off before it exploded in a burst of light.

Before Eli could get up, the wolf he summersaulted under kicked him in the back sending him sprawling forward. Taking advantage of the other wolf's attack, another wolf jumped into the air to pounce on Eli. Gathering his wits rapidly, Eli rolled on his back with his sword facing up. The wolf that had pounced gave out a cry of recognition as it could not veer from its course and exploded into light as it impaled itself on Eli's sword. The blue light flashed close to Eli's face, temporarily blinding him. Unable to see his attackers and prepare for the blow, Eli had his sword knocked out of his hand by a powerful swipe of the wolf's paw. A strong paw grabbed Eli around the neck, and ripped him off of the ground. Eli placed both hands on the wolf's wrist in an attempt to keep from being strangled as he dangled in the air. The wolf smiled, thinking that Eli was done for, when Eli threw his head into the wolf's face, smashing the face of the wolf with his helmet of salvation.

Light poured from the gash in the wolf's face and the wolf howled in pain and dropped Eli. Eli turned to grab his sword only to see the last wolf leaning down to pick it up.

"I wouldn't do that if I were you." Eli warned.

The wolf snarled at Eli and grabbed the sword. Blue flames erupted off of Eli's sword and raced over the body of the wolf as if the wolf was covered in gasoline. Howling in pain, the wolf dropped the sword and ran away but soon burst into light as the flames consumed it.

Eli picked up his sword and turned to the last wolf that was still holding its face in agony.

"It's over, wolf, your path of destruction ends here. You are trespassing on the King's land, you have attacked and destroyed the King's sheep, and you have severely wounded one of the King's under-shepherds. Your lies, schemes, and attacks have caused great damage to the lives of those who love the King."

"But your days of devouring are over. The King has sent me to take heed to His flock and bring peace back to this land."

The wolf lowered its paws, revealing a widening wound with light pouring out, and opened its mouth to speak but instead of the wolf's voice, Zephyr's voice emerged.

"Now that's how you deal with a pack of wolves!"

Immediately the wolf, the prairie, and the sheep all disappeared leaving Eli standing in the pure white space of the training room. The training room reminded Eli of the room of thorns from the mausoleum in that it was a vast empty space that could morph into any landscape with any creatures in it. It was inside this training room that Eli had spent a great deal of time since his return from the throne room preparing for his next mission from the King.

Hovering in front of him, where the wolf was standing moments ago, was Eli's guardian Angelos, Zephyr. Eli sheaved his sword.

"Thanks Zeph. But why did you end the simulation early? That wolf was wounded but he was far from finished."

"No way man, after watching you defeat the entire pack, that last wolf was finished. But I stopped the simulation because of an urgent message from Michael."

"An urgent message? What do you mean, 'an urgent message'? I thought everything was urgent with Michael. "

"Yes it seems that Michael always serves the King with a sense of urgency, but this time there is something seriously bothering him. He wants to see you in the war room immediately and I think we should hurry, I have never heard Michael so distressed before."

Eli's mind automatically thought about Michael's great size, strength, and power.

"What could possibly cause someone as powerful as Michael distress?"

"I'm not sure but we are about to find out."

chapter 2

a state of emergency

Rushing to the door, Eli's mind was running through countless scenarios of what could be going on and how it could involve him. By the time Eli made it to the training room door, he was completely stressed out. Opening the training room door, Eli looked up at Zephyr and felt a calm brush over him. Zephyr and Eli had developed a strong bond through training and Eli knew that whatever was going on, he and Zephyr would face it together.

Eli had always felt a strong familiarity with Zephyr even before he knew that Zephyr was his guardian Angelos, but since the beginning of Eli's training, the two had become inseparable. The strengthening of their relationship began when Zephyr flew into the atrium after Michael and Eli returned from the throne room. It was then, that Eli saw the change that Brutus and Zephyr had alluded to if Eli were to be successful in his endeavor to become a defender for the King.

Zephyr's whole appearance had changed. Zephyr's hair, wing, and eye color, that was orange when Eli first met him, was now deep radiant blue same as the accent color on Eli's armor. Zephyr's skin had also changed color and turned the same brilliant metallic silver coloring of Eli's armor and sword. The change in Zephyr's appearance was so shocking to Eli, that when Eli first saw him, all he could do was stare blankly as Zephyr knocked him over hugging him in congratulations for his victory in the cemetery.

At first, the change in Zephyr's appearance made Eli feel guilty. Eli knew that if he were the one who changed color and had silver skin that he might feel resentful against Zephyr. When Eli talked with Zephyr about the change, Zephyr told him that contrary to human thinking, guardian Angelos see the unifying of their appearance with a defender as one of the greatest honors in life.

"Resentful? Not one bit Eli, we guardian Angelos dream of having the opportunity to team up with the human we have been given responsibility for and work together against the Enemy. To us, the change in color is a privilege not all Angelos enjoy."

Zephyr partnered with Eli during his time in training, sometimes going through the simulations with Eli and sometimes watching from the background. After each simulation was over, Zephyr would accompany Eli back to his room where they would watch a replay of the mission on the large screen televisions mounted on the wall and talk about how to improve while lounging on the sectional munching on snacks.

At other times, Zephyr would display the different lands and creatures found in the spirit realm on the large screens and try to educate Eli on what was out there and how to survive. During these times, Eli felt he was in a real-life version of one of his role playing video games he loved so much. Even though Eli learned about some terrifying creatures and some intimidating lands, he had to admit that the time he had spent with Zephyr in training was the most exciting and fun time he could ever remember.

"It is no wonder Grandpa called the last five years the most exciting of his life" thought Eli after one of his mission debriefings with Zephyr.

Eli's thoughts filled his mind as he stood holding the door to the training room open for Zephyr.

"Are you okay Eli?"

Zephyr's voice brought Eli back to the present and his sense of urgency returned.

"Yeah, I'm good. I'm just waiting on you to get in gear so we can see what has Michael all stressed out."

Zephyr motioned for Eli to walk in front of him, "After you, my friend."

Eli exited the training room and stepped into the atrium. The training room door was located on the wall of the atrium just to the side of the small white gazebo that took Eli to the Cemetery of the Old Man. Because of the frozen and colorless state of the atrium when Eli first arrived, he did not notice the door during his first visit to the atrium. However, after Eli returned from the cemetery successfully, the color flooded back into the section of the room and the door was one of the first things he noticed.

Stepping into the atrium, Eli quickly ran past the small white gazebo with the emblem of the helmet still floating above it, ran over the crystal bridge and up the path toward the door. As Eli approached the door, he closed his eyes and concentrated on the doorway to the war room.

Now that Eli was a defender and had possession of the helmet of salvation, the Illuminator, and the Sword of the Spirit, he had the ability to turn any doorway in the castle into a portal to any other doorway in the castle. This saved Eli a great deal of walking time throughout his time in training.

The doorway filled with the blue light of Eli's sword. Not hesitating at all, Eli stepped through the glowing blue doorway and into the war room.

Usually when Eli would return from a mission the war room would be filled with the applause and congratulatory remarks of the Angelos, but there was no such welcome this time. The war room was in a state that Eli had never seen it before.

The atmosphere was one of utter chaos, as Angelos flew around the room and through the walls at great speed. The gigantic screen that covered the left wall of the room was fixed on a war-torn looking city with a crimson sky. The city was dark and shrouded in shadows. All of the smaller holographic screens located on the Angelo's desks were also all fixed on that same city.

Eli heard an Angelos cry out.

"Sir, they have taken the tower of conviction!"

There was a collective gasp among the Angelos.

"Sir, the tower of acceptation has just fallen!" cried out another Angelos on the other side of the room.

Flintrock, one of the higher ranking Angelos flew into the air, "Get me a visual on the tower of direction!"

"Yes sir!"

The giant screen zoomed in on a tall lighthouse-looking tower. The tower stretched high into the dark crimson sky. A powerful beam of light flew into the top of the lighthouse and the lighthouse reflected the beam of light all throughout the land. The light was beautiful and mesmerizing to Eli, though he could not figure out why. Suddenly, a terrifying roar that gave Eli chills exploded from the darkness around the lighthouse and a giant ball of dark energy clashed with the light reflecting off of the tower. After a few moments of the two elements clashing, the dark ball of energy covered the reflector tower cutting off the light beam to the lighthouse and allowing the dark shadows to fill the screen. Just before the screen in the war room went dark, Eli caught sight of a terrifyingly large profile stomping towards the lighthouse. The large screen went black as haunting laughter echoed through the darkness.

"Sir," came the weak voice of the Angelos, "it appears as though they have taken the tower of direction."

"Not on my watch!" yelled Flintrock as he drew a sword and flew up to the top of the tower. "To war!"

As a whole, the Angelos drew their swords and flew into the air to join Flintrock.

"To war!"

Flintrock turned to fly out the tower window when Michael's powerful voice silenced the room.

"Stand down!"

Flintrock and all the other Angelos immediately stopped moving and looked to their commander.

Michael stood outside of his door at the top of the tower in the war room. Radiating with bright yellow light, the gigantic angel was a picture of power and control. With the war room in silence, Michael pointed to the screen.

"What you see on that screen has only come about through the King's permission. I too desire to travel to the Desolate City and reclaim the towers for the King, but the King has given a decree against it. The King has declared that this battle is not a battle for Angelos to fight, but a battle for the King's Defender."

All the Angelos in the room sheaved their swords and looked to Eli.

"Eli." continued Michael, "Return to your room and prepare for battle. Your training has ended and the time of your next great adventure is upon us. As for the rest of you, return to your stations and collect as much intelligence on the situation as you can. Eli will need as much information as we can gather. Now, let's get to work!"

The Angelos immediately returned to their desks and the room filled with chatter as they compiled intelligence. As for Eli, he slowly walked toward the door of the war room wondering what terrible event he had just witnessed, what kind of creature could roar like that, and what, if anything, he could possibly do about it.

chapter 3

lions and lambs

Approaching the large arched doorway of the war room, Eli closed his eyes and pictured the door to his room in the castle. Bright blue light filled the doorway ready to transport him to his destination. Still feeling surreal, Eli stepped through the door and into his room in the castle. Zephyr followed immediately behind him and soon they were both moving towards the sectional facing the wall full of large flat-screens.

With his mind racing and his heart pounding, Eli could not help but fidget with his sword to distract himself. As he held his sword and ran his fingers down the smooth blade that proceeded out of the lion's mouth, a question that had been nagging him for a while popped into his mind.

"Hey Zeph, I have a question for you."

"Go for it, but I have to tell you I don't know what roared on the screen or any details about your mission to come."

"That's okay. My question actually has to do with the Enemy and the King."

“Okay then, what’s your question?”

“Well, I’m confused. The hilt and the pommel of my sword are made in the likeness of a lion. The blade of my sword is designed to look like it is coming out of the mouth of the lion. Throughout the castle I’ve seen banners and decorations with pictures of a lion or a lion’s head including the stone lion heads in the atrium. However, the only lion I have come across so far is the Enemy. The King’s Word even describes the Enemy, ‘as a roaring lion’. I guess my question is, why are there so many representations of a lion when the only lion I have seen is the Enemy?”

“That is a good question.” boomed Michael from behind Eli.

Eli jumped at the sudden appearance of the large angel.

“What are you trying to do, Michael, give me a heart attack? That is, if that is even possible here in the spirit realm.”

Eli looked over to Zephyr who was trying not to laugh.

“Whatever, you know what I mean. You’re really quiet for a being your size, you know that?”

Michael walked around the leather sectional and stood in front of the large screens.

"I apologize for startling you, but your question is a valid one. If you don't mind Zephyr, I will answer this question."

"As you wish, General."

"The first thing you need to know, Eli, is that the King uses two different animals to symbolize His relationship with mankind: a lamb and a lion. The lamb represents the King's role as deliverer and the lion represents the King's role as conqueror. Though both symbols are intimately intertwined, the Enemy wants nothing to do with the role of a lamb. This choice is a great illustration of the great differences between the Enemy and the King."

"How so?" asked Eli.

"After mankind fell into sin, man did not need a conqueror, he needed a deliverer. Sin had conquered man and put man under its reign of death. The King's Word describes the cycle of sin's reign as such, 'Wherefore, as by one man sin entered into the world, and death by sin; and so death passed upon all men, for that all have sinned'".

"In order for the King to deliver man from the consequences of sin, it behooved Him to come in the likeness of a lamb. You see, the King was, is, and always will be perfect and free from sin. The King had already conquered sin, but sin had conquered man. The King was not under the penalty of sin, but man was. The King's perfection meant that the King would not face the penalty of death, but the King's freedom from sin could not change the King's declaration, 'the wages of sin is death' that condemned all mankind."

"Mankind was lost in sin, condemned to die, and utterly helpless to save itself. Man did not need a conqueror, man needed a deliverer, a substitute, an atoning sacrifice. Looking at an eternity separated from His beloved creation, the King chose to 'endure the cross despising the shame' for the joy of spending eternity with man. When the King took on human flesh and dwelt on the Earth, He did so to perform the ministry of a lamb. As a lamb, Jesus took upon Him the condemnation of man and shed His blood to fulfill the requirements of the King. Up to this point, the world of man knows Him as 'The Lamb of God which takes away the sin of the world.'"

"Currently, the King is ministering to the peoples of earth as a lamb, providing His atoning blood sacrifice to all who will accept it. However, a time is coming in which the King will take upon Him the role of conquering lion. And it is the future role of lion that is represented on your sword and throughout the castle. It is a role the King has earned through His actions as a lamb, as the King's Word attests in the Revelation given to the defender John."

"The King allowed John to see into the future to a time when a book will be created in the heavens that no one is worthy to take or to open. When John saw this he wept because no one could take the book or open it. That is when the King appears, the King who sacrificed Himself for the sins of the world. You see, that act of sacrifice is what makes Him worthy to take the book and open it. The King who sacrificed Himself to be worthy to take the book is described as, 'The Lion of the Tribe of Judah'. When the King appeared with the title of Lion of the Tribe of Judah, John records, 'And I beheld, and lo, in the midst of the throne, stood a Lamb as it had been slain'".

"The sacrifice of the King is what makes Him everything the Enemy wants to be, and yet, the sacrifice of the King is the very thing the Enemy cannot understand."

"What do you mean?"

"The Enemy does not see sacrifice as strength but weakness. However, the King has declared in His word, 'Greater love has no man than this, that a man lay down his life for his friends'. The Enemy sees love as weakness, but the King knows that love is the most powerful force in creation. Therefore if there is no greater show of love than sacrifice, then it is true that there is no greater source of power and no greater reason for praise than the ultimate sacrifice the King gave to mankind."

"This is why the choice of the King to be known as the Lamb of God is so significant." added Zephyr.

"You see, The King who is all-powerful and has every right to seek honor and glory for Himself and present Himself as a lion, chose to first be the sacrificial lamb for the sins of mankind. The Enemy mocked Him and saw the choice to born in the physical realm as a fragile human as a mistake. Yet, it was the King's choice to come as the sacrificial lamb that gained the ultimate victory over the Enemy."

"The Enemy desires to be as worthy and honored as the King, but he will never be because he only cares for himself. The closest the Enemy can come to being like the King is to take the form of a lion and prey on weaker beings."

"If it will help," interjected Michael, "think about the difference between the illustration of the lion of the King and the Enemy's portrayal of a lion like the difference between the lions affected by sin in the physical realm and the lions free from sin here in the spiritual realm."

"The lions affected by sin are predators who use their power to kill, devour, and benefit themselves in whatever way they desire. In the same way, the Enemy attempts to use his power to prey on others and benefit himself. The lions here in the spiritual realm without the taint of sin are powerful, yet, loving, kind, and will only use their might against others to protect the ones they love from harm. In the same way, the King used His power to sacrifice Himself for the lives of man and uses His might to benefit and protect others."

"To answer your question, Eli, the Lion represented by your sword and honored throughout the castle is the Lion of the Tribe of Judah who came first as the Lamb slain before the foundation of the world but who will reign forever as the King of kings and Lord of lords. The lion form the Enemy takes upon himself is nothing more than a vain delusion of a defeated being who will one day bow to the rule of the True King. Do you understand now Eli?"

"Yes, thanks guys."

"Good." said Michael turning his attention to a gold file-folder in his hand, "Now, let's get down to business."

chapter 4

the briefing

Michael opened up the large golden file-folder he was carrying and with a wave of his massive hand, the screens on the wall lit up with different images. Some of the screens had images of different creatures while other screens had images of the war-torn city nestled under a dark crimson sky, the same city Eli saw on the giant screen in the war room. Now that Eli was able to get a good look at the city on the screen, Eli saw how massive the city was. Looking like a normal physical-realm city, the city stretched as far as the eye could see. This city, however, looked as though it had been bombed or burned. From tall skyscrapers with half of the top of the building missing to smaller buildings completely gutted from fire, everything looked destroyed and vacant.

In addition to the desolate state of the city, Eli noticed that the city had two main streets. The first street was a broad street that ran through the heart of the entire city. This street looked several times larger than any street or highway Eli had ever seen in the physical realm and it was packed full of people walking in an almost trance-like state. The entire scene creeped Eli out as the ruined buildings and zombie-like state of people reminded him of a post-apocalyptic movie.

The other street Eli saw, running parallel to the broad street, was a much narrower street. This street had only a few people walking down it, but these people seemed much more alert and walked with a purpose. Contrary to the dark state of the broad street, this street seemed to glow with the bright light of the King.

On the highest screen, Eli saw an image that looked like a fortress. Nestled underneath the same dark crimson sky, surrounded by the eerie glow of the land, the fortress was vastly different than all the other buildings and structures. This fortress glowed with light, was completely intact, built on top of a high hill, and had gigantic walls made out of pure white stone. In the middle of the fortress, stretching high into the air, was a large lighthouse structure with a massive crystal orb that shone with a brilliantly bright light at the top. Seeing the light again, Eli recognized the light as the light that filled the throne room of the King.

Michael walked up to the screens and pointed to the screen with the war-torn city on it.

"This is the Desolate City and it is where you must go for your next mission."

"Why does it look like that? You know, all destroyed and ruined like it has been through a war or something?"

"The Desolate City looks like it is in ruin because it is. It is a place without meaning, without purpose, and without hope because it is a land largely devoid of the new life the King offers to all mankind. The Desolate City is where the spiritual lives of the people wander who have yet to accept the new life the King offers through Jesus Christ."

"So those people walking like they are in a trance are real people in the physical realm who are not saved?"

"Correct. The people you see wandering the broad street represent real people who are currently alive in the physical realm. The broad street they are walking on leads to the lake of fire."

Eli looked back at the screen to see if he could see what the lake of fire looked like, but all Eli could see was the broad street stretching across the city.

"But when does the street end? It looks like it goes on forever."

"The broad street ends at different places for different people. Every human has a pre-determined life-span that ends precisely when the King has decreed. If that person still wanders the broad street when his life on earth ends, the soul of the person vanishes from the street and awaits its eternal destination in the grave."

Eli took a moment and looked at the screen with all the wandering lost on it. As he looked at the countless number of souls walking toward their own destruction, a feeling of desperation overwhelmed him.

"We have to do something! We can't just let them walk to their destruction without warning them. Please tell me this is my mission. Please let me go and warn them!"

"Seeing the souls on the broad street can be terrifying, yes, but the broad street is not the only path in the Desolate City. The Desolate City is the place where the souls of the lost wander, but it is also the place where the light of the gospel shines. The broad street leads to destruction, but there is also a narrow street that leads to salvation. Even here, in the Desolate City, the King has established a way for the souls of the wandering lost to find their way to the place of salvation. And yes, your mission has everything to do with reaching the wandering lost with the gospel and leading them to the City on a Hill."

Eli pointed to the screen with the fortress city on it.

"Are you talking about the fortress with the lighthouse in it?"

"Indeed I am. That is The City on a Hill and it was built by the King Himself to shine forth the saving light of the gospel. Because of the fall of man into sin in the garden, at a certain age, the soul of every person born in the physical realm walks the broad street. Every single soul that has ever set foot on the broad street and every soul that will set foot on the street is loved by the King with a perfect love. The King's Word tells us that the King is not willing that any one of these souls perishes, and so He established the City on a Hill to shine the gospel light of salvation throughout the Desolate City. When the light of the gospel reaches the hearts and minds of the lost, they follow the light, enter the gates of the city, and find the new life of the King."

"So if everyone the light touches comes to the King, why doesn't the King just shine the light on everyone all at once and end the war?"

"Zephyr, since you have more experience with this question, I would prefer you to answer him."

"Absolutely sir. Eli, when the light of the gospel touches the lives of the wandering lost, it awakens the person's need for the life of the King. When that person feels the awakening of the need, that person then must choose to follow the light to the source or to pursue the filling of that need in the world. This decision is difficult enough for humans to make, but to make matters worse, this land is full of the Enemy's minions who are constantly looking for wanderers whom the light of the gospel has awakened. These enemies take every opportunity to seize enlightened wanderers and prevent them from finding their way to the City on a Hill. So, no, not every person who sees the glorious light of the gospel comes to the King. Many wanderers seek to meet their need in the world while others are deceived by the Enemy's servants."

"Well said Zephyr. These enemies are the reason why your next mission lies in the Desolate City. There are three common enemies that roam the

Desolate City: wolves, which you are already familiar with, watchers, and tares."

"The wolves," continued Michael as he pointed to a screen on which a wolf, dressed in a lavish, mobster-looking suit, lifted a golden goblet in celebration with other wolves, "are led by their pack leader, Filthy Lucre. You are already familiar with their tactics. They disguise themselves as King's sheep and at times under-shepherds from the City on a Hill to deceive enlightened wanderers. Lucre's wolves aggressively seek to hinder the awakened souls from entering the City on a Hill through the deceitfulness of riches and what they call the pursuit of happiness."

Michael pointed to another screen on which a picture of a person with a creepy-looking blindfold walked down the broad street. The blindfold, which wrapped all the way around its head, was made of what looked like iron with screws attaching it to the person's skull. The person also had an iron collar around its neck with a loop to attach shackles on the front of it. What made the person even more bizarre to Eli was the fact that along with the horror-movie iron blindfold and collar, the creature wore a full-piece black suit with a white button up shirt and a black tie.

"This is a watcher. The watchers are perhaps the bitterest of the Enemy's servants in the Desolate City, and are by far the most complicated to understand. The watchers are enlightened spirits who were ensnared by a despicable group known as the watchtower. The watchtower was formed by one of the vilest spirits of the Enemy, a spirit known as Taze, for the single purpose of twisting the King's Word in order to condemn the souls of man. Once the watchtower ensnares an awakened soul, that soul is taken inside the watchtower."

Michael paused for a moment looking at the screens until he pointed to a screen that contained a picture of a black-iron tower that looked like a rook on Eli's family's chess board surrounded by a ring of white military-styled barracks.

"There we are. This is the watchtower fortress, this is where the enlightened souls are taken. Once inside, the soul is blind-folded and convinced that it must now live as a slave in order to gain its salvation. In order to gain their salvation, the watchers must obey the watchtower without question and search diligently for spirits that have been awakened in order to convert them."

"So, once a spirit is converted to a watcher, is it beyond the reach of the King?"

"No. There are many glorious accounts of watchers entering the City on a Hill and being converted. No person is beyond the light of the gospel, not even watchers. However, because of the wicked enslavement forced upon them in the watchtowers, re-opening their eyes to their need through the light of the gospel is often a slow and painful process. It takes a defender or a harvester with a special love for the watchers and a powerful knowledge and skill in the King's Word to successfully take the blindfold off their eyes and free them from their life of enslavement."

"What's a harvester?"

"Good question, I apologize for getting ahead of myself. A harvester is a citizen of the City on a Hill who has been commissioned by the King to work in the broad street of the Desolate City. Many of these workers are humans who, like yourself, work for the King in both the physical and spiritual realms. In fact, I believe you might just run into a harvester or two whom you recognize. However," said Michael as the surprised look on Eli's face communicated that Eli was about to ask a question about the harvesters, "that is something that you will have to discover on your own."

"Now where was I, oh yes, the third common enemy you will find in this land is a tare. Tares are the most effective of all the enemies because they have been designed by the Enemy to imitate the citizens of the City on a Hill. Tares present the awakened souls with a gospel made to look like the King's gospel but a gospel that denies the completed work of Jesus Christ."

"These three enemies have been around for many years, however, it is due to recent events that the King is sending you to the Desolate City. Though all three of these enemies fight against the City on a Hill, they do not get along and have also been known to fight each other. Recently, however, the Enemy has sent one of his most ancient and powerful servants to unify these enemies and war against the gospel light. That enemy is the reason why you must go to the Desolate City.

When Michael said this, all of the screens on the wall changed from the images they were showing to images of one large creature. The screens all acted like puzzle pieces showing the different parts of the massive creature with the feet of the creature on the bottom screens and the head of the creature on the top screens.

The creature was terrifying. Towering over his surroundings, the creature was obviously a giant. When the creature first appeared it looked like a gigantic humanoid stone giant. The stone giant looked as if he were created for war. His body looked like a statue of a Greek god; with gigantic muscles and no body fat whatsoever. The giant wore only a leather loin cloth with a leather belt. Decorating the belt like diamond studs were the skulls of men. Further, the giant carried a large spiked club. The giant's face looked like an orc from one of Eli's computer games with a bulging forehead, oversized walrus-like teeth protruding up from his lower jaw, and small dark eye sockets blazing with green fire.

As if the giant's war-like appearance was not enough, the giant laughed and in a flash of darkness, the giant's appearance changed completely. The giant now had a slender black body with the head of a snarling dog. In place of the large spiked club, the giant now carried an odd looking scythe in his hand. The only thing that had not changed on the creature's body was his eyes that were blazing with the odd green fire. Eli did recognize this form as Anubis, one of the gods the ancient Egyptians worshipped. Another flash of darkness, and again the giant's appearance changed. Now the creature looked like a giant Middle-Eastern man. The man wore a turban and robes, and carried a long sword with a curved blade in one hand and a large book in the other hand.

Michael's voice broke Eli's hypnotic stare at this shape-shifting enemy.

"This," said Michael with obvious disgust in his voice, "is Polytheist. Polytheist is one of the Enemy's oldest and vilest servants. Polytheist was created by the Enemy with the ability to change his appearance in order to appeal to the minds of the wandering lost. Since the early days of creation, Polytheist has aided in the destruction of countless souls that have rejected the King by providing gods that fit the desires of the lost. This unique ability of Polytheist to adapt to the desires of man is perhaps his greatest strength but it is also his greatest weakness. Remember that when the time comes for you to battle him."

"Having said that, do not underestimate this enemy, Eli. Polytheist is cruel, wicked, merciless, and extremely skilled in combat. Further, Polytheist is extremely intelligent in human wisdom. He has spent thousands of years watching and observing to find the best ways to corrupt the minds of the wandering lost and keep their minds in a vale of darkness."

"Since arriving in the Desolate City, Polytheist has united the wolves, watchers, and tares, and has successfully captured the three reflector towers of the gospel light."

"They have captured the gospel light?"

"No. They have captured the reflector towers. No person or being can ever capture the light of the gospel established in the City on a Hill. The King decreed when He established the City on a Hill that not even the gates of hell could stand against it. However, there are three reflector towers in the Desolate City that amplify the gospel light and make the gospel clear to the wandering lost. These towers are the towers of conviction, acceptation, and direction, and currently, all three are in the hands of the Enemy's forces.

"It is obvious from the Enemy's choice to send Polytheist to the Desolate City at this time that the Enemy wants you defeated. Only a creature as vile and powerful as Polytheist could unite the wolves, watchers, and tares and demand the attention of the King's defender. Knowing that you are still young in your experience as a defender, the Enemy has created what he perceives as a stacked showdown between a young defender and one of the oldest and most powerful servants of darkness. I think the Enemy believes with the combined forces of the land and the power of Polytheist that you will be destroyed."

Michael paused giving Eli a chance to comprehend what he had just said. Eli, who's face communicated that he understood, spoke slowly as if he were trying to find the right words.

"Let me get this straight. You believe the Enemy has sent Polytheist to unite the enemies of the Desolate City as a way to set a trap to destroy me, but, you are going to send me there anyway? Why?"

"Simply put Eli, the recovering of those reflectors is the number one priority for the servants of the King. As a child of the King, your greatest call is to enlighten the wandering lost with the light of the gospel. By attacking the light of the gospel, the Enemy has attacked the very heart of the King. Never forget that the Enemy can do nothing without the permission of the King. The King has allowed this attack because He knows you are able to gain the victory. With the King's Word in your possession, His Illuminator in your heart, and His helmet of salvation on your head, you have the ability to gain the victory and recover the reflector towers."

"I understand that, but we're talking about a giant who is thousands of years old!"

"Granted the battle will not be an easy one, and it will test you in ways that you cannot imagine. But the King believes in you, I believe in you, and I know Zephyr believes in you."

"You bet I do, Eli!" exclaimed Zephyr.

Michael handed Eli the large golden file-folder that contained the mission information.

"I can see the concern on your face, but you need not be concerned. You have only to ask yourself one simple question."

"What question is that?"

"Do you believe what the King's Word says is true?" replied Michael as he looked directly into Eli's eyes, "Because if you do, then you will find the truth that leads to victory."

chapter 5

finding direction

Eli sat on the sectional looking at the golden file-folder and starring at the screens. The screens returned to their original images showing the different enemies and places in the Desolate City. Michael had left and asked for Zephyr to accompany him leaving Eli alone with his thoughts.

What does he mean, if I believe what the King's Word says I will find the truth that leads to victory? thought Eli, *Of course I believe the King's Word! I'm a defender.*

Eli glanced back up at the pictures and then at the screen that contained the constant changing form of Polytheist and placed his face in his hands.

I wish Michael would just tell me what he wants me to find out.

Eli stood up and lay the file-folder on the sectional.

"I need some air."

Eli rose from the couch and walked to the door. Eli knew that he needed some time away from the screens to sit and meditate upon his mission the same way he had meditated on his training when things got rough. Knowing where he needed to go, Eli closed his eyes as he approached the now glowing door and stepped through the doorway and into the Courtyard of Eden.

The King's light had an immediate impact on him as it seemed to instantly lift the burden of his mission off of his shoulders. Eli made his way down the white-stone path toward the large golden fountain in the center of the courtyard. With his fears melting away with every step, Eli felt quite at peace when he sat down on the side of the fountain.

This was Eli's absolute favorite place to be in the castle. He could sit here enjoying the benefits of the light of the King as the sound of the running water calmed him down and allowed him to re-evaluate whatever was bothering him.

After a few moments of Eli heard the soft thud of approaching steps and felt a large furry snout nuzzle his left arm. Eli gave in to the nudging and began petting the large head and mane of the lion. Immediately the large animal purred and laid down next to him.

Eli remembered the first time he encountered the lion, back when Zephyr and Brutus were escorting him through the courtyard his first day in the spirit realm, and how the lion walked up to Eli and how uncertain he was as he pet the lion.

Since that day, it seems every time Eli comes to the courtyard, the lion finds Eli and listens to him as he talks about the struggles and victories in training. Sitting on the fountain petting the lion, Eli chuckled to himself as he realized just how much of a friend he sees the lion as.

"Hey buddy, I knew I could count on you to cheer me up."

The lion looked up at Eli and licked his face with its large sandpaper-like tongue nearly knocking Eli backwards into the fountain.

"Easy buddy, I love you too."

At that moment Zephyr flew up and sat beside Eli on the rim of the fountain.

"So have you thought of a name for your friend here?"

"No, not yet. I am terrible at choosing names. Besides, it is not like he belongs to me."

"So, how are you feeling about *our* new mission from the King?"

"Well, I'm not sure. Wait, did you say '*our new mission'* like yours and mine? Like you are going to come with me?"

"That's exactly what I mean! When Michael asked me to speak with him after the briefing, he informed me that I am to accompany you to the Desolate City and make sure you get to the City on a

Hill alive. Apparently the Enemy's servants are anticipating your arrival, and Michael thinks there is a high chance of confrontation before your arrival in the City on a Hill."

"That is fantastic! And a little scary at the same time, but to be honest with you, I'm very frustrated by how anxious I am about this whole mission."

"What do you mean?"

"Throughout training, all I have wanted to do is fulfill a meaningful mission for the King and retrieve the next piece of armor. We have trained, prepared, and waited for our orders excitedly. Now we have a mission, but instead of being excited, I'm nervous and afraid. I just feel like I need something a little easier than to go and battle an ancient servant of darkness like Polytheist and a mixed army of wolves, watchers, and tares. I just don't feel ready for a mission like this. Especially a mission with so much at stake."

"Your reaction is understandable, but is exactly why, I believe, the King has allowed the Enemy to send Polytheist to the Desolate City and unify the wolves, watchers, and tares. You're facing this type of mission now because if you want to be the defender the King desires you to be, you need to face a mission that is far beyond your ability to overcome."

"I don't understand, Zeph, why do I need to face a mission of this magnitude?"

"Because, Eli, if you want to survive this mission, then you need to not only know the truths of the King's Word, you need to claim their power in your life. You know how important it is for the light of the gospel to be restored to full power. You know how needful it is for the light of the gospel to reach the wandering lost. You also know that you are no match for Polytheist or his army. To accomplish this mission will require a power and skill that is far beyond anything you can boast."

"This mission is needful for you to progress as a defender because it is going to force you to ask yourself what is true; *really* true. Is it true that the King is the all-powerful God of creation? Is it true that the King is in control of all things even the difficult tests in life? Is it true that the wandering lost need the light of the gospel and deserve it no less than you did when the light awakened you? Is it true that all the servants of darkness including Polytheist, the wolves, watchers, and tares, have no power to overcome the King? Is it true that you have the King's Word in your possession and that the King's Word grants you the power you need to overcome any and all obstacles the Enemy can throw at you?"

Not able to contain himself any longer, Eli cut in, "Yes, of course I believe all of these things!"

"Aw, but do you really? If you truly believed all of these things, then this mission would not intimidate you the way it does. There is a difference between knowing something to be true and claiming it as truth in your life. For you to be a mighty defender for the King, you must not only believe these things to be true but claim them as true in your life. We call this type of mission a claiming because in order for you to gain the victory, *the* truths of the King's Word must become *your* truths from the King's Word."

Zephyr hovered up into the air and looked up into the glow of the King's light.

"The light of the King is truly an amazing blessing. A blessing that all creation ought to have the ability to experience, don't you think? Take some time, listen to the King's Spirit, and search your heart concerning what we have talked about. When you are ready to meet this new mission head-on, I will be waiting for you. Until then, may the King's face shine upon you."

Zephyr flew back into the castle leaving a trail of blue and silver light in his path. Eli sat there a minute longer scratching the lion behind the ear and thinking about Zephyr's words. Leaning over, Eli looked at his reflection in the large fountain. There glistening in the light of the King was the helmet of salvation firmly fixed upon his head. Though Eli did not feel like he was wearing any helmet whatsoever, every time he saw his reflection in the castle or in the fountain he would see the brilliant silver helmet with a majestic blue crown of thorns wrapping around the helm sitting on his head.

Seeing the helmet on his head reminded Eli of all the King had done to empower him to overcome the Cemetery of the Old Man and claim that helmet for his own. Pondering these memories spurred his sword to vibrate with energy. Eli stood up from the fountain and drew his sword. As soon as Eli held his sword in the air, the Illuminator filled Eli's being with a bright light. Closing his eyes, Eli concentrated waiting to see what message the Illuminator would bring from the King's Word. After a few brief moments of blinding light, words materialized in Eli's mind.

"Now faith is the substance of things hoped for, the evidence of things not seen...But without faith it is impossible to please him: for he that cometh to God must believe that he is, and that he is a rewarder of them that diligently seek him."

The familiar rush of warm confidence that washed over Eli every time he connected with the King's Word flowed through him dispelling all of his fears and anxieties about the mission.

"It's true, I don't know how the King will empower me to be able to overcome Polytheist and his army, but I have seen how the King has empowered me to overcome all of the other obstacles I have faced. I know that He can, and if I want to please Him, then I must believe that He will."

Eli sheaved his sword and lifted his head toward the light of the King allowing the light to warm his face. Eli then dropped his head and looked at the lion that was still nudging him for attention.

"What do you think, buddy, do you think that we should hog all of this incredible light for ourselves or do you think we should go and make sure as many people as possible have the opportunity to feel the light of the King?"

The lifted lifted his head and nudged Eli's chest several times.

"I don't know: it's going to be difficult."

The lion rose to his feet, lifted its head to the sky, and roared loudly.

Trying not to laugh, Eli turned around and faced the fountain, "I hear what you are saying, I just, when I look at all that I have here, I just don't know if I want to leave this for the Desolate City and"

Eli never got to finish his last sentence as he was shoved forward, over the edge of the fountain into the sparkling clear water. Jumping up out of the water, Eli turned around to see sitting on its hind legs looking like it was smiling at him. Realizing what happened, Eli laughed and climbed out of the fountain.

"I was only playing! Of course I'm going to go to the Desolate City and follow the King's command. How ungrateful would I have to be to receive the light of the King and not do everything he could to share it with others who are in darkness? Besides, the Enemy ought to know better than to mess with the light of the gospel. Obviously the Enemy wanted to pick a fight. Well, let me tell you, if it is a fight he wants, then it is a fight he is going to get."

The lion walked up to Eli and placed its face right up against Eli's face, as if to communicate to Eli that the horse supported him.

"Thanks boy. You know what, I think I have a name for you. How do you like the name Compass? Although your methods are a little unconventional, you have helped me find the right direction."

Compass lifted his head up as if he were pondering the name, and then roared at the sky. The lion then crouched on the ground and looked at Eli expectantly.

"What is it boy? You want me to get on your back?"

The lion nodded

"Okay, if you say so."

Eli cautiously threw one leg over the lion's back and sat down as if Compass were a horse. Compass rose to his feet, and Eli had just enough time to wrap his arms around Compass' neck before the lion took off down the path and toward the nearest archway.

chapter 6

final preparations

Michael sat in his office holding a piece of parchment looking at a holographic map of the Desolate City. In his hand was the response from the King sent by the hand of his fellow servant, Gabrielle. When Polytheist and his make-shift army of wolves, watchers, and tares launched their assault on the reflector towers of the gospel light, Michael immediately sought permission to go and fight against Polytheist personally. Michael knew that he could gain the victory and smash Polytheist into as many pieces as the different false gods he spawned throughout history. However, the answer from the King stayed his hand.

Beloved Michael. I rejoice to see your zeal for the restoring of the light of the gospel. I understand your heart, and I know that seeing the workings of the Enemy in the Desolate City has stirred your soul to take action and strike back. My heart is also grieved at this attempt to strike at Me; however, you need to trust Me when I tell you that I have allowed all of this for a reason. As difficult as it is for you to sit back and watch, I need you to allow Elijah to strike back and confront Polytheist and his army. For Elijah to become the defender I desire him to be, he must learn the lessons I have planned for him through this mission. This mission is designed to be a claiming for him as victory will require him to take the truths he knows about Me and make them real in his life.

Michael sat back and watched as images of Polytheist celebrating his victory with his make-shift army flooded across his desk. Michael knew better than to question or doubt the King, for eternity had shown Michael that the King had the ability to work everything out according to the King's pleasure. Michael felt frustrated, though, because of Elijah's hesitation and fear.

Though Michael understood the need for humans to go through a claiming in order to become great defenders for the King, it nevertheless baffled him.

Elijah has defeated his flesh, thought Michael, *and has experienced the commission of the King. How can he still doubt his ability to overcome in the task ahead of him?*

Michael's frustration with Eli's hesitation and fear began to swell up again just as his doorway glowed with light and Eli stepped into his office.

Michael rose to his feet in surprise and spoke to welcome Eli when Eli quickly cut him off.

"Before you say anything, I need to say something to you. I'm sorry that I have been so self-centered. I'm sorry that my first reaction to the King's mission was a reaction of fear and hesitation.

I know how important the light of the gospel is and I know that every moment I sit in faithlessness is a moment in which the souls of real people are in danger. I'm sorry I let you down. You have trained me well and you have given me everything I need to be able to answer the mission with immediate confidence. I know I let you down, and I know I let the King down. I have already confessed my failure to the King but I also wanted to apologize to you. The Enemy is looking for a fight and I want to meet the challenge in the name of my King."

Tears welled up in Michael's eyes as he once again witnessed the ability of the King to work all things out for the good of creation.

"Well then." said Michael as he sat back down behind his desk, "We have a few final preparations to make before you go on your way. Please, pull up your chair."

Michael waved his hand and, as it happened the first time Eli visited this office, a smaller stone chair appeared facing Michael's desk. Eli sat down in the chair and scooted it up next to the large stone desk. Michael then tapped the holographic map making it larger for Eli to be able to see well when someone knocked on Michael's office door.

"Come in." called Michael.

The door opened and a jubilant looking Zephyr flew into the room.

“Zeph! How did you know I was in here; I just arrived a few seconds ago?”

“Well you might have only just arrived, but I received word from the King shortly after I left you in the courtyard that you would be sitting here making final preparations for your mission.”

“Really?”

“Yes, really. You might have doubted yourself, but the King never doubted you for a moment. He knew that you would make the right choice and that you would follow His orders.”

“I’m glad you’re here.” said Michael, “Pull up a chair.”

Michael waived his hand and another chair appeared. This chair was made out of the same white stone but was taller than Eli’s chair to help Zephyr see over the desk. Eli smiled at the difference in height and Zephyr could sense what Eli was thinking.

“Not one word, Eli, not one.”

Eli did his best to contain his laughter.

“I’m hurt that you would think I would say anything.”

“Yeah right, save it for the jury.”

“Gentlemen,” interrupted Michael, “I give you the Desolate City.”

The holographic map on Michael's desk filled with a picture of a gigantic city that spanned the entire planet. This city had many high rise buildings, skyscrapers, and residential areas. Again, Eli noticed that these buildings looked as if they had been through a war. The tops of some of the buildings were broken off and crumbling, some buildings looked as if they had been gutted by fire, and most of the building's windows had all been broken out.

"The Desolate City spans the entire physical realm world. Your mission, however, does not include the entire Desolate City, but this particular section here."

Michael tapped his gigantic finger on his desk and the holographic map zoomed in to reveal a familiar looking set of high rise buildings.

"Wait a minute. That looks like the downtown city buildings where I live."

"It ought to." Zephyr answered, "Because it is the downtown buildings of where you live."

"Really?"

"Yes." continued Michael, "Though the King desires all the lost land to be saved, He does not send one person to reach the entire population. He sends each defender into his own part of the Desolate City to reach those the defender already has contact with."

Michael paused for a moment to give Eli a chance to acknowledge that he understood. When Eli nodded, Michael pointed to the top of a medium-sized building in the middle of downtown.

"Here is where the portal will take you. Your first objective is to make your way over here." said Michael as he placed his hand on the right side of the map and moved his hand across his chest causing the map to spin.

"This is your destination, the City on a Hill. Here you will meet with the Council of Light that you will be given information on your mission and the enemies' whereabouts. Be warned, this will not be an easy journey. There are a lot of enemies looking for you. You and Zephyr must move quickly and stealthily if you hope to reach the city without an all-out battle. Do you have any questions?"

Eli paused for a moment as he looked at the location of the City on a Hill as he felt a nagging in the back of his mind.

"I do. I hate to sound like a coward, but why don't you all just send me into the City on a Hill through a portal? That way we can skip the whole problem of having to make it to the city alive."

"That is a fair question. The City on a Hill is a very unique place and we do have the ability to transport souls directly into the city, however, there is one condition that you have yet to meet. In order for you to transport directly into the City on a Hill, you must first have been in the City on a Hill. The first time any person enters the city, that person must walk through the gates of the city. Seeing you have not visited the City on a Hill yet, you cannot simply get transported into the city. The closest we can get you is the location I have shown you."

The word, "location" triggered Eli's mind and he realized why the location of the City on a Hill caught his attention.

Eli pointed to the City on a Hill on the holographic map and then moved the map back and forth with his finger.

"Look at that, I know where the City on a Hill is located. It's where the Open Door Church is located in my town. I was just there for my grandfather's funeral."

Eli laughed to himself, "I had no idea. How crazy is that? Wait, my dad said that no matter how many people came to the funeral that my grandfather wanted to have his funeral at that church. Is that because he knew that the City on a Hill was there?"

Michael leaned back in his chair with a contemplative look on his face.

"It is a very good possibility. Master Granite loved the City on a Hill and spent a great deal of time striving to reach the population of the Desolate City in both realms. One of the trademarks of your grandfather's legacy as a defender is the fact that he never forgot his time wandering the broad street and he used that time as a motivator to do everything he could to reach those wandering toward destruction.

"This discussion is a good time for me to bring up an aspect about this mission so that it does not catch you off guard. You are going to see places that are familiar to you from the physical realm but this is not the physical realm. Do not forget this fact. Just because the land looks familiar to you does not mean that the danger is less. There is an army of wolves, watchers, and tares, scouring this land waiting for your arrival.

"Further, you will see the souls of people you know. Some of these souls you will see wandering in the street toward destruction. When you see these souls, you must not stop to try and help them. The only way to help them now is to restore the light of the gospel. Once the light is restored, and the enemies defeated, then you may venture into the streets with more security.

"Finally, the souls of people you know from the physical realm will not all be lost souls. You are not the only one from your town who ventures into the spirit realm. You will find some allies in the City on a Hill. I am telling you this now so that when you see them you will not think it is some trick of the Enemy."

"So, I'm not the only one; there are others like me. That's exciting!"

"Yes it is." said Zephyr, "And the best part is that these others will not only be your allies here in the spirit realm, but can also be your allies when your mission requires you to return to the physical realm. This mission will absolutely change your life."

"Zephyr's right, this mission can change everything in both realms. If you do not have any more questions for me, then your preparations are complete. Zephyr, Eli, it is time to make your way to the atrium."

The three of them stood up and immediately Zephyr's and Eli's chairs disappeared. Zephyr and Eli then made their way to the door of Michael's office. As they walked, Eli was picturing the Atrium of Ephesdammim and the door was already glowing. Just before they stepped through the door, Zephyr turned to look at Michael who was still standing behind his desk.

"Sir, are you coming with us?"

"Yes, I will be right behind you. There is one more thing I need to look to here before I join you. Go ahead and I will see you shortly."

"Yes sir."

Turning around, Zephyr and Eli stepped through the glowing door and into the atrium.

With Zephyr and Eli gone, Michael picked up the parchment he received from the King informing him to allow Eli to go on the mission and denying Michael's request to go personally.

"As always, LORD, You are right. You knew Eli would make the right choice and You have prepared him to gain a glorious victory. Now I ask Your protection upon him as he discovers the true power of Your Word. Thank you for your wisdom and decision."

After Michael had finished speaking, he tossed the parchment into the air and it disappeared in a burst of light. Having made right his frustration at the situation, Michael transported himself into the atrium.

chapter 7

the desolate city

When Michael arrived in the atrium, Eli and Zephyr were waiting for him by the bridge to the second gazebo. The light of the atrium had already drawn a line from the pathway, over the crystal bridge, and to the second gazebo on the left.

Eli and Zephyr looked expectantly at Michael as he appeared in the atrium. Eli cupped his hands around his mouth and called out.

"Any final advice for us?"

"*Be strong and of a good courage. Be not afraid, neither be thou dismayed: for the LORD thy God is with thee withersoever thou goest.* These are the same words the King spoke to Joshua when the King sent Joshua into the land of Canaan for his own claiming. Like you, Joshua had to face armies, obstacles, and giants. He too battled with the feelings of fear and anxiety that you are wrestling with. In the same way that you have accepted your mission, he accepted and he saw the King work amazing miracles to grant him the victory."

"These words contain all the power and encouragement you need to gain the victory over

Polytheist and his army, for in them lie the truth from which your victory will come."

Michael paused and looked at the second gazebo. Lifting his massive arm, he pointed from Eli to the gazebo.

"The Desolate City awaits you and the wandering lost need you, Elijah Storm, Defender of the King. Go now and claim the belt of truth. And while you are at it," said Michael with a smile on his face, "Give Polytheist my warmest welcome. And by that, I mean smash him to pieces for me."

"That's what I'm talking about!" laughed Zephyr.

"Nothing would make me happier." said Eli.

Eli and Zephyr made their way over the bridge to the second small gazebo on the left side of the room. When the two entered the gazebo, the light of the atrium that formed the line to the gazebo flooded the gazebo the way it did when Eli entered the gazebo that took him to the Cemetery of the Old Man. The light shot from the top of the pillars to the center forming a large ball. That ball formed into a belt and the image of a belt shone on Eli's ring he received from his grandfather. In an instant, the belt of light shot two more beams of light that connected with Eli and Zephyr. After the light had engulfed them both, the light sucked them into the portal and the atrium returned to its previous state.

Though Eli was tempted to get lost in the excitement of travelling through the portal, he tried to concentrate on the mission ahead of him so that he would be prepared for anything when he arrived. Soon the amazing sensation of being shot through space subsided as his feet landed on solid ground. Slowly the light faded from his body leaving Eli standing on top of one of the smaller business buildings in his town looking at the dark crimson sky of the Desolate City. Walking over to the edge of the roof, Eli took his first in-person look at this dark land.

Though the sky was a dark shade of red with no visible light source, like a sun or a moon, the sky did give off a dark glow that somewhat illuminated the land enough for Eli to see. Nestled in the middle of a familiar looking downtown, Eli felt as if he were in an entirely foreign place. The buildings that Eli knew so well from the physical realm were all present and in the same locations they were from home, but they looked so dead and foreboding in their post-war condition.

The element that caused Eli the most pause was seeing the broad street, full of wandering lost in their zombie-like state. The building Eli landed on bordered the broad street. Standing on the roof, Eli was only about five stories away from the countless souls walking toward their destruction.

He knew from the holographic map that there would be a lot of people walking toward their destruction, but Eli had no idea there would be so many souls from his own town who were lost. Looking down at the jam-packed broad street, Eli realized the great need for the gospel in his town.

Driven by the need of his town for the gospel, Eli looked left toward the direction he knew the City on a Hill to be to see if the light of the gospel was still shining. Sure enough, Eli could see the tall lighthouse structure and could see the beams of light flickering over the broad street. The light was at times causing several of the wandering lost to stop and look around, but because the light's brightness was rather dim, it did not seem strong enough to awaken many if any of the wandering lost to their great need.

"It's a sobering sight isn't it?" said Zephyr as he hovered next to Eli.

"Yeah it is. There are just so many who need the gospel in my own town! I feel sick to my stomach that I have never taken the time to think about people I know who are on their way to an eternity in the Lake of Fire. I feel like seeing this in person has set my heart on fire. Is that normal?"

"Yes it is, especially for defenders of your bloodline. Your grandfather spent more of his time as a defender working alongside the harvesters here in the Desolate City than he spent anywhere else. I remember Krane telling us how your grandfather would go out into the streets weeping for the lost souls of the people he knew striving to enlighten them with the light of the gospel."

"As painful as it is to see them wandering the streets toward destruction, remember, the best thing you can do to reach them right now is to restore the light of the gospel to its most brilliant brightness. In order to do that, we must make our way to the City on a Hill and meet with the Council of Light."

Eli looked passed the broad street and saw the narrow street just on the other side of the buildings that bordered the broad street.

"You're right, I say we make our way over to the narrow street and follow it to the gates of the City on a Hill."

At that moment, Eli saw movement and heard the echo of voices coming from the street below. Running down the alley that connected the narrow street and the broad street between two buildings opposite Eli was a mixed group of watchers and wolves. Instinctively, Eli ducked down to where only his head was sticking up over the edge of the building. Because the building was not very tall and because the Desolate City was eerily quiet, Eli could hear the words of these creatures with startling clarity.

"Right over there, that building right there!" said a watcher as he pointed to the building Eli landed on. "I saw a flash of light coming from the top of that building. I bet anything that the defender is up there."

Seeing a watcher in person gave Eli the chills. There was just something about the blind-folded watcher being able to see that creeped him out.

As Eli attempted to process the watcher, a nearby wolf, visibly frustrated spoke up.

"Hold it! Are you telling me that you just made us run from our nice hiding spot all the way down here because you think you 'saw' a light from a portal? I hate to break this to you, but you're wearing a blindfold! This is ridiculous! I say we go back to the narrow street and wait for the defender to show himself. I'd bet anything that his plan is to follow the street all the way to that cursed city."

The watcher walked over to the wolf and stood as close as he could to the wolf without touching him.

"I can see fine, wolf, and I am telling you that the defender Polytheist wants us to capture is on top of that building!"

"Really?" exclaimed the wolf in an exasperated voice, "So where is he? Do you think he is just on top of the roof enjoying the sights? Maybe he is making himself at home somewhere inside. If he landed up there, he would be down here by now, but I don't see him. I say you're crazy."

The wolf stood up as tall as he could, now towering over the watcher who compared to the seven-foot tall wolf looked small and weak.

"And one more thing, freak; if you don't get out of my face, I am going to tear you to shreds."

The escalation of the argument between the watcher and the wolf split the group in half. Following the wolf's threat, all four of the other wolves moved over to stand behind the wolf growling and snarling at the watchers. In turn, the watchers produced large iron chains from their suit jackets with a large iron ball on the end of the chain, and held their weapons in a threatening fashion at the wolves.

Seeing the tension between these two supposed allies of Polytheist's army gave Eli hope that the union between these former enemies was not as strong as he had once thought.

Just when it looked like a fight was going to break out between the wolves and the watchers, two tares stepped out of the darkness of the alley and stood between the two sides. These tares did not look scary, yet, both the wolves and watchers responded to their presence in fear. The tares looked like normal men wearing nice dress pants and a short-sleeved button up black shirt with a backward white-collar. The only obviously odd aspect about the tares, as far as Eli could tell, was their jerky movements. When tares walked or moved their heads and arms, their movements looked unnatural, as if moving was uncomfortable for them.

"Gentlemen." began one of the tares in a smooth voice as he jerked his head back and forth to look at the wolf and the watcher who were arguing, "I hope we are not going to start fighting again. Do you remember how Polytheist settled the last argument?"

The way both the wolves and the watchers reacted to this reminder told Eli that however Polytheist dealt with the last argument was meant to send a message to the parties involved.

"Now," continued the tare slowly, "I don't think anyone here would want that to happen again would we?"

Both groups of watchers and wolves shook their heads and squirmed uncomfortably as they were reminded of the incident.

"I didn't think so. Now, here is what we are going to do. You, watcher, you think you saw a light coming from the top of that building over there. I want you to take two of your watcher friends and two wolves with you and go check out the top of that building.

"You, wolf, you're sure the defender will be travelling down the narrow street, are you? Well then, you take the remaining two wolves and watchers with you and return to our hiding spot."

One of the wolves in the back of the group growled, "What about you two, what are you going to do?"

The wolf's demeanor, which started as aggressive and accusatory, quickly changed as the wolves standing in between it and the tare stepped aside so the tare had a direct line of sight with the wolf. Looking at the tare's eyes, the wolf quickly lowered his head and changed his tone to a much softer tone as he tried to clarify his point.

"I mean, it's just that we could definitely use your help if we come across a defender. I have no doubt that we could capture him on our own, it's just that it would be easier if you all came with us."

The tare took a few jerking steps toward the wolf who spoke up.

"Yes it would be easier to capture this defender if we all worked together. However, Polytheist instructed us to make sure you all did not kill each other before you found him. Now that you have your orders, we are going to prepare a surprise for our young defender if by chance he escapes your," the tare paused and looked at the large wolf with an arrogant disdain, "capable hands I guess we will call it."

Having backed the wolf down, the tare looked to his friend, "Come on, let's go get the surprise ready."

As the two tares walked jerkily away, the leader turned back one last time to address the group of wolves and watchers.

"What are you waiting for? You have your orders. Go find that defender and bring him to Polytheist. Once that is done, things might just go back to normal around here and we can all continue hating each other."

The leader turned back and continued walking down the sidewalk of the broad street as the wolves and watchers smiled at each other nodding their heads.

"Okay." said the lead wolf who was arguing with the lead watcher, "Let's work together and capture this defender. Then, when all is back to normal, we can continue this discussion later."

"Agreed." said the lead watcher, "Since this is the last time we will be working together, let's make the most of it. Let's find this defender and take all of our anger out on him."

The whole group of watchers and wolves spoke up in agreement before breaking up into the two groups and heading in their directions.

Shocked by the dynamics of the union between these foes, Eli whispered to Zephyr, "What kind of trap do you think the tares were talking about?"

"I'm not sure, but right now, we have bigger things to worry about. Right now we have Polytheist's welcoming committee about to enter this building looking for us!"

chapter 8

fight and flight

Eli looked down to see the group of watchers and wolves make their way through the wandering lost toward the entrance of the building. Rolling away from the edge of the building so not to be seen from below, Eli quickly stood up and looked around the roof to see if there was a place to hide or a way to exit the roof. On the roof were several large air conditioner units and several metal pipes that looked like a periscopes. The only entrance or exit Eli could see was a door on the far side of the roof. Eli ran over to the door and swung it open. The door led to a staircase, which Eli assumed stretched all the way down to the ground.

"Okay, Zeph, here's the plan. I say you hide behind that large air conditioner over there. I will wait by the door to the stairs and will slice the first thing that comes out of that door and will then slam the door shut. That will give me a moment or two to run to the unit you will be hiding behind. When the rest of the group bursts out of the door they will likely try to surround me. When that happens, you come out of hiding and slice the ones with their back toward you and I will charge the ones in front of me. How does that sound?"

"As far as a battle strategy goes, that is not a bad one. However, I don't think fighting is our best option at this point. There are three watchers and two wolves coming our direction. That means we will be outnumbered five to two. Those are not good odds in any situation."

"True. But after I slice the first thing that comes out of that door, it will only be four to two. And we will have the element of surprise on our side. Besides, you are an Angelos, I bet they don't have anything like you on their side."

"Eli, listen to me. I know you hate the thought of running away from a battle after you have spent so much time training for this, but look at our situation. We are miles away from the City on a Hill, which means we are miles away from any form of back-up. There is not only a group of five enemies coming up our stairs, but there is also another group of five enemies not far away and who knows how many other groups of enemies are lurking not far from here. I guarantee you that once we are discovered, the first thing one of the watchers will do is to sound the alarm. If we are able to defeat this first group, the second group will be upon us shortly as will many more re-enforcements not limited to the army of wolves, watchers, and tares."

"Whoa, hold on! What do you mean? Are there more enemies here?"

"Yes, of course there are. Think about it. When the Enemy rebelled, one-third of all the King's ministers went with him. Many of the former servants of the King are eternally stationed in the Desolate City by the Enemy to counter the light of the gospel. Once the alarm is sounded, we run the risk of not only facing a countless number of wolves, watchers, and tares, but we also risk battle against other Angelos, known as the Arkhay' and possibly even Polytheist himself."

"You are a great warrior," continued Zephyr, "and I know that you have what you need to gain the victory in this mission. However, I do not think risking a battle of two against all the forces of the Enemy at once is a wise decision. I say we find a way down from this building and make our way to the City on a Hill trying to avoid detection. Once inside the walls of the city, we will have safety, allies, and knowledge of the situation."

"You're right. Okay, let's find a way off this roof."

Eli walked over to the door to the staircase.

"Do you think we still have time to go down the stairs or hide on one of the levels before they get up here?"

Eli cracked the door open to see if he could get a glimpse down the staircase to spot the group of enemies. To Eli's shock, he could already hear the group jogging up the stairs. Quietly, Eli closed the door and looked at Zephyr to communicate the stairwell was not an option.

A little more frantically, Eli examined the layout of the roof but could not see a place he could hide. Thinking he might have to fight the wolves and watchers, Eli saw one last option that might help him get down off the roof. On the side of the building opposite the broad street, the top of a rain gutter stuck over the edge of the roof.

Eli ran over to the rain gutter and looked down. To his delight, the entire gutter was intact and reached all the way down to the ground. Hearing the voices and steps of the welcoming committee grow louder, Eli wasted no time in swinging his legs over the edge of the roof and grabbing hold of the gutter with his hands. Shimmying down the gutter, Eli thought he had caught a break when the first brace attaching the gutter to the side of the building snapped off and fell to the ground.

Before Eli could react all of the braces above Eli snapped off the gutter and the top of the gutter bent down away from the wall. Almost instantly, Eli found himself falling toward the ground at a dangerous speed. Acting out of instinct, Eli pushed himself off of the gutter towards the brick wall of the building.

Freefalling towards the ground, Eli did the only thing he could think of; he drew his sword and plunged it into the brick. The sword cut right into the brick and quickly reduced the speed in which he was falling. By the time he came to a stop, Eli was only about five feet from the sidewalk.

In an instant, Zephyr was right beside him.

"Praise the King that you are okay, but what were you thinking? I'm not sure letting go of the gutter was a good idea. What would have happened if you dropped your sword, or if you could not draw it in time?"

"You might be right, but we can talk about this later! Hold me up a second so I can pull my sword out of the wall."

"Sure thing."

Zephyr held Eli up as he pulled his sword out of the wall and then Zephyr slowly lowered Eli to the ground.

The instant Eli's feet hit the ground, the group of enemies burst through the door out onto the roof. Eli sheaved his sword and looked around for a hiding place. Seeing an awning over the back entrance to the building, Eli motioned for Zephyr and they both took cover under the awning.

The moment they were under the awning one of the watchers commanded the group to look over the sides of the building to see if they could spot the defender.

Breathless, Eli pressed his body as close to the side of the building as he could get and cautiously looked up through a small rip in the awning. Soon Eli saw the long, ferocious snout of a ravenous wolf sticking over the side of the building. Eli could tell that the bent rain gutter had caught the attention of the wolf, but Eli could not see where the wolf's eyes were looking. Every moment felt like an eternity as Eli waited to see if they would have to fight. Eli had faced many different situations in training, but nothing Eli faced in training had prepared him for what happened next.

"Do any of you see anything? Any sign of the defender?" called out the watcher's voice from the roof.

Eli stood silently as he heard three other voices reply negatively from the three other sides of the building but hearing no reply from the wolf looking down on this side.

"You, wolf, did you hear me? I said do you see any sign of the defender?"

Eli froze waiting for the response and he could feel the tension in Zephyr's body as they huddled together underneath the awning. Hoping that the broken and bent rain gutter would not stand out from the rest of the war-torn surroundings, Eli heard the wolf reply with the words he was afraid to hear.

"Yes, I heard you, and yes I do see signs of the defender. In fact, he's standing right there!"

chapter 9

a gigantic close encounter

Excitement erupted on the roof and soon Eli saw several other shapes join the wolf looking down over the edge. Anticipating a fight for his survival, Eli's heart raced so fast he thought it would burst out of his chest. Instinctively Eli reached for his sword, but Zephyr stopped him by gently grabbing his arm. Eli glanced over at Zephyr and saw Zephyr shake his head slightly as if to say, "not yet". Eli nodded his head and looked up through the rip in the awning trying to not shake with anxiety.

Eli could see the group looking down at the bent gutter and scanning the area for any sign of life.

"Where, where is he?" demanded the watcher, "I told you all I saw a light! Now where is he?"

"Over there!" yelled the wolf as he pointed not at the awning but at a random empty space in the alley-way behind the buildings.

Eli could see all the heads of the watchers and wolves turn and look in the direction the wolf pointed.

"What?" continued the wolf, "Don't you see him? He is standing right there. Oh wait, no maybe that was the light you saw on the top of this building, you blind boggart! You never even saw a light, did you? You made us all run up five flights of stairs because you thought you saw something but you're wearing an iron blind-fold!"

The wolf speaking and the other wolf in the group growled threateningly and walked toward the watcher.

"Now wait just a minute." squeaked the watcher as he backed up from the edge of the roof and out of sight with the other watchers at his side, "We're allies! Remember what happened to the last group of wolves and watchers who fought? Let's just regroup and go find this defender. I bet your friend is chasing him right now. Let's just go and help. Okay?"

Part of Eli wanted to stay there and listen to whatever was going to happen next, but at that moment, Zephyr pulled on his arm.

"Come on, now is our chance to get moving."

"You're right." Eli whispered back, "But we can't follow the narrow street like we had planned. We know now that there are scouts watching it."

"Agreed. So tell me, do you know of any other way to get to the City on a Hill?"

"Yes, there is another way. I used to ride my bike to the arcade just down the street from here. If we can make it to the city park there is a jogging trail that leads right past the City on a Hill."

"Sounds good to me, lead the way."

Eli waited until he heard the yelling of the wolves and watchers recede into the stairwell leading off of the roof above and then swiftly crossed the alley-way behind the building and ducked behind a large dumpster. Cautiously, Eli peaked over the top of the dumpster to make sure the roof was clear of its former inhabitants.

"I think the coast is clear." whispered Eli, "Let's roll."

"Good idea, which way?"

Eli pointed to the left and was about to take off when the ground began to shake.

"Oh no!" whispered Zephyr.

The look on Zephyr's face told Eli everything he needed to know. Squeezing himself as close to the dumpster as possible, Eli lifted his head just high enough to see a giant dark silhouette running down the street toward the building he had just come off of. Every time one of the giant's feet would hit the ground, the ground would reverberate with its impact. In a matter of seconds, the giant had arrived and was looking down at the street on the other side of the building. Polytheist, who was currently in the form of a giant man with the head of a goat, carrying a long staff, stood glaring down at the entrance to the building. This form of Polytheist was familiar to Eli because it looked like the representation of Satan from the statue recently erected at the state courthouse. Polytheist was so gigantic that Eli could still see his head and shoulders over the five-story building.

"Where is he?" bellowed Polytheist apparently at the group of wolves and watchers who had just come out of the building.

"Where is the defender? I saw the portal open from my fortress. This is where he entered the Desolate City and this is where you were told to patrol. So, where is the defender?"

Apparently Polytheist's presence unnerved the group of wolves and watchers, because all Eli could hear was sputtering.

"Answer me!"

"Your terribleness." Eli finally heard what sounded like the lead watcher answer, "We were right over there. Yes, and I saw the portal open. But the wolves refused to believe me and they said that the defender would be travelling somewhere along the cursed narrow way. So, they argued and delayed and by the time I convinced them to come to the rooftop with me, the roof was empty with no sign of the defender at all."

The green fire in Polytheist's eyes erupted and green smoke rose from his eye sockets.

"Fools!" bellowed Polytheist and he took his staff and battered the top-half of the building.

Bricks and stones tumbled down across the side street and hammered into the dumpster behind which Eli and Zephyr hid.

"If you do not stop fighting like children and find the defender before he reaches the City on a Hill, I will make an example of you so terrible that the spirit realm will never forget it. Do you understand me?"

"Yes, my liege."

"Yes, your terribleness."

"We'll find that defender!"

"Come on guys, let's go. He could not have gotten far."

As the group of wolves and watchers left, Polytheist shook his head in disdain.

"Morons! I'm surrounded by morons."

Polytheist turned and scanned the alleys and roof-tops all around him before stomping back out of sight.

The pain in Eli's chest told him that he had been holding his breath for too long. Eli slowly exhaled and turned toward Zephyr.

"That was close!"

"Yes, that was really close."

Zephyr opened his mouth to speak but stopped suddenly when the voices of the wolves and watchers echoed through the alley-way.

"We're checking the alley-way first because if he came down off that building, he did not go out the front door." Explained the lead watcher in a tone of frustration.

"Don't get cocky with me." came a growling wolf's voice, "You may have been right about the portal but that doesn't make you the leader."

"Would you look at that," came another voice that Eli had not heard before. The voice was more human than wolf and so Eli assumed it came from one of the watchers. "It looks like that defender cut his way down the side of the building."

The wolves let out a threatening growl in unison. The growls were close and Eli knew the group was likely standing in the middle of the alley-way not 20 feet from the dumpster he was hiding behind.

"I wonder," said the unfamiliar watcher's voice, "if he is still around? If he had to slice his way down from the roof, I bet he could not have gotten far before we were on top of the roof. One thing I will say about our friends here is that with all their shortcomings, they do have keen eyesight. I believe our friend here would have seen him running had the defender tried to run away."

"That's right!" replied the lead wolf with surprising appreciation.

"So you think the defender is hiding somewhere in this alley?" replied the lead watcher in a mocking tone. "Well then, why can't your new friends here pick up on his scent? Don't wolves have amazing sense of smell?"

"Of course we do!" growled one of the wolves, "But I can't smell anything with all this dust in the air from Polytheist smashing the top of that building."

"Oh, how inconvenient." snapped the lead watcher. "So instead of going out looking for tracks, you all are sitting here hoping the defender is going to be miraculously hiding in this dumpster."

Eli slowly drew his sword as he heard the steps of the lead watcher walk over to the front of the dumpster. Eli ducked as the lid of the dumpster was thrown open and crashed against the back of the dumpster where his head was a moment before.

"Oh look." continued the lead watcher, "No defender in here. I guess he is not just going to fall into our laps. It looks like we might actually have to go looking for him. The defender is likely getting closer to the City on a Hill as we speak. Need I remind you what Polytheist said about making us an example? Now, let's get real. The defender is not in this dumpster or any other dumpster in this alley and we are not going to waste any more time standing here waiting for our doom! I was right about the portal and I am right about this! Let's move."

With grumbles of frustration, the group turned up the alley in the direction of the City on a Hill and began scouring for signs of Eli.

chapter 10

a dry and thirsty land

Eli waited until the sounds of the watchers and wolves could no longer be heard echoing down the alley. Moving slowly so as not to make a noise, Eli turned his head and looked at Zephyr.

"What just happened?"

"What just happened is the King gave us an opportunity to make it to the City on a Hill. Let's not wait and give the King another chance to bail us out. Let's get moving!"

"About that." said Eli, "The fastest way to the city park is the direction of the welcoming committee. If we want to get to the park, we will need to go to the right and enter the park where it borders the bank. It will take longer to get to the park, but at least that particular search party will not be a problem."

"I don't think we have any other options. Lead the way."

Swords drawn, Eli and Zephyr ran down the alley in the opposite direction of the search party. Eli and Zephyr travelled down the alley staying as close to the buildings on the right side of the alley as possible. Finally, they arrived at the building that bordered the backside of the city park. In the physical realm, the street on the front side of the building which ran parallel to the alley that Eli and Zephyr had just traversed was one of the city's busiest streets. Here in the Desolate City, however, this street looked abandoned. The building Eli was hugging was one of the city's large bank buildings with large sliding glass doors in the front and back. In the Desolate City, these doors had been shattered giving Eli a clear line of sight through the main lobby of the building into the abandoned street bordering the park.

"Let's go inside," whispered Eli, "we will be able to see where to cross the street and if there are any enemies out and about."

Eli walked over the shattered pieces of glass as softly as possible trying to not make any noise, but every crunch of glass under his boots echoed in the otherwise silent building. Entering the lobby area, Eli saw all of the offices that lined the walls of the lobby completely ransacked and destroyed. All of the desks and office furniture that decorated the bank building in the physical realm looked as if someone or something hacked them all to pieces with an ax. The only thing in the lobby that looked untouched for the most part was the large stone fountain that sat in the middle of the lobby.

Voices outside of the building's entrance broke through the silence. Knowing he was completely exposed in the empty lobby Eli frantically looked for cover. The only cover Eli could see was the fountain. Eli took off toward the fountain and was about to jump over the side of the fountain and hide inside the fountain when Zephyr suddenly grabbed Eli's clothes and jerked him backward onto the lobby floor.

"What did you do that for?"

"Quiet! I will explain in a moment."

Eli squeezed next to the fountain's brim and peeked over the edge. A small pack of three wolves walked down the street in front of the shattered glass doors of the bank building. Their voices bounced off the empty street and the walls of the lobby making it impossible for Eli to make out what they were saying, but Eli could see that they were annoyed with their task of walking the deserted streets of the Desolate City. After a few moments, the wolves had walked passed the front entrance and out of sight.

Feeling it was safe to talk, Eli looked at Zephyr.

"Now, would you please tell me why you went all commando on me?"

"I would not call that commando, I would call that saving your life." Zephyr answered as he pointed to the inside of the fountain.

Remaining on the ground in case the wolves walked back, Eli put his hands on the brim of the fountain and lifted his head high enough to see over the edge. The fountain had no bottom. Where the water pooled in the fountain in the physical realm, was only a bottomless pit of darkness.

"First. Thank you. Second, why is there a bottomless pit of darkness in the middle of the bank building?"

"It is not just in the bank building, anywhere there is a significant source of water in the physical realm is a bottomless pit of emptiness here in the Desolate City."

"But why?"

"It is one of the reasons the Desolate City is so desolate. Water has always been a source of life not only for people in the physical realm, but also here in the spirit realm. In the spirit realm, water is often used by the King as a means of spiritual refreshing and giving of life. But we are in the Desolate City, a place of no refreshing, of no hope, and no life-giving streams of water. The bottomless pits of emptiness are reminders that a land devoid of the King's life is a land of eternal drought and thirst."

"That's really depressing."

"Yes it is, and you are not the only one to think so. In fact, David, yes *the* David, after he spent some time serving the King in his own Desolate City, was inspired by the Desolate City to pen one of the more commonly known passages in the Psalms.

'O God, thou *art* my God; early will I seek thee: my soul thirsts for thee, my flesh longs for thee in a dry and thirsty land, where no water is'"

Eli thought about that for a moment.

"You know, I have never thought about the place David was describing as an actual place."

"You would be amazed at how many of the references made in the Scriptures are references to real places found throughout the spirit realm. "

Eli paused for a moment as a thought crossed his mind.

"So let me get this straight; everywhere there is water in the physical realm there would be bottomless pits of emptiness here?"

"Yes, why do you ask? Is that going to be a problem?"

"No." said Eli as he walked to the front of the building, "I don't think so."

That is, unless they are guarding the bridge.

chapter 11

watchers in waiting

Eli stood just to the side of the shattered glass-front entrance of the bank building looking across the street to the city park. Bordering the edge of the city park was a concrete fence. The city park had two main entrance gates, one located on each side of the park, however, Eli was nowhere near one of the entrances.

Fortunately for Eli, the concrete fence had not escaped the war-torn state of the Desolate City and sported several large cracks. Directly across from the bank entrance, Eli saw a crack just wide enough that he thought he could squeeze through.

Knowing that the street between the bank and the park was being patrolled, Eli knew that he and Zephyr needed to cross soon. Walking out of the building, Eli looked one more time down both sides of the street before running down the front steps of the bank building and across the street.

Eli knew he was in trouble when he arrived at the wall. The crack still looked wide enough for Eli to fit through but it was not as wide as it looked across the street. Now out in the open with no cover, Eli knew he had no other choice but to begin squeezing through the crevice. Immediately Eli started wiggling his body through the crack one piece at a time starting with his left arm. Eli had managed to get exactly half of his body through the crevice when he heard the wolves' voices returning from down the street they had walked earlier.

Panic struck Eli as he realized he could not even fight the wolves at this point with half of his body and his sword on the other side of the wall. Zephyr, who had stayed on the other side of the street to act as a look-out was waiving his hands frantically trying to communicate to Eli that he needed to hurry.

"I know! I'm trying!" mouthed Eli back to Zephyr, "But I'm stuck!"

"Don't move!" mouthed Zephyr to Eli as he pointed toward the intersection and the appearance of the wolves. Eli froze, not moving and trying his best to keep his breathing calm and under control. Zephyr disappeared into the building and Eli hoped that he had a plan.

"Bloody bad luck we all have," complained one of the wolves, "getting stuck walking up and down the same boring street hoping the defender will just show up."

"Forget that defender." answered another wolf, "I'd love to get my paws on one of those arrogant little watchers."

The three wolves all grunted their agreement before one of the wolves stopped in his tracks in front of the bank building entrance.

"Hey, do you smell that?" asked the wolf as he lifted his snout into the air and sniffed.

The other wolves followed suit and soon they were growling.

"It smells like this assignment might not be so boring after all."

A loud crash exploded in the alley behind the bank building as it sounded like something knocked over the trashcans.

"What are you waiting for?" yelled one of the wolves, "Don't let him get away!"

The three wolves dropped to all fours and sprinted into the bank building lobby. As soon as they went into the lobby, a blue and silver streak flew over the building and right up to Eli. Eli's eyes widened as Zephyr did not slow down.

"No, no no!" whispered Eli as he realized what Zephyr was going to do.

Eli's pleading did not stop Zephyr as he flew into Eli at high speed and shoved the rest of Eli's body through the crevice.

Eli rolled on the ground clasping his chest that the stone crevice scraped as he was pushed through.

"I'm sorry you're hurt, but we do not have time to sit here. The wolves will not take long to follow your scent back through the lobby and figure out where you have gone. They will be on our trail soon, we need to get to the City on a Hill as fast as possible. Where is that jogging trail?"

The desperation in Zephyr's voice moved Eli to action. He stood up off the ground and looked around. The part of the city park Eli and Zephyr had crossed into was a heavily wooded section with plenty of vegetation to conceal them. Eli knew that the vegetation would conceal them from sight, but the wolves would be able to sniff them out. Fortunately Eli was very familiar with where they were, they were right next to the jogging trail that lead by the Open Door Church in the physical realm which happened to be the City on a Hill in the spirit realm.

"Over there."

Eli pointed to a dirt path not far from where they were standing.

"That's the jogging trail that leads to the City on a Hill."

"Praise the King!" exclaimed Zephyr, "Go, go, go, go!"

Eli and Zephyr took off down the trail and for probably the first time in his life, Eli was glad he lived in a small town. They had not been running very long and already, Eli knew they were drawing closer to the City on a Hill. As Eli had predicted, the jogging trail seemed abandoned and they had not run into any patrols whatsoever. But as the two raced down the trail, there was still a nagging thought in the back of Eli's mind about the bridge.

The city park was designed around a small river that flowed through the town. The original founders of Eli's town first settled here because of the abundance of fresh water. Now, over a hundred years later, the town had spread out from the river, but the city park had been designed to preserve the river that brought the settlers here. Unfortunately, there was no way to avoid crossing the river on the jogging trail as it lead to a large arched bridge. As long as the bridge was clear, Eli knew that they could make it to the City on a Hill. Originally, Eli thought that if the bridge was guarded, he and Zephyr could simply go downstream and cross at an unguarded section. Ever since he learned the truth about water in the Desolate City, he could only hope the bridge was not guarded.

"Hey Zeph." huffed Eli as they ran, "I need to tell you about a possible problem."

"Let me guess, there's a large bridge and you think it might be guarded by a garrison of enemies?"

"Yes that's it exactly! How did you know?"

Eli did not need Zephyr to answer because at that moment the large bridge came into sight, and as Eli had feared, it was guarded with a garrison of watchers.

Eli quickly ducked into the brush and crept up slowly to get a better picture of what lay ahead of them. Eli's heart sank as the clearing in the brush allowed Eli to see the towering walls of the City on a Hill maybe half a mile passed the bridge. But that bridge was going to be a problem. Ten watchers meandered around the entrance to the bridge looking bored. The bridge spanned a large bottomless crevice of emptiness at least twenty feet wide. Eli knew there would be no jumping over it. The only way for him to get to the City on a Hill was to somehow cross that bridge.

Though the watchers did not look like they were expecting a fight, Eli could tell they were ready for battle because they all carried the dark iron chain with an iron ball on the end of it. Unlike the wolves, the watchers did not have bulging muscles one would assume they would need to carry such weapons, but Eli was sure the watchers could swing their weapons with more than adequate force to cause injury.

"Any ideas?" asked Zephyr.

"Not yet, but give me a minute and I will come up with something."

Before Eli could finish his sentence, the sound of wolves howling echoed down the jogging trail.

Instantly the watchers all looked down the trail.

"What do you suppose those oversized-beagles are yapping about now?" asked one of the watchers.

"Who knows?" answered another watcher, "Perhaps they have discovered their own tails and are in the process of chasing them down."

The group of watchers burst into laughter and continued walking around, but Zephyr had a very different reaction to the howling.

"It sounds like the wolves figured out where we went. Eli, we don't have a minute."

Eli drew his sword, "Well, then, we attack!"

With his sword drawn, Eli closed his eyes and concentrated. *What truth can I use to defeat the watchers*? Thought Eli as he connected with the Illuminator. Soon his answer came in bright burning letters in his mind.

"But there were false prophets also among the people, even as there shall be false teachers among you, who privily shall bring in damnable heresies, even denying the Lord that bought them, and bring upon themselves swift destruction."

Eli and his sword burst into blue flame and Eli felt the pain of the Spirit at the work of the watchers who snatch up the spiritually enlightened and teach them to deny the very God who awakened them. Without making any plans or giving Zephyr any type of warning, Eli opened his eyes and charged the camp of watchers.

The closest watcher looked up just in time to see Eli's sword slice across his chest. Instantly the physical body of the watcher disappeared and the watcher's spirit, now free from the bondage of the blindfold and shackles flew back to the broad street. Though Eli was surprised at what he just witnessed, he continued his attack with ferocity.

Choosing to attack the group of watchers on his right, Eli turned toward them and made it to the first two watchers before they had the opportunity to get their weapons swinging. Two more quick slices and the broad street had two more wandering lost residents. The last two watchers on the right side were ready for Eli. Eli turned toward them just in time to dive to his left to avoid the first watcher's ball and chain. The second watcher anticipated Eli's move and had his ball and chain aimed directly at Eli's head. Just before the ball were to crush Eli, Zephyr flew in front of it and batted it away with his sword. With the watcher unarmed, Eli dispatched the watcher without delay. Eli turned toward the last watcher but could feel the other watchers running toward him. Knowing there were another five watchers coming up right behind him, Eli could not focus on the last watcher on his right. Pouring all of his zeal from the Spirit into his sword, Eli turned and slashed a broad swing toward the group of oncoming watchers. A powerful wave of blue light spread through the air sending another five wandering lost to the broad street.

But Eli knew he was in trouble. He could sense the oncoming attack and could hear the large iron ball whistling through the air. Eli turned around just in time to see the large iron ball crash into his head.

Eli stood there with his eyes closed. Slowly he opened them to find, to his great surprise, pieces of the large iron ball laying all around his feet. The iron ball connected directly with Eli's head and smashed to pieces without harming him. Eli was surprised but not near as surprised as the watcher. The watcher backed up slowly shaking his head in disbelief.

"I don't understand." stammered the watcher, "How could you withstand that attack without any damage?"

"It is the helmet of salvation." answered Zephyr, "You see, watcher, true salvation and true power is found in the gifts of the King, not the watchtower. Against the power of the King's helmet of salvation, your weapons are powerless."

As the watcher backed up, something interesting began to happen. The shackle around his neck fell to the ground and bolts began popping out of his iron blindfold like popcorn in a popcorn machine. The blindfold fell off and immediately a beam of light from the City on a Hill struck the eyes of the watcher. Instantly, the watcher was transported from the entrance of the bridge back to the Desolate City, but this time, Eli could see that the watcher did not return to the broad street but the narrow street.

"Did that just happen?" asked Eli in wonder, "Did we just rescue that watcher?"

"Technically, the King and His light rescued that watcher, but yes, you just witnessed a watcher being rescued."

Before Eli could respond, a growling voice interrupted their conversation.

"You may have rescued that watcher, but who is going to rescue you?"

Eli spun around to see the three wolves from the abandoned street standing in the opening of the trail followed by a whole pack of wolves. Behind the wolves Eli could see a large group of watchers sprinting down the trail trying to catch up to their faster allies. The three wolves from the street howled and charged.

chapter 12

a race to the gates

The first wolf reached Eli in a matter of seconds, but Eli was ready for it. Lunging forward with his sword in a jab position, Eli was able to stab the wolf before he could rise up on his hind legs and attack. The wolf disappeared in an explosion of light and the two other wolves from the street backed off from their charge.

After dispelling the first wolf, Eli's sword once again was aflame with fire. Eli stuck his sword in the ground and drew a semi-circle in the ground creating a flaming barrier between him and the enemies.

With the barrier temporarily stopping the advance of enemies, Eli slowly backed up onto the bridge with his sword in striking position. The flames died out and the entire group of wolves and watchers slowly advanced in a semi-circle formation, completely closing Eli onto the bridge. The wolves barred their fangs at Eli and the watchers in the back of the group swung their weapons in the air like lassos.

"What do you think Zeph? Can we make it to the City on a Hill if we run for it?"

"Not likely. The wolves are too fast, unless we can somehow slow them down, you won't make it."

"What about you? Could you hold them off while I run to the City on a Hill?"

"That won't work either. Remember, I am a guardian Angelos, I do not have permission from the King to attack any of the creatures unless you are in immediate danger. Besides, Eli, if I enter the conflict, I will open the door for the Enemy's Angelos to enter into the conflict. Trust me when I say, that right now, that is the last thing we want to happen."

Eli had reached the center of the bridge when one of the watchers to Eli's right flung its ball and chain at Eli. The iron ball struck the side of the bridge and crushed the guardrail near Eli sending pieces of the bridge tumbling into the bottomless emptiness below. Already in a war-torn state, the bridge shook and several cracks formed all around the point of impact.

"Stop it you fool!" cried one of the wolves nearest Eli, "You will bring the whole bridge down with your stupidity!"

"So what?" replied the watcher, "At least the defender will be gone."

"The wolf's right." answered another watcher, "As much as it pains me to say it, Polytheist wants the defender, or at least his body, in hand. If he falls into the emptiness below, we will all feel Polytheist's wrath."

The wolf in the front of the pack of enemies growled at Eli.

"Give it up boy! You are hopelessly outnumbered. You can't defeat all of us and you cannot out run us. If you come peaceably, I promise no harm will come to you by our hands. We will take you to Polytheist in one piece. If you choose to reject my offer, I can promise you that you will still go to Polytheist, but your condition will be much more painful. Put your sword down, and come with us. You have to the count of three before we charge! One. Two."

"Okay, okay, you win. You want me to put my sword down, I will put my sword down."

The wolf smiled in satisfaction until he saw what Eli was doing. Eli lifted his sword high into the air with the point facing down. Then Eli plunged the sword into the center of the bridge. The sword cut right through the bridge and the impact shook the already war-torn structure.

Large cracks rapidly spread across the entire width and length of the bridge. The wolves jumped backward onto the ground avoiding the cracks. Before Eli could lift his sword out of the bridge, the center of the arch had already began crumbling and falling into the vast emptiness below. Eli turned and ran as fast as he could to the other side of the bridge but had a difficult time getting a good grip because the bridge underneath his feet was rapidly crumbling.

"This was your plan?" shouted Zephyr as he flew by Eli's side.

"It's all I could think of. At least the wolves are not able to follow, right?"

"Yes, technically you're right, but what good will it do you if you find yourself falling into dark emptiness?"

"Positive thoughts, Zeph, think positive thoughts!" was all Eli could yell back as the remainder of the bridge crumbled into the darkness below forcing Eli to jump in desperation to make it to the other side of the shore. With visions of the Room of Fire from the mausoleum flashing in his mind, Eli could only flail his arms and legs as it appeared he would fall short of the other side. Suddenly, something struck Eli from behind pushing him forward to where he landed safely on the other shore.

Turning around, Eli saw Zephyr hovering close to the shore fixing his helmet that had somehow gotten knocked crooked.

"I totally would have made it."

"Totally. That is if your goal was bottomless emptiness. You totally would have achieved your goal."

Angry howls and calls of frustration from the other shore brought Eli back to attention.

"Come on, Eli, we need to go before they figure out a way across!"

"Way ahead of you."

Eli rose to his feet to run down the trail when a terrifying howl grabbed his attention. One of the wolves had attempted to jump the chasm only to come a few feet short and fall into the emptiness below.

Eli turned and ran down the trail toward the City on a Hill when several loud thuds and cheering from behind Eli caught his attention. Eli looked over his shoulder and saw several large iron balls embedded into the shore with the chains connected to the balls creating a type of chain bridge. Starting across the chain bridge as fast as they could without falling were several wolves with their eyes fixed on Eli. Eli knew it would only be a few moments before the wolves would successfully cross to Eli's side of the chasm.

"Run!" yelled Eli as he ran as fast as he could toward the City on a Hill.

Eli ran down the jogging path jumping over roots and at times ducking under low-lying branches. Not long into his run, Eli heard the howling of the wolves signaling they had made it to the other side and were in pursuit of their prey. Knowing the great speed of the wolves pushed Eli to press on toward the city with all he had. With every turn Eli ran around and with every hill Eli climbed, the giant fortress city grew closer.

Howls from the wolves exploded extremely near Eli and he could hear the sound of massive paws running on the path directly behind him. Eli took his sword and began slicing every tree, tree branch, and any other vegetation on the side of the path hoping they would fall on the path and slow the wolves. The plan worked, but though Eli bought some time, the wolves were still gaining on him. Finally, the jogging trail opened up to the clearing that bordered the City on a Hill.

Spilling into the clearing at full speed, Eli could see an almost invisible barrier, like a large wall of bubble solution circling the great walls of the City on a Hill.

"There, Eli, we must cross the barrier!" shouted Zephyr, "That is the King's barrier and it protects the city from all enemies. If we can cross that barrier, we will be safe."

Eli tried to respond but involuntarily cried out in pain as one of the wolves struck Eli in the back with his massive paw. Eli could feel the razor sharp claws cut through his uniform and slice his body.

"Eli, no!" cried Zephyr as he immediately flew behind Eli and engaged the wolf.

Eli kept running knowing that Zephyr could handle himself in a battle. A bright burst of light from behind him told Eli that the wolf that struck him was no longer a threat. Hobbling a little as the searing pain of the wolf's claws throbbed on his back, Eli was mere feet from safety. All Eli had to do was cross between two large trees and he would be able to cross the barrier. Just feet away from the barrier, Eli leapt forward, head first, into the barrier. But he never made it. Standing behind the two trees were the two watchers who cast a glowing net between the trees that caught Eli and held him inches from the barrier.

Eli struggled to get free but the tares moved fast, wrapping the net around him, pulling him away from the barrier, and pinning him to the ground.

The surprise! thought Eli, *I can't believe I forgot about the surprise!*

Eli struggled violently, but to no avail. In no time he was completely surrounded by the pack of wolves who helped hold him down.

A flash of blue and silver cut across Eli's vision and one of the tares evaporated into a burst of chaff into the air.

"Arg!" grunted the other tare, "where are those Arkhay'? Don't they know we have an Angelos to deal with?"

At that moment, Zephyr made another pass and this time three of the wolves holding Eli down where picked up and thrown into the air as they exploded in light. Eli's hopes sprung up as he was free enough to draw his sword and cut the net off of him. Looking up, Eli could see Zephyr diving down one last time to give Eli enough freedom to cross the barrier when several dark flashes intercepted Zephyr and threw him to the ground. These three flashes produced a glowing net of their own and cast it onto Zephyr.

"NO!" yelled Eli as the net wrapped itself around Zephyr pinning him to the ground.

This momentary pause in Eli's actions allowed the remaining wolves to tackle him and hold him down.

Too worried about his guardian Angelos to care about his predicament, Eli lay there in shock as the three flashes came to a halt hovering over Zephyr. Seeing these new enemies for the first time in his adventures in the spirit realm, Eli lost hope of ever making it to the City on a Hill.

chapter 13

familiar faces

"Look here boys." laughed one of the three creatures hovering over Eli and Zephyr in a surprisingly human sounding voice.

"Yeah." answered another one of the creatures, "It looks like we caught ourselves a defender and his little Angelos slave."

These creatures looked like they could be kin to Angelos, but definitely not Angelos. These creatures were about the same height of Zephyr, but looked malnourished and starved. Instead of muscles, these creatures looked like skeletons covered with a thin layer of colorless skin. The eyes and hair of these creatures, which if they were Angelos would be a unique and full color, were also pale and colorless. These creatures had wings in the same place on their backs that Angelos had, only their wings were only made up of bones, having no skin and no feathers. For clothing these creatures wore a black body-suit much like the armor the Enemy wore when he appeared to Eli in the Cemetery of the Old Man. Hanging on the belts of these creatures were long, crooked-bladed, black swords.

"Now." spoke up the tare with his branches still wrapped around Eli, "I hope you tell the Master who it was that actually caught the defender. I don't want to share the glory with any of the wolves or watchers who failed to stop the defender from traversing the Desolate City."

The wolves growled at the tare, but their annoyance only seemed to encourage the tare's rant.

"If you ask me, the Enemy would do well to rid himself of their incompetence."

"Easy there plant-man." cut in one of the three creatures that resembled Angelos, "Be careful how you evaluate the choices of the Master. The Master knows what he is doing and his servant Polytheist has found profitable uses for the wolves and the watchers outside the realm of scouting parties."

"The Master?" called Zephyr in a mocking tone, "Did you just call the Enemy, 'the Master'?"

The flying creatures reacted to Zephyr's words with obvious rage, "Yes I did, *slave,* and what is that to you?"

Zephyr responded in an almost laughing tone, "Well, it is just that with all the shame and condemnation following the Enemy has caused you, I find it absolutely astonishing that you would still follow him. I just thought that after all these years of shame knowing that your doom awaits you for serving that wicked traitor that you would at least have enough dignity to not continue serving him."

"Wait!" blurted out Eli, whose curiosity got the best of him even in this dire circumstance, "So you three used to be Angelos?"

Immediately the three flying creatures turned their attention toward Eli as one of the creatures spat, "Don't ever call us that cursed word again. We are not mere messengers for the corrupted King; we left that life of weakness long ago. We are now the Arkhay'; the principality, the powers."

"Or you can just call them the shamed, the defeated, those awaiting their punishment for rebelling against the King."

Eli had never seen Zephyr so bold, but then again, Eli had never seen Zephyr encounter the traitorous group of Arkhay' who used to minister alongside of him before the rebellion. The Arkhay' who had first spoken to the tares glared at Zephyr for a moment and then smiled a twisted and wicked smile.

"Bring the wagon up! We will load this pathetic excuse for a defender and take him to Polytheist. I'm sure Polytheist will enjoy playing with his new toy."

Another one of the Arkhay' whistled and a large wooden wagon that reminded Eli of the prison wagons from the old western movies his grandfather watched rolled into sight from down the street that led from the Desolate City. Pulling this wagon was a team of four skeletal horses, being driven by two watchers, and the wagon was surrounded by a pack of wolves.

"Well, Zeph." whispered Eli as he evaluated their situation, "It's your turn to come up with a plan?"

Zephyr struggled to turn his head and look at Eli. Instead of a grim look, Zephyr actually was grinning and he winked at Eli.

"Patience Eli, I have a feeling we are not the only ones who were not expecting a surprise attack."

"As for this one," continued the Arkhay' as he pointed toward Zephyr, "we will take him back to our Master and then we will see just how brave he really is."

At that moment, the wagon exploded in a burst of bright yellow light destroying the watchers driving the wagon and sending their spirits back to the broad street. Several of the wolves accompanying the wagon also disappeared while the other wolves ran away with their fur singed from the light. The team of skeletal horses galloped away dragging the remaining pieces of the wagon straight through the crowd of wolves and watchers gathered around Eli knocking several to the ground.

Eli watched as a glowing spear of yellow light flew into the air from the other side of the barrier. This spear of light landed directly on top of the tare's branches that wrapped around Eli. The tare yelled in pain but was silenced when the spear erupted like a light grenade and turned the tare into a pile of chaff.

Now free from his bonds, Eli quickly picked up his sword, and turned to face the rest of the group of enemies. To Eli's amazement the enemies, at least what was left of them, were retreating back into the jogging trail and the Desolate City as arrows of yellow light and more light spears where raining down on them.

"Cursed citizens!" screamed the lead Arkhay' as a group of people clad in glowing armor launched their own ambush from the other side of the King's barrier.

Eli quickly turned to try and free Zephyr when a brave group of three watchers advanced from the chaos with another attempt to bind Eli. Eli stood in between Zephyr and the advancing watchers ready to defend his friend, but he did not have to. A flash of black and gold flew over Eli and landed in front of the middle watcher slamming the watcher in the head with a large staff sending the watcher's spirit back to the broad street. The man's staff captured Eli's attention because it reminded Eli of his sword. The staff was made from some sort of black steel with a golden ribbon wrapping itself up the staff in the same way Eli's sword had a majestic blue ribbon on the blade. When the man wielded the staff, it glowed with the bright yellow light of the King.

As for the rest of the man, he looked like a ninja-shepherd mix. This guy had on robes that looked like the garments shepherds who live in the Middle-East wear, and had a head piece that covered his entire face except for his eyes. The robes and hood were a solid black but had golden accents such as the belts, face covering, head bands, and boots.

Before the other two watchers could react, the shepherd thrust his staff to either side sending the broad street two more former watchers.

With the wolves and watchers in full retreat, two other citizens came out and stood next to Eli facing the Arkhay'. These two citizens caught Eli off guard because they were not adults like the shepherd but were younger more like Eli's age. There was one boy and one girl, and they looked absolutely astonishing.

The girl was wearing the same white elastic-like clothes Eli received from the castle covering her from her ankles to her neck and down each are to her wrists, but her attire included glowing neon-purple armor. The girl's armor looked and glowed as if it were metallic. The armor included a female-cut breastplate and back plate connected with two shoulder straps that stretched off to the girl's sides covering the tops of her shoulders, a pair of arm guards that covered her arms from her wrists to her elbows, a skirt that covered her waist to her knees, and knee-high boots. Strapped across her back was a large, glowing purple quiver full of glowing light arrows, and in her left hand, she carried a beautiful metallic neon-purple bow.

The boy citizen looked equally impressive standing looking like a renegade motorcycle warrior. The boy too had a basic layer of elastic white clothes but his armor included black and gold camouflage pants tucked into glowing gold boots and held up with a glowing gold belt. The upper body armor included a form fitting black leather vest zipped up to his neck. On his head, the boy wore a black motorcycle helmet with a transparent yellow light visor and a Mohawk made from golden spikes. In his right hand, the boy held an intimidating spear made of pure yellow light.

Eli's new allies looked terrifying, but it was their faces that Eli could not look away from. The reason for Eli's fascination was the fact that these two terrifying warriors were friends of Eli's from the physical realm. Ella and Aiden Thomas were old friends of Eli's from when his family used to attend The Open Door Church. Eli's mind raced with all the possibilities of what this meant and a million different questions for his friends, but his thoughts were interrupted by the cruel voice of the Arkhay'.

"What do you all think you are going to do? You know that you do not have the power to kill the Arkhay'."

True." shouted back the adult citizen who sounded, to Eli's amazement, a lot like Pastor Thomas, "And you know that the Arkhay' do not have the authority to enter into conflict with the citizens of the King's city. Your doom, which is already appointed by the King, will come swiftly if you so choose to break the command of the King."

The lead Arkhay' drew his crooked bladed sword with confidence while the other two Arkhay' looked around nervously as they drew their crooked bladed swords.

"Have it your way, keep your defender. We captured him once, we can capture him again. However, we will take our prize and be off."

With lightning quickness the lead Arkhay' grabbed the glowing net which imprisoned Zephyr and rose in the air laughing pointedly at Eli.

The sight of Zephyr trapped in the metal netting in the grasp of the wicked Arkhay' was more than Eli could handle. Zephyr was not only Eli's guardian Angelos, he was also Eli's best friend. Eli did not know what he could do against three Arkhay', but Eli did know that he wasn't going to allow these wicked traitors to kidnap Zephyr without a fight.

Eli was so focused on saving Zephyr that he did not realize his whole body was glowing with the powerful blue light of his sword. Upon seeing Eli radiate with the light, Ella and Aiden cautiously backed away from him and the Arkhay' stopped laughing.

"I don't know what you are thinking, boy, but if you are thinking of trying to save your friend, you better think twice. We are more powerful than you can imagine. Our power comes directly from the Enemy himself. Any attempt to save your Angelos will end in your death."

Eli knew the Arkhay' was not bluffing. He knew that the King created His ministers with powers far superior to that of humans. Eli knew that to attempt to save Zephyr he would be risking his life. But he also felt the Illuminator fill him with power. Focusing on the power of the Illuminator, Eli closed his eyes and allowed the King's Word to fill his mind. As the King's Word burned into his mind, Eli spoke with powerful confidence.

"Your power is great and I can see the malice of the Enemy in you. However, you are about to learn a lesson that your master had to learn the hard way."

"Oh, really?" mocked the lead Arkhay' as black energy erupted around him, "And what might that be?"

As Eli spoke the words that were burned into his mind, he instinctively pointed his sword directly at the lead Arkhay' who was holding Zephyr.

"Greater is He that is in me, than he that is in the world."

As soon as Eli finished speaking the King's Word, a powerful blue ray of light erupted from Eli's sword and blasted the lead Arkhay' sending him sprawling backwards through the air. The impact of Eli's attack knocked Zephyr's net out of the Arkhay's grasp. Eli ran over and caught Zephyr before he hit the ground. Still glowing with the power of the King's word, Eli ripped open the metal netting with his sword freeing Zephyr from his bonds.

As soon as Zephyr was free, he drew his sword and the light that was radiating off of Eli instantly exploded off of Zephyr as well. The two nodded at each other and then turned their fierce gaze to the Arkhay'.

Smoke sizzled off of the lead Arkhay' as he recovered and faced Eli. Though it looked like Eli's blast had stung the lead Arkhay', he was far from defeated.

"You will pay for that, defender!" screamed the lead Arkhay' as he lifted his sword and radiated with black energy.

"Sir." shouted one of the Arkhay', "We do not have permission to attack the defender at this time. You risk the".

The lead Arkhay' cut off the other Arkhay'.

"Silence! I know what I am risking, but this boy deserves it. No one strikes me and lives!"

At this point, the lead Arkhay' was completely engulfed in a powerful sphere of black energy. Yelling insanely, the lead Arkhay' pointed his crooked-bladed sword at Eli and released a massive beam of black energy. Eli lifted his glowing sword in front of him and prepared to defend himself, but he did not have to.

In an instant, a massive glowing wall appeared in front of Eli blocking his view of the Arkhay' and the black beam. The next thing Eli knew, the black beam had been deflected toward and harmlessly absorbed by the King's barrier. As Eli attempted to figure out what was going on, a familiar voice boomed from the glowing wall in front of him.

"Arkhay', by the command of the King, you do not have permission to engage in conflict with the King's defender nor the citizens of His city. You have broken the King's command and now you must suffer the consequences."

Eli stumbled backwards until he was able to see the Arkhay' looking terrified. Eli did not blame the Arkhay' because he too would have been terrified if an angry and powered up Michael had just condemned him. Eli had never seen Michael like this; radiating with light and power. His massive frame was tensed and ready for a fight and his white robes were overlapped with golden battle armor. Michael grasped his gigantic golden spear in his right hand and had it pointing at the lead Arkhay'.

"No, wait!" sputtered the lead Arkhay' as he visibly shook in fear, "It's not fair, he".

"Silence, traitor!" commanded Michael, "The King's command forbid you from engaging the defender. *You* broke the command, and now you will pay."

At that moment, a powerful blast of light exploded from the tip of Michael's spear and struck the lead Arkhay'. The blast was so powerful that it knocked Eli backwards onto the ground. When Eli recovered and looked up, the lead Arkhay' was gone and his crooked-bladed sword was falling to the ground. The sword clanged on the ground and the other two Arkhay' raised their hands in surrender.

"Do not fear." said Michael to the remaining Arkhay', "You have not broken the King's command at this time. You will not face judgment now. Leave my presence and await your time of judgment elsewhere."

The two Arkhay' nodded their heads and then flew toward the horizon leaving only a streak of black in their wake.

chapter 14

the red brick road

The group watched the trail of the Arkhay' until it disappeared into the crimson sky.

"That was totally awesome!" yelled Aiden, "You blew that Arkhay' right out of the sky Michael!"

"Thank you for that assessment, Aiden. But I must say that I am more impressed with the courage you all showed today and especially with the power Eli was able to harness. Very well done Eli, very well done indeed."

Eli had no idea where to start. He wanted to question Ella and Aiden and figure out how they got to the spirit realm and what they did here. He also wanted to check to make sure that the ninja-shepherd guy was Pastor Thomas, but the first question that surfaced from the ocean of questions swirling in his head was to Michael.

"What do you mean? What was so impressive about what I did? It looked like I nearly got myself killed."

"Allow me to explain, but as I explain let's get you inside the King's barrier."

As the group walked to the barrier, Michael continued.

"You made a choice. A choice that incorporated the greatest elements and sources of power in all creation."

"I did?"

"Yes you did. You knew you were outnumbered and weaker than the Arkhay', yet you still chose to engage them. You did so because of your love for Zephyr. Knowing that you could not gain the victory in your own power, your love for Zephyr pushed you to make a choice to sacrifice your life in order to try and save his. Are you following me, because this is exactly what we have talked about all through your training? Love and sacrifice are two of the three most powerful elements in creation. Tell me, what is the third?"

Eli thought for a moment about all of his training and all of the lessons he had learned from his time in the Spirit realm.

"Faith. Love, sacrifice, and faith."

"Exactly. When your love for Zephyr fueled your willingness to sacrifice yourself for him, you engaged a superior enemy depending on the King and His Word for the power to win the victory. When you put all three of these elements into play, the Illuminator opened a powerful truth from the King's Word that, in fact, gave you the power to gain the victory and save Zephyr. The reason for your mission is for you to learn how to do what you just did."

The group had walked up to the barrier and Ella, Aiden, and Pastor Thomas all crossed over the barrier, but Michael stopped outside the barrier.

"Aren't you coming in?"

"No, I was sent to defend you from the Arkhay' and execute the judgment of the King upon its disobedience. Now that you are safe, I am needed elsewhere."

"Can I ask you just one more question?"

"Sure, Eli."

"You said that the reason for this mission is for me to learn how to do what I just did. This is something that I keep hearing but I don't quite understand. Can you please explain what this whole claiming thing is?"

"Of course. The claiming is a type of right-of-passage for a defender. When a defender faces a claiming, that defender faces enemies far greater in number and in power than the defender. Understand that you cannot gain the victory and accomplish your mission on your own. The only way for you to be successful is to do what you just did: to literally stake your life upon the truths of the King's Word. It is only as you abandon your reservations and place complete faith in the truths of the King's Word that you will discover the true power of the King's Word and gain the power you need to overcome. Farewell Eli, and may the King's face always shine upon you, *master* defender."

Michael winked at Eli as he emphasized, 'master', and then disappeared in a burst of bright light. With Michael gone, Eli crossed through the barrier. As he did, the wounds he incurred from the race to the city healed instantly. Inside the barrier, Eli found an ecstatic looking Ella and Aiden Thomas standing next to their father, Pastor Thomas. Pastor Thomas' gold face covering was pulled down so Eli could clearly see that it was in fact the Thomas family he knew from the physical realm.

"I don't even know where to begin." said Eli as he shook his head and smiled, "Hi, I guess."

The Thomas family looked at each other and then back at Eli chuckling. Pastor Thomas stepped forward and extended his hand to shake Eli's.

"Welcome, defender. It's an honor to finally meet you. After the promotion of your grandfather, we have been praying diligently that the King would send this region a new defender. I must say that I'm both surprised and pleased with the choice of the King."

"It's so amazing to see you here Eli!" Ella jumped in, "I mean, one moment Aiden and I are heading to the celebration of your grandfather's life and the next moment we are pulled into the sprit realm and told about this new defender who has already conquered the Cemetery of the Old Man and is on his way to the City on a Hill."

"Yeah." added Aiden, "Then, all of a sudden, dad comes up and tells us that the new forces of the

Enemy here in the Desolate City have set an ambush outside the King's barrier for the defender and we were going to set an ambush for their ambush."

"So we get in place." cut in Ella, "And who do we see running toward us? You! I almost yelled for joy and gave away our position!"

Eli had no idea how to respond to all he was seeing and hearing.

"I can't believe you all are here! I mean, you all here in the spirit realm. Not only are you all here, but you're warriors, really terrifying looking warriors!"

Eli turned and looked at Zephyr.

"Zeph, did you know about this? Oh, by the way, Zeph this is Ella, Aiden, and Pastor Thomas. Thomas family this is Zephyr my guardian Angelos."

"It is nice to meet you all." said Zephyr, "And to answer your question, yes Eli I did know about the Thomas family and their presence in the spirit realm, but I did not know to what extent your mission would bring you into contact with them."

"Ella, Aiden." said Pastor Thomas, "Please run ahead into the city and tell the Council of Light that we will be arriving shortly. I would like to escort Eli and Zephyr into the city alone.

"Yes sir." the siblings said in unison.

Before taking off, Aiden acted like he was whispering to Eli, "A little advice for you man, watch out for that staff, it definitely smarts if he hits you on the head with it."

"Should we give Eli a demonstration son?"

"No sir, on my way, see you all in a little bit."

Aiden and Ella jogged into the city.

Laughing at his son, Pastor Thomas put his right hand on Eli's back, "Come Eli, I want to talk with you a little."

The two began walking slowly up the narrow road that lead to the City on a Hill's gates.

"I don't know if you are aware or not, but your grandfather and I were very close after his salvation. In the physical realm our friendship was a short-lived one, but here in the spirit realm, your grandfather and I spent many years working side-by-side striving to reach the wandering lost of the Desolate City. I remember when your grandfather became a defender. I remember when your grandfather faced his own claiming and I want to encourage you Eli."

"I don't know what all awaits you out in the Desolate City, but I do know that in all the years I have worked here as a harvester and under-shepherd, I have never encountered such a powerful grouping of enemies as is present in the city now."

"That's not all that encouraging."

"No, it's not, but I am not finished. I want you to know that even though you are going to face difficulties like you have never faced before, I know that you can be successful. I have heard rumors that Polytheist himself is in the Desolate City and leading this new army, and if that is the case, then I cannot imagine the struggle that awaits you. However, you are not the first defender to face impossible odds, every defender has faced them in his or her own claiming and those who have relied on the power of the King have found victory. And Eli, it is imperative that you gain the victory here."

Pastor Thomas stopped and spread his arms toward the Desolate City.

"Look out there in the Desolate City. There are thousands of wandering souls walking to their destruction. The need to reach them with the light of the gospel is great, but the King has allowed our enemies to dim the great light. The light is more than sufficient to reach the lost when at full power, but we need to re-claim the reflectors and return the light to full strength as soon as possible."

"Eli, I wanted to talk to you before we enter the City on a Hill because I wanted you to know two things. First, I want you to know that whatever your mission and however impossible it may seem, you have our full support. We will help you in every way possible. I cannot tell you how excited my children are to finally have someone else they know in the physical realm join them in their work for the King. Second, I wanted to tell you that the Desolate City was your grandfather's personal ministry passion. Your grandfather was known for his passion to reach the wandering lost. Every opportunity he had, he spent walking up and down the broad street striving to awaken the eyes of the wandering lost. His passion was so powerful that whenever he walked the streets, the wolves, watchers, and even the tares steered clear of him. I just wanted to tell you Eli that when your mission gets difficult, remember that you are not only representing the King, the City on a Hill, and all the harvesters working in the Desolate City, you are also fulfilling your grandfather's greatest passion in ministry. I figured you would like to know that."

Tears filled Eli's eyes as he listened to Pastor Thomas talk about his grandfather and his passion for the wandering lost.

"Thank you, Pastor."

Eli walked in silence as he considered all that Pastor Thomas had told him. After a moment of reflection, Pastor Thomas stopped walking and spread his arms toward the City on a Hill.

"I present to you, the great City on a Hill."

The City on the Hill was a fortress built on a mountain-like hill. Eli had seen pictures of the city during his briefing, but seeing the massive fortress in person took his breath away. The massive fortress city had towering walls of pure white stone that radiated the golden light of the gospel. The only entrance to the city was through a massive set of gates with a deep red coloring.

The narrow street led all the way from the Desolate City to the very gates of the City on a Hill. Now, almost to the gates, the Narrow Way turned into a red-brick road that matched the color of the gates. When the company set foot on the red-brick road, a sign appeared to the left of the road:

"Welcome weary traveler, to the Path of Grace"

The sign intrigued Eli, but soon his attention was demanded elsewhere as he approached four large, brass statues with large square brass bases lining the Path of Grace. The statues were symmetrical with two statues on each side of the way lined up perfectly with the statues on the other side of the way. As he approached, Eli noticed that the first two statues included a statue of a brass net and a statue of a brass ship. Curious, Eli walked up to the first statue on the right side of the path, the statue of the net, and read an inscription engraved into the base of the statue.

"Passions"

"And they straightway left their nets and followed him."

Immediately, Eli walked over to the statue on the left side of the road, a statue of the ship and read that engraving.

"Possessions"

"And when they had brought their ships to land, they forsook all and followed him"

Eli looked up at Pastor Thomas.

"Go ahead and read the other two and then we can discuss them."

Eli consented and approached the second statue on the left side of the path, the statue of a large pot.

"Past"

"The woman left her water pot, and went her way into the city"

Finally, Eli made his way over to the last statue on the right side of the path, the statue of an elegant man standing looking proud.

"Pride"

"We *are* fools for Christ's sake...we *are* weak...we *are* despised."

Eli took a moment to think about each of the statues before turning back to Pastor Thomas.

"These are all things that a person must let go of in order to come to Christ aren't they?"

"Very good, Eli. These statues represent the things that often hinder people from coming to Christ. As a soul approaches the City on a Hill, that soul is encouraged to lay each of these burdens down and enter the gates."

Pastor Thomas walked up to the statue of the nets.

"The nets represent the passions of people. The passage engraved on the base comes from Matthew 4 when the Lord called for Andrew and Peter to follow Him. Fishing was their passion, it was what they loved doing and had planned to do for the rest of their lives. But when Jesus called them to Him, they left their passion in life behind."

Pastor Thomas walked over to the statue of the ship.

"The ship represents possessions. That passage engraved on the base comes from Luke 5 when the Lord called James and John. Not a lot of people know this, but James and John came from a wealthy family. Their family owned ships and slaves, and yet, when Jesus called them to Him, they forsook all of their possessions."

"The water pot," continued Pastor Thomas as he walked to that statue, "represents a person's past. That passage comes from John 4 when Jesus is dealing with the Samaritan woman who had a terrible, tragic, and wicked past. When Jesus called her to Him, she left her past behind as represented by her water pot and became a great witness for Him."

Pastor Thomas walked over to the last statue of the man looking proud. Nodding his head knowingly as though he related with the statue, Pastor placed his hands on the base of the statue.

"The man is an image of Paul, when he was still Saul, and represents pride. Saul was a rising star among the Jewish people. He had fame, praise, and honor. According to the religious elite, Saul had a bright future of respect ahead of him. But when the Lord called Saul to Him, Paul left his life of prestige for a life of ridicule, suffering, and humility."

"These statues are here to help the wandering lost who are awakened by the light of the Gospel understand that a commitment to citizenship is a commitment to Jesus Christ above all else. One must be willing to set aside all passion, possessions, past experiences, and pride and seek entrance on the Path of Grace through the Gates of Faith. It is only as one enters the city holding to nothing but Jesus that they will be granted the life the gospel brings."

Eli, Zephyr, and Pastor Thomas continued up the path of Grace toward the city gates.. When the company approached the large red gates, Eli noticed writing that he thought was engraved on the gates, but then the gates opened and he realized the writing was hanging in the air at the entrance of the Gates of Faith.

"For by grace are you saved through faith, and that not of yourselves: it is the gift of God: not of works lest any man should boast"

The words made Eli's soul burn inside of him and he knew immediately that these words came from the King. Eli walked under the words and through the Gates of Faith. As soon as his foot crossed the threshold, Eli was overwhelmed with an intense blast of the King's light which filled the City on a Hill.

"Welcome defender Elijah Storm," announced Pastor Thomas, "to the King's City on a Hill."

chapter 15

the city on a hill

"Wow. Just wow!" announced Eli as the light of the King energized his spirit.

"Yeah," said Aiden who was waiting for them just inside the gates, "it's pretty alright. That is if you like that whole awesome-fortress-of-the-King-filled-with-the-powerful-life-giving-light-of-the-gospel-thing."

"Well, it just so happens I do."

The City on a Hill looked like an ancient Italian city enclosed behind the massive fortress walls. There were only two colors found throughout the city that gave it the Italian feeling: white and red. All of the structures, including the massive walls were constructed out of a beautiful white stone with specks of rock that sparkled in the light of the King, whereas all of the roofs, doors, and the brick road matched the deep red color of the Path of Grace.

The city was circular with several different tiers of buildings ascending up to the large lighthouse structure in the center of the city. The red brick road wound around in circles leading higher up into the city and ended at the base of the large lighthouse structure. Part of the red brick road connected the city gates with the lighthouse structure making it possible for a person to walk directly to the lighthouse structure from the gates. The layout of the city reminded Eli of an upside-down funnel with the mouth of the funnel the walls and the stem of the funnel being the light tower.

Lining both sides of the street were white structures of all different sizes and shapes. The more Eli looked at these structures the more he realized that these structures were various church buildings with architectures from all around the physical realm world. Eli saw large cathedrals, gigantic modern buildings, small country-looking buildings, third-world hut-like structures, and countless other types of church buildings.

"I tell you what, kids, why don't you two show Eli around the city and get caught up while Zephyr and I go meet with the council and prepare a plan to reclaim the reflector towers? How does that sound? What do you think Eli?"

"That is fine with me, if it is fine with Zeph. Is it Zeph?"

"Absolutely Eli. I am eager to get an understanding on the situation and I believe it is important for you to get caught up with your friends here."

"It's settled then." said Pastor Thomas, "You two take Eli around the city and then bring him to the light tower where we will be waiting with the council."

"Okay dad." The siblings replied in unison.

With that the group split in two with Eli, Aiden, and Ella going left down a street that circled around the walls, and Zephyr and Pastor Thomas going directly up the street to the lighthouse.

Eli had dealt with a lot of interesting situations during his time in the spirit realm, but walking with two friends from the physical realm through the streets of the City on a Hill was one of the most awkward moments to date. Ella and Aiden Thomas were the children of Pastor Thomas, who currently pastored the Open Door Church. Ella and Aiden were twins, and were two of Pastor Thomas's five children. The other three children, Elliot, Judah, and Loraine, were several years younger than Eli. Eli used to be really close to the Thomas family but drifted away when his family left the Open Door Church. Even though Eli dropped his friendship with the Thomas children and even though Eli had been living contrary to the way the Thomas family lived, Ella and Aiden were always kind to him and invited him to all of their birthday parties and church activities. Now that he was walking next to them in the City on a Hill in the spirit realm, Eli felt very ashamed of how he treated them and how he lived before he was saved.

"Listen." said Eli as he broke the silence, "I just want to say that I'm sorry for the way I stopped being your friends. And I'm sorry for the way that I acted in school."

"Oh hush." said Ella, "How in the world are you going to focus on your past life in the physical realm when we are walking down the streets of the City on a Hill? We know that you were not saved and we know that has changed. Who you were before you were a child of the King doesn't matter; all that matters now is that you are a King's defender and our ally in the battle against the Enemy."

"Seriously man." added Aiden, "You don't understand how cool it is for us to see you here! We've been working with your grandfather for years and all through those years, your grandfather begged us to pray for your salvation. When your grandfather learned of his promotion, he made us promise that we would do everything in our power to keep trying to reach you with the light of the gospel. Your grandpa always envisioned us teaming up with you and becoming a powerful force in the spirit realm and in the physical realm."

"So you actually worked with my grandfather here in the spirit realm? That's so cool. And he told you that I wasn't saved?"

"Yes." said Ella, "In fact, there were several times in which your grandfather went out into the streets of the wandering lost looking for you."

"So those people wandering the streets *really* are the people of our city?"

"Yes, Eli," continued Ella, "you should have been briefed on that."

"I was, it's just that I am still adjusting to the truths of the spirit realm. So did my grandpa ever find me in the broad street?"

"Yes he did. I remember him finding you on several occasions and one in particular, not long before his promotion."

"Yeah, I remember that too." said Aiden, "We were out in the streets and saw him walking slowly crying and praying. When we walked up to him, we saw that he was walking next to you crying and praying that you would see the light of the gospel. It was intense, man. I don't remember seeing anyone so distraught over another person's soul."

"And yet," said Eli shamefully, "I ignored my grandfather's words over and over again. I was so stubborn that it took his earthly passing for me to listen to what he was trying to tell me."

"That reminds me," exclaimed Ella, "You have to tell us about what happened to you at your grandfather's celebration party after the funeral. After the funeral, Aiden and I came to your house with the specific purpose of telling you about Jesus. We were going to fulfill our promise to your grandfather by not leaving until you made a decision for Jesus, when we were suddenly pulled into the spirit realm. We entered the city in time for dad to tell us about the ambush."

"The next thing we know, you are running toward the barrier with an army of enemies hot on your tail." added Aiden. "So, tell us, when did you enter the spirit realm, what happened, and how much do you know about everything going on?"

Eli related to them his adventures beginning with the way God was working on his heart during the funeral. By the time Eli had finished up his adventures in the Cemetery of the Old Man, the group had circled the city and were approaching the street that led directly to the light tower.

"I have been in training ever since." continued Eli as the group turned up the street that led to the light tower, "Then, out of nowhere, I get informed about this mission. All that I know is that the Enemy has sent Polytheist to unite the wolves, watchers, and tares and take possession of the reflector towers. I'm here to reclaim the reflector towers from the enemies and send Polytheist back to his master."

"Yeah buddy!" chuckled Aiden.

Eli gave Aiden a high-five,

"Now that I have told you all about my adventures, you've got to tell me about how you and your father have become harvesters and what that means."

"Well, sis, go ahead, tell the man what he wants to know."

"With pleasure. As you know, dad is the pastor of the Open Door Church. What you may not know is that dad used to work as the youth pastor and assistant pastor at Grace Gospel Fellowship."

"Wait. Your dad used to work at the church I go to now?"

"Yep."

"But GGF is like a huge church with a lot of people. Why would your dad want to leave there?"

"I was getting to that before you interrupted me."

"Oh, I'm sorry."

"It's okay. I will forgive you this time but the next time will cost you."

"Dude, she's not joking. Interrupt her again and you might just get an arrow in the bum."

"Excuse me, boys, I'm trying to tell a story. Anyway, where was I? Oh yes, you see, not only was dad the assistant, but he was supposed to take over the senior pastor job when he chose to leave to pastor the Open Door Church. Dad loved ministering at GGF and God blessed his ministry in many ways. But a few years before dad left, he started seeing a terrible trend in the upper leadership of GGF. I don't know everything, but one thing dad told us was the senior pastor and the other assistant pastor were making choices that valued their own personal bank accounts more than the welfare of the congregation.

Further, these two decided the reputation of the church was more important than the reputation of the King. As such, dad was placed into a situation in which he was forced to decide which was more important to him: his job at GGF or his calling from the King."

"Though dad tried to do everything to reconcile and remain at GGF, the senior pastor refused to listen to him or the deacon board. Finally, the senior pastor gave dad an ultimatum; keep quiet and keep employed, or stand up for what he believed in and lose his job."

"No way!"

"Yes, well, dad was torn because he loved the church and the people, but he had a responsibility to the King to serve and honor Him above all else. It was as he was praying that the former pastor of the Open Door Church called dad and asked him if he would take over. You see, dad did not know it at the time, but Pastor Griffith, the former pastor of the Open Door Church, was also a harvester who worked for years in the fields of the wandering lost. When Pastor Griffith knew his promotion was coming, he asked the King to direct him to a man who would continue the work. One day, the King brought the two together here in the City on a Hill and dad agreed to take Pastor Griffith's place.

"Our family has been at the Open Door Church ever since. Aiden and I have been harvesters for about three physical realm years. Our citizenship began when dad hosted a mission's conference and

Aiden and I both surrendered to do whatever we can to see the lost won to Jesus Christ. That night as we were dedicating our lives in prayer, we opened our eyes to find the City on a Hill in front of us and dad standing at the entrance to the city overjoyed inviting us to enter."

"I remember that conference! Grandpa tried desperately to get me to go. He said that a missionary who had spent years in prison over in China would be speaking about his life. That's so cool."

"As harvesters, Aiden and I have answered the call of the King for laborers to work in the harvest field of the Desolate City. The missionary at the conference spoke on Matthew 9:35-38 in which Jesus saw the crowds and had compassion on them. Jesus' words ignited a fire in us and it was as if Jesus Himself was speaking to us about the need for laborers in His harvest field. When I went to pray, all I could hear was the words of Jesus, 'The harvest truly is plenteous, but the laborers are few; pray ye therefore the Lord of the harvest, that he will send forth laborers into his harvest.'"

"Me too!" announced Aiden excitedly. "It was as the words of Jesus rang in my ears that I knelt to pray and when I opened my eyes, there before me was the City on a Hill! I remember walking through the gates, dad hugging us and explaining everything to us, and then working in the Desolate City."

"So do the wolves and watchers ever attack you guys?"

"Sometimes." admitted Aiden, "But more often than not, they keep their distance and usually just yell at us or try to discourage us from a safe distance."

"I can understand that. After all, you both look terrifying in your spirit realm gear. Besides, it looked to me like you have been well trained in the use of your weapons."

"Thanks for noticing." said Ella, "Michael helped train us when we were preparing to go into the Desolate City. When we are here, we always take time to help sharpen our skills."

"Yep," said Aiden, "and it's easy to practice when what you are practicing is blowing darkness away with the powerful light of the King."

"So, how do you practice? I mean, where did your weapons come from and how did you learn to use them?"

"Our weapons," answered Ella, "are a lot like your sword. The power of our weapons come from the King's Word. The way we learn to use our weapons here in the spirit realm is by learning more about the King's Word in the physical realm. The greater our knowledge and application of the Bible, the more powerful and accurate our weapons are here in the spirit realm. Our weapons are also empowered by the Illuminator, the Holy Spirit, Who takes our knowledge of the King's Word and translates it into the power we need to gain the victory."

"That. Is. So. Cool! So when you guys come back to the spirit realm, do you always come through the gates of the city, or how do you get here?"

"Naw, man," answered Aiden, "after a person becomes a harvester, or a defender in your case, when the person enters the City on a Hill, they travel through the door that represents the King's church they are a part of."

When Aiden said this, he pointed to the different structures that lined both sides of the red brick road of the City on a Hill.

"So these buildings are not just replicas of the churches in our town or around the world, they actually represent those churches?"

"Yep, in fact, when we return to the City on a Hill, no matter where we are when we are called, we always come through The Open Door Church's door."

Aiden pointed toward the lighthouse structure.

"The Open Door Church's doors are just up there, by the lighthouse."

Eli looked at all the structures again, "So what about these other church buildings, you know, the ones that look like they are from Africa or somewhere; what are they doing in the City on a Hill in our town's region?"

"Good question." Aiden said as though he were a host on a gameshow, "Eli, the Desolate City spans the entire globe. In every region of the Desolate City, there is also a City on a Hill. Though there are many different Cities on a Hill, they are not separate cities, but rather they are all connected through the body of Christ. More often than not, the King calls harvesters and defenders to minister in their own local region of the Desolate City, but there are times when the King will call harvesters and defenders to minister in regions all across the Desolate City. You know, like missionaries and evangelists."

"Remember that Chinese missionary your grandfather was talking about at the mission's conference? Well, he too was a harvester whom your grandfather worked with right here! In fact, I don't know where the church representing his ministry in China is right now, but it has an entrance in this City on a Hill!"

"Amazing!" answered Eli, "This place just keeps getting cooler and cooler!"

"Well," announced Ella as the group walked up to the base of the lighthouse, "here we are."

Waiting for the group, standing outside of the lighthouse's massive base, was Pastor Thomas, Zephyr, and four adults: two men and two women wearing glowing white robes. One of the men in white robes stepped forward to greet them.

"Welcome, Elijah Storm, defender of the King. We are the Council of Light and we have much to discuss with you,"

chapter 16

the council of light

The Council of light was a group of two men and two women all dressed in clothes that reminded Eli of the clothes martial artists wear: white wrap-around tunics with a deep red belt and white flowing pants with deep red boots. On the left breast of their tunics, where Eli's clothes had the blue cross, was a pair of golden hands holding a golden open-book.

The man who welcomed Eli spoke again.

"I am Aquila, lead member of the Council of Light, and a man who dedicated his physical realm life to the planting of churches and partnering with the defender Paul to spread the gospel light. To my right is Philip the Evangelist, a man whom the King used in a mighty way to spread the gospel during his time in the physical realm."

Philip stepped forward and extended his hand to shake Eli's.

"Welcome brother."

"Thank you." replied Eli as he shook Philip's hand.

"To my left is my wife and partner from the physical realm, Priscilla. Without her love for the gospel and willingness to risk her life, my ministry in the physical realm would have been far less than what it was."

"Welcome Eli, it is an honor to meet you." said Priscilla as she stepped forward and shook Eli's hand."

"Thank you, it is an honor to be here."

"And finally, this is Tabitha, a woman known for spreading the light of the gospel throughout her life by means of her good works, death, and earthly resurrection."

"Welcome defender, we have been eager for your arrival."

"Nice to meet you." said Eli as he shook Tabitha's hand. "Did I hear Aquila right? You spread the gospel through your earthly death and resurrection?"

"Yes, defender, you heard him right. In my physical realm life, the King allowed me to suffer a sickness and die so that Peter could show the mighty power of the King by resurrecting me."

"That's incredible, but why have I not heard this story before? I know I am not a pastor or anything, but I am sure I would have remembered a story like yours."

"Well, Eli, perhaps you would recall my story if Aquila were to refer to me by my other name; a name that seems to attract more attention from young English speaking children. My other name is Dorcas."

Instantly Eli's mind raced back through memories of hearing his teachers tell Tabitha's story and Eli and his friends laughing at her name. Standing in front of Tabitha now, Eli felt embarrassed at his earlier reaction.

Tabitha smiled knowingly at Eli, "It's okay, Eli, nothing to be ashamed of. If I lived in an English speaking nation in your time, my name would be very out of place."

"Come, Eli." Aquila cut in, "There is much to discuss."

The Council of light turned and walked up the street to the entrance of the lighthouse. Eli followed but hesitated when he saw the Thomas family not following.

"Aren't you all coming?"

"Sorry Eli, I believe this is where the kids and I say goodbye for now. But if you ever have need of us, we will be ready to assist."

"Actually," responded Aquila, "your time together is just beginning. Please come with us."

Ella and Aiden's faces lit up with excitement as they looked up to their dad for direction.

"Never mind, it appears our journey together is just beginning."

Eli smiled at his friend's excitement and at the possibility of sharing more of this adventure with them. Eli and Zephyr then followed the Council of Light into the lighthouse with the Thomas family walking behind them.

As he approached the base of the lighthouse, Eli was overwhelmed at its massive size. The lighthouse stretched high into the sky with a large crystal orb at the top from which three powerful beams of light shot out into the darkness of the Desolate City. The base of the structure was a gigantic square block with a large arched-entrance without doors. Etched into each side of the square base, in giant golden letters each the size of Eli, was this passage from the King's Word.

Matthew 5:14-16

14 Ye are the light of the world. A city that is set on an hill cannot be hid.

15 Neither do men light a candle, and put it under a bushel, but on a candlestick; and it giveth light unto all that are in the house.

16 Let your light so shine before men, that they may see

your good works, and glorify your Father which is in heaven.

Eli walked through the doorway not knowing if he would find a luxuriously decorated inside like the inside of the castle or if he would see a plain inside that matched the other structures in the City on a Hill. To Eli's surprise, the inside of the lighthouse was extremely plain, save for the source of the gospel light.

The walls of the lighthouse matched the brilliant white plain stone of the outside of the lighthouse. There were no pictures, decorations, or any type of color on the walls of the lighthouse: it was just plain white stone. The red brick from the Path of Grace formed the floor of the lighthouse which had no furniture, rugs, or anything other than the source of the gospel light on it.

The only thing in the entire lighthouse was the source of the gospel light: a large white-stone octagon, about the size of the octagons in which Eli's favorite mixed martial arts fighter fights, standing in the center of the lighthouse. Inside the octagon was a gigantic golden statue. The bottom of the statue was two gigantic hands with the palms pressed together and the hands and fingers stretched out like moose antlers. The hands were so large that the span from the fingers on one hand to the fingers on the other hand filled the entire circumference of the octagon. The base of the statue was the hand's wrists giving the appearance that the hands protruded out from the floor.

In the palms of the hands was a large open-book also completely made of gold. The book was so large that the span of the pages reached the base of the fingers on both hands. Surrounding the edges of the octagon, and continuing all the way up the tower, was a thick layer of perfectly clear crystal. Exploding from the open pages of the book and completely filling every millimeter of space inside the crystal all the way up to the top of the tower was the most powerful light Eli had ever seen.

The light exploded out from the pages of the open book with such force that it reminded Eli of the time the local river flooded due to heavy rains. The tremendous force of the flood water terrified Eli as he knew if he fell in he would be swept away. As Eli stood near the light of the gospel, Eli could feel the great force of the light shooting up into the tower.

The only decorations in the entire lighthouse came from five white-stone triangles that originated from the five points of the white-stone octagon pointing out. Curious, Eli walked over to the triangles to see if they had any significant purpose.

As he approached, Eli could decipher writing engraved in each triangle inlayed with gold. The writing included a caption followed by a passage from the King's Word. The first triangle Eli approached had this caption and passage:

"POWER"

"For I am not ashamed of the GOSPEL OF CHRIST for it is the POWER OF GOD unto SALVATION"

Eli could feel the power of the Word fill him and he felt a powerful connection to the light that was exploding up the tower. Without stopping to speak with the council members whom he could tell were watching him, Eli continued around the octagon reading each triangle.

"MESSAGE"

"Moreover, brethren, I declare unto you the GOSPEL...that CHRIST DIED FOR OUR SINS according to the Scriptures; and that HE WAS BURIED, and that HE ROSE AGAIN THE THIRD DAY according to the Scriptures"

"NEED"

"But if our GOSPEL be hid, it is hid to them THAT ARE LOST"

"WARNING"

"But though WE, OR AN ANGEL FROM HEAVEN, preach any OTHER GOSPEL unto you than that which we have preached unto you, LET HIM BE ACCURSED"

"MISSION"

"Go ye into all the world and PREACH THE GOSPEL TO EVERY CREATURE"

When Eli finished reading each of the triangles, he could feel an overwhelming sense of power growing inside of him. Before he knew it, his body was radiating with the powerful blue light that he radiated with during his fight with the Arkhay'.

Eli walked back over to the Council of Light, "I'm sorry for walking away like that, I was just so mesmerized by the light."

"Do not be bothered by that my brother." replied Philip, "It's refreshing to see someone with your youth so enthralled with the gospel light."

"Yes." agreed Aquila, "And that light is the reason why you are here. It is time you get a clear picture of the mission ahead of you. Come with us."

Aquila signaled and the Council of Light lined up in a single-file line in front of the crystal octagon of light. After a moment's pause, a set of stairs appeared in front of the Council of Light next to the octagon. There were about ten steps and the stairs reached the top of the fingers of the statue. Philip, Tabitha, and Priscilla all walked up the steps and stood for a moment. Then, Philip stepped through the crystal barrier and shot up the light beam like a blast from a roman candle. Soon both Tabitha and Priscilla joined Philip at the top of the lighthouse and Aquila motioned for Eli to step up next.

"Because you have the light of the gospel already inside of you, the crystal barrier will not prevent you from entering the light. When you step into the light, the light will carry you all the way to the top of the lighthouse. When you get to the top of the lighthouse, simply exit the light beam by pushing yourself out of it. Do you understand?"

Eli looked to the others who all shook their head communicating that they understood.

"I think so." replied Eli.

"Good. I will go last to make sure that there are no issues. Eli, I would like you to go up first."

“Sounds good.” said Eli as he walked up the stairs to the edge of the crystal octagon followed by Zephyr and the Thomas family.

Once again, Eli could feel the tremendous force of the light exploding upward out from the open book in the palm of the statue. A feeling of excitement rushed through his body as he anticipated the thrill he was about to experience. Looking up the light beam one last time, Eli took a deep.

"I love the spirit realm!" thought Eli then he jumped through the crystal and into the light beam.

chapter 17

the mission ahead

Eli shot up the lighthouse tower like a bullet coming out of a gun. He soared up the tower with lightning speed and jumped off to his right when he saw the top of the tower approaching. When Eli left the light beam, his body floated over to the side of the tower where the other members of the Council of Light awaited him. The top of the tower of light was a gigantic crystal globe with a crystal walkway lining the wall of the globe.

The light of the gospel filled the crystal globe and then split into three smaller beams that shot out the right and left side of the globe running along the border of the Desolate City, as well as a beam that shot directly into the heart of the Desolate City.

While waiting for the others to make their way up the light tower, Eli walked up to the edge of the crystal globe and looked out over the Desolate City. Eli could see the light of the tower illuminating the whole of the Desolate City, but Eli could also see that something was wrong. Eli could tell that each of the light beams were dissipating when they reached their destination instead of reflecting and further illuminating the Desolate City. With the light dissipating and dispersing, the light was too dim to effectively reach the entire city.

"That, Master Storm," said Aquila as he followed Eli's gaze from light beam to light beam, "is the reason you are here. The King has established three towers in the Desolate City to reflect the light of the gospel. Each light beam is sent from the City on a Hill to its specific tower which is designed to then reflect the light beam into the whole of the Desolate City. When working properly, these reflectors illumine all areas of the Desolate City with an intense glow of gospel light. Currently, those reflectors have been captured by Polytheist and his army of darkness. With those reflectors in the hands of the Enemy, the light of the gospel is being hindered greatly in both realms. You have been brought here to reclaim the reflectors and restore the light of the gospel."

"I see. Could you please explain to me more about what these reflector towers are, what they do, and how exactly the enemies were able to take control of the reflectors so that I could have a better idea of what I am going to face?"

"There are three reflector towers: the tower of conviction, the tower of acceptation, and the tower of direction. The tower of conviction is located to our right. It is this reflector that helps the wandering lost awaken to the fact that they are lost and have a need and that need is for the gospel. This reflector has always been a target of wolf attacks, but with the help of Polytheist, the wolves were able to erect a den of sorts over the tower and thus block the reflector from the light of the gospel.

"The tower of acceptation resides to our left. It is this tower that communicates to the lost that the life the King offers is a free gift birthed in grace and delivered through faith and not something to be earned. This reflector tower has always been the target of the watchers. Though the watchers have raged against this tower non-stop, they have failed in capturing this tower until their new treaty with the wolves, tares, and Polytheist. The watchers have attempted to turn the tower into another one of their watchtowers, but all they have accomplished in reality is simply to construct a watchtower around the reflector tower.

"The third tower is the tower of direction. This tower lies at the very edge of the Desolate City in a direct line out from this tower. When all three towers are in use, they form a gigantic triangle of light with the lighthouse. The tower of direction receives the light of the gospel and illumines the narrow way with tremendous radiance. It is this reflector that shows the awakened lost the only way to enter into the City on a Hill is through the King's sacrificial blood that colors the red bricks on the Path of Grace. As you can imagine, this tower is one that Polytheist hates above all other towers. As such, when Polytheist and his army captured this tower he built his personal fortress around this reflector. Within the walls of his fortress, Polytheist stands vigil with orders from the Enemy to defend his fortress at all costs."

"What about the Arkhay'? Will I be battling them as well?"

"I highly doubt it. After seeing your boldness toward them and Michael's reminder that you are under the protection of the King, I doubt they will trouble you again."

"Besides," added Zephyr, "The Arkhay' were only able to enter into the conflict because of my intervention on your behalf. Now that you have arrived at the City on a Hill, my task from the King has been accomplished. I have received orders that I am to remain with the Council of Light until further notice. With me out of the picture, the Arkhay' would risk immediate destruction at the hands of Michael for any involvement whatsoever."

"Well there is some good news." replied Eli, "Although I am totally bummed that you and I won't get to go out and reclaim these towers together, Zeph."

"I feel the same way, but the King has given you even better allies than myself."

"Are you saying we get to go with Eli?" Ella asked in shock.

"Not all of you." answered Aquila, "Only Ella and Aiden. The King has another mission for Pastor Thomas that will help aid you three in your mission. The reason why the King has brought you all together at this time is to allow you to fight hand-in-hand for the wandering lost in your own Desolate

City. You each have skills and abilities that the King knows will aid Eli in his mission to restore the light of the gospel."

"This is going to be great!" said Aiden as he walked over next to Eli, "Not only am I going to go to battle with a friend who happens to be a defender, but I also get to go to battle with my own sister! I pity the fools in the Desolate City who stand against us."

"So," asked Eli trying to contain his excitement, "how are we going to get to the towers? Are we going to have to fight our way through the Desolate City or is there a secret way we don't know about?"

"You don't have to fight your way through the Desolate City but the way is not very secret. Any defender or harvester has the ability to ride the light beam of the gospel anywhere and in any direction. I recommend that when you are ready to travel to the towers, you simply jump into the light beam and soar over the Desolate City to your destination. When you complete your mission and free each tower from the grasp of the Enemy, you simply return to the lighthouse by riding the beam back."

"But the beam is so high in the air." observed Ella, "How will we get back into the beam once we have left it?"

"That is a good question, Ella." answered Priscilla, "To re-enter the light beam of the gospel, simply look up toward the light and jump into the beam."

"But that is like jumping from the city street up to this crystal globe! There is no way we can jump that high."

"Not in the physical realm, no, but remember you are in the spirit realm. The light beam of the gospel will act as a giant magnet to any harvester or defender. If you look up to the light and jump, the light beam will draw you in."

Ella nodded her head in understanding. There was a short period of silence as the group contemplated what lay before them. Not wanting to waste any time, Eli addressed the Council of Light.

"Well, I guess that about sums it up. Is there anything else you think I should know before we head out?"

"Yes," replied Aquila, "You need to understand that this is not going to be a simple task. The Enemy has given specific orders to Polytheist regarding these battles. All of the defenses of these towers are designed to ensnare you and destroy you. Do not underestimate your enemies."

"Having said that, do not underestimate the great power you wield. You are the King's defender. You will face nothing out there that you do not have the ability to overcome. No matter what you see, hear, or face out there in the Desolate City, never forget that in the power of the King, you can conquer it all."

"Thank you. So, which tower will we be going to first?"

"The tower of conviction." said Philip.

"And that is the tower that the wolves took over?" asked Eli.

"Yes. Its light provides the wandering lost with the initial ability to see their need for the King's salvation, a need which the wolves attempt to fill with the things of this world. For that reason, it will be the first tower that you must go and reclaim for the King."

"Sounds like a game plan." replied Eli.

Facing Ella and Aiden, Eli asked, "You guys ready to rumble?"

"Yes, absolutely!" replied Ella.

"Are you kidding?" replied Aiden, "I was born for this!"

"Then what are we waiting for? Let's ride this beam and pay the wolves a little visit from the City on a Hill."

Eli, Ella, and Aiden walked over to the side of the globe and stood underneath the light beam of the gospel that shot toward the tower of conviction.

"I'm so proud of you all." said Pastor Thomas as the three stood under the beam, "I will pray that the King will give you great success. Be careful out there, these enemies are playing for keeps. Take care of them Eli."

"Thanks dad." replied the Thomas children.

"I will Pastor Thomas." replied Eli. "Now are we ready to go?"

"No, not yet!" cried Aiden desperately.

"Why not?" asked Ella, "You're not backing out now are you?"

"Of course I'm not sis! I just realized that we do not have a cool team name. We can't go stomping through the Desolate City dominating the servants of the Enemy without a cool name that strikes fear into the hearts of our enemies."

Ella rolled her eyes, but Eli laughed.

"Okay, Aiden." said Eli, "What do you have in mind?"

"I'm glad you asked. It just so happens that as I was riding the light wave up the tower that a perfect name came to mind. Are you ready? Here it is; I think we should call ourselves the Light Train of Pain."

"Oh brother." said Ella as she turned so Aiden would not see her smile.

"I like it!" said Eli, "Now is there anything else we need before we jump into this light beam and reclaim the reflector tower of conviction?"

No one said a word.

"Light Train of Pain," said Eli, "let's roll!"

Eli, Ella, and Aiden all joined hands and with a running start, leapt into the light beam and sped toward the tower of conviction.

chapter 18

a way in

Soaring through the air over the Desolate City, Eli felt that one of his greatest dreams had come true. Since Eli was a young boy, he had always wanted to fly. Eli would spend hours imagining what it would be like to have the ability to fly, but now he did not have to imagine anymore as the light of the gospel propelled him through the red sky of the Desolate City. With Ella on his left and Aiden doing his best superman impression on his right, Eli felt a powerful peace knowing that he was not going into battle alone.

"Hey." Eli called out to Ella, "What happens when we get to the tower? How are we going to get inside? Do you think we need to make a plan?"

"I'm not sure how we will get inside. As for a plan, I like to plan to make things up as we go."

"Those are the only kind of plans I make." Eli said with a smile.

Soon the trio approached the wolves' den and though Eli did not have any expectations of what the wolves' den would look like, he was sure whatever he would have thought would not look like what was before him. The wolves' den looked like a large business tower built directly in front of the reflector tower that resided on the highway exit to Eli's town. The outside of the wolves' den was covered in glass windows that were all tinted gold. At the top of the tower was a large golden spire with a large golden ball at the top of it. This golden ball intercepted a majority of the light of the gospel and reflected the light into the golden windows of the den. At first Eli was puzzled by this and then he realized that the awakened lost who were attracted to the light of the gospel were being directed into the den of wolves.

A single road ran in front of the wolves' den with war-torn looking gas stations on either side. Both the street and the gas stations looked war-torn but the wolves' den looked immaculate. Walking down the street away from the Desolate City was a steady stream of awakened lost following the light of the gospel that was now radiating from the wolves' den.

The group slowed to a stop just on the other side of the street that ran in front of the main entrance to the den.

"That's sick!" said Aiden, "They're using the gospel light to ensnare the awakened lost!"

"We have to do something." said Ella, "We have to bring that tower down."

"I know." replied Eli, "But first, we have to find a way into the tower without being captured."

"The front entrance is the only way in I see, and it is too heavily guarded for us to sneak in." replied Ella, "I don't see another way in."

The main entrance to the tower looked like the entrance to an amusement park. Connecting the front entrance to the war-torn road was a golden ramp. Where the ramp met the road, the wolves had construction a large gold-brick arch-way with the words, "The Pursuit of Happiness" etched into the top of the arch-way and inlayed with what looked like diamonds. Lining the sides of the ramp were large arrow signs pointing to the wolves' den with words like, "Happiness this way", "Your new life just ahead", and "Everything you need to be happy and so much more!"

The ramp lead all the way to the entrance to the golden-tower, which consisted of tall, gorgeous sliding glass doors. Standing directly in front of the glass doors was what Eli guessed was supposed to look like a female tour guide, but was obviously a wolf dressed in a human-looking costume.

The tour lady wore a bright red pants suit complete with a blazer, shoes, a scarf, and gloves. The tour lady's face gave Eli the creeps. The mask was obviously not made to fit the long snout of a wolf and was therefore stretched tight distorting the facial features. The tour lady's eyes and mouth looked like they were stuck in a perpetual smile and her nose was stretched completely flat and molded to the wolf's snout lying under the mask. Even with the scarf, gloves, and shoes, Eli could still see patches of wolf hair sticking out of the costume. Nevertheless, the awakened lost who approached her reacted to her as though they did not see anything amiss. She would greet them, write something down on her clipboard and send them through the door.

"How are the awakened lost fooled by those costumes?" asked Eli.

"Those disguises are specially crafted to deceive the minds of those who do not have the Illuminator to show them the truth. We have the King's Spirit so we can see them for what they are, but the minds of the lost are clouded and deceived by them." answered Ella.

Flanking the tour lady were two lines of wolves stretching down the length of the tower on both sides. These lines of wolves were dressed in similarly creepy looking security guard costumes. Looking at the wolves' setup, Eli knew that they could not go in through the front door without setting off alarms.

The group scanned the building for any other way in when they caught sight of a pair of wagons, like the wagons the Arkhay' called for to capture Eli, exiting from the highway and rolling towards the golden tower. These wagons were also being pulled by skeleton horses but were being driven by wolves. As Eli looked through the bars of the wagons, he could see what looked like security guard clothes and bars of gold. The wagons pulled off of the road on the side of the tower before getting to the front entrance. Curious, Eli hovered around to the side of the light beam to see where they were going. On the side of the building, Eli saw a large commercial door designed for deliveries roll open preparing for the wagons' arrival.

"Right there!" exclaimed Eli, "That is our way into the den! Come on, we have to hurry."

Eli pushed himself out of the light beam and soared through the air toward the wagons with Ella and Aiden right behind him. The wagons had come to a stop waiting for the door to open all the way. When the door was finished opening, the wagon drivers snapped the reigns and the skeleton horses jumped forward. Seeing a way to land on the wagons without being detected, Eli motioned to Ella and Aiden to time their landing in unison on the second wagon when the driver snapped the reigns. They nodded in agreement and as soon as the second driver snapped his reigns, the trio landed on top of the wagon as the horses jerked forward.

"Easy there you lags." growled the wolf driver as the wagon shook with the impact of their landing. "The master won't be happy if yer pull the front off his wagon."

The wagon entered into the delivery section of the den and the commercial door rolled closed behind. Once the door closed, all the light of the gospel disappeared. The inside of the delivery section of the tower was dimly lit with flickering fluorescent lights. The wagons came to a halt and two wolves, one normal size and the other much larger, both in security guard costumes, approached the wagons.

"Point of origin, cargo, and delivery number." growled the smaller wolf not even looking up from his clipboard.

"What's this all about, you? You know who we are! We're the only drivers Lucre trusts to deliver such precious cargo."

The smaller wolf looked up from his clipboard, obviously angered, "I said point of origin, cargo, and delivery number! I don't care who you are, Lucre has given strict orders to examine all deliveries while that cursed defender is still on the loose. Now either give me your name and delivery number or Benny and I will rip you to shreds."

Benny, the much larger wolf smiled at the driver revealing his large teeth and cracked his knuckles.

The driver, now obviously intimidated, responded, "Okay, okay. No need to get all violent and stuff. This is another load from one of Lucre's top generals, Mr. Steen. He sends yet another shipment of disguises made from the very spinner of Deceit. Ten in all." said the driver as he pointed to the second wagon, the one on top of which Eli, Ella, and Aiden were hiding.

"Very nice." admired the smaller wolf as he walked around the wagon examining the security guard clothes and wrote on his clipboard.

"Yes, and yet there is more. As always, Mr. Steen gladly sends Lucre's portion of all his gains. In this wagon, driven by none other than yours truly, is no less than fifty gold bars!"

"Not a bad haul at all!" admired the smaller wolf as he looked longingly at the gold in the first wagon. "That Mr. Steen always had a knack for sniffing out suckers. Everything looks in order, all I need now is your delivery number."

"No problem, 7990."

"Looks like you are cleared for entry. Pull up to the loading docks, give them your invoice, and they will unload your wagons and give you a receipt. Move on out."

"Gladly."

The driver snapped his reigns and the wagons lurched forward.

"Those disguises." whispered Eli, "I think they are our way into the tower. Do you think they will work for us?"

"Absolutely." responded Ella, "If they are truly spun by Deceit, then they will allow the wearer to appear in whatever manner the wearer so chooses. In the same way the wolves use them to appear as sheep and under-shepherds in the physical realm to deceive the King's people, we can use them to infiltrate the wolves' den."

"But won't the wolves be able to see through them?"

"No, only those who have the King's Spirit can see through them. Well, them and the more powerful enemies, but these wolves don't remind me of the type who can see through them."

"Whatever the case, I think it's worth a shot." answered Eli. "We need to get them fast. Any ideas?"

"Of course I have ideas." whispered Aiden, "Dude, I'm like the idea factory. Grab my feet and hold me over the back side of the wagon. I will use my spear to grab the disguises and pull them through the bars. In. Out. Easy."

Eli looked over to Ella and raised his eyebrows.

"It sounds as good as anything I can think of." responded Ella, "Besides, we don't have much time."

Ella pointed in front of the wagons at a large loading dock with several wolves wandering around pointlessly.

"Okay, let's do this." said Eli as he and Aiden scooted toward the back of the wagon.

Eli grabbed Aiden's feet and Aiden dangled off the back of the wagon. Using his spear, Aiden was able to pick up and bring out three disguises. One by one, Aiden lifted them up for Eli to grab and pass to Ella. The group was just able to lift Aiden back on top of the wagon as the two wagons arrived at the dock.

"Quick, put these on!" whispered Eli.

"Invoice please." snarled a wolf sitting on a stool outside of a small security booth.

"With pleasure."

The driver handed the wolf the invoice he received from the first smaller wolf.

Both drivers dismounted their wagons and walked around the front of the horses to wait for the inspection. The wolf who asked for the invoice opened up the first wagon and counted all the bars of gold. Once he was satisfied there were fifty bars, he ordered several wolves to begin unloading the gold bars. The wolves were so enamored by the gold bars that they did not notice three dark figures jump from the top of the one wagon onto the top of the security booth.

The wolf with the invoice then walked over to the second wagon, opened the door and counted the disguises.

"Hold on a sec." he snarled, "The invoice says you have ten disguises, but I only see seven."

"You're as blind as you are ugly." replied the driver of the wagon. "We just had em checked out and there are ten."

"Oh really?" replied the wolf with the invoice, "Then why don't you come over here and count them yourself?"

"Gladly." snarled the driver as he walked next to the wolf with the invoice and counted the disguises.

"Now aint that something?" said the driver in amazement as he counted seven disguises, "There is something fishy goin on around here. I picked up ten disguises and checked in ten disguises up front. Now all of a sudden, three of them have gone missing. I say you're a thief and when Lucre finds out he is going to string you up by your paws."

The group of wolves unloading the gold bars took offense to this comment and immediately growled in a threatening fashion as they put the gold down and walked up next to their boss.

"Did you really just call me and my crew a bunch of thieves right in front of our faces? Are you really that stupid?"

The main driver and his partner stepped up to the wolf with the invoice and snarled back in return.

"What I am saying is that I know there were ten disguises and we counted ten disguises up front. I counted them and so did Benny. If you are calling me a liar, then you are calling Benny a liar too. I tell you what, why don't we get old Benny over here to settle this?"

The wagon driver turned toward the commercial door and yelled, "Hey, you two. These guys are saying that your invoice is wrong. They think that you messed up and are threatening us to keep quiet."

"What?" hollered the first smaller wolf, "Come on Benny, let's go see what's going on!"

The addition of two more wolves, including one very large wolf, seemed to calm the loading crew of wolves down.

"Calm down." said the wolf with the invoice as Benny and the smaller wolf arrived looking ready for a fight, "Let's not get hasty. All I said is that the invoice says ten disguises and there are only seven."

"Can't be!" argued the smaller wolf from the entrance, "I counted them myself. There were ten up front, if there are only seven now, that means the disguises disappeared as soon as your loading crew came into contact with them."

Once again the loading crew of wolves snarled, but quickly backed away when Benny snarled back.

The arguing continued and was soon followed by shouting but Eli, Ella, and Aiden did not stick around to find out what was going to happen.

"Now's our chance." said Ella as the wolves continued their argument. "Remember, imagine yourselves to be wolves and then I say we make for the door to the main floor."

Ella pointed toward a door on the side of the wall that said "Main Floor".

"Sounds good." said Aiden.

"Okay, one more time." replied Eli, "You're telling me that all I have to do is imagine I am a wolf and this disguise will make me look like a wolf?"

"Exactly." said Ella, "We don't have time to explain now, but if Deceit really made these disguises, they have the ability to manipulate the minds of the creatures you come in contact with."

The trio then hopped off of the security booth and walked casually to the door. Right as they reached the door, a loud crashed followed by a painful howl erupted by the wagons. The group turned in time to see the second wagon get knocked over by the wolves who were now fighting.

"Move. Now!" said Eli knowing that a large brawl like this would attract a lot of unwanted attention.

Eli put his hand on the door and swung it open. Eli, Ella, and Aiden then ran through the door and right into the security headquarters of the tower. The room was full of monitors that showed every level of every section inside the wolves' den. Not only was this room full of security monitors, it was also full of security wolves. Soon, Eli, Ella, and

Aiden were completely surrounded by a room full of wolves in security clothes. A large wolf wearing a black suit, white shirt, and a black tie that reminded Eli of a secret service agent walked up looking curiously at the group.

"Well, well, well, what do we have here?"

chapter 19

the pursuit of happiness

Well, this is it, thought Eli as the large group of security clothed wolves growled and approached the trio, *so much for sneaking into the wolves' den.*

The group of security clothed wolves stood in a semi-circle around the trio with the wolf in the business suit standing in the center of the semi-circle.

To Eli's amazement, the wolves did not attack or call for help; they just stood there looking confused.

"Where'd you three come from?" asked the wolf dressed like a secret service agent, "I don't remember seeing you before?"

"Of course not." said Ella in the deepest voice she could muster, "That's because we are transfers. We just arrived with the shipment from Mr. Steen."

This explanation seemed the satisfy several of the wolves who nodded their heads as if Ella's brief explanation settled all their questions.

"Mr. Steen, huh?" said the wolf in the business suit, "Let's see."

The wolf walked over and picked up a clipboard and ran his claw down the page. "Hmm, so you all just arrived huh? You were supposed to have two wagons, one with gold and one with extra disguises, right?"

The way the wolf said the word "disguises" made Eli uncomfortable as if the wolf had an idea that they could be imposters. But Ella did not seemed phased at all.

"That's correct, sir, and I am sure we can cover all the details as soon as we deal with what we came in here to tell you."

"And what is that?"

"A fight broke out between the drivers, the large wolf named Benny, and the loading crew. It appears that the loading crew miscounted the inventory and accused Benny and the drivers of stealing the goods."

The wolf in the business slammed the clipboard down angrily and the other wolves backed away. At first, Eli thought that Ella had said something that gave them away, but soon learned that Ella had hit a lucky cord.

"That is exactly why you don't hire your family! I promised mother that I would look after Bane, but everywhere I put him he is always causing trouble. I mean seriously, what kind of idiot accuses Benny of anything?"

“Fang.” snapped the wolf in the business suit as he pointed to a wolf in the security uniform, “Take your crew and go break up that fight before Lucre hears of it and punishes us all.”

“But sir, we’re supposed to begin our floor shift now.”

“I said go! These three can more than take your place.”

“Yeah.” said Ella, “We could use a break from riding on the wagons. My crew can more than cover the floor patrol for you.”

“Fine.” growled Fang as he glared at Ella. “Let’s go boys.”

Two other wolves followed Fang as he walked out the door and started yelling at the brawlers.

Eli knew they needed more information about the floor patrol but he also knew that he could not ask. Eli learned in training that in every pack of wolves, no matter the size, there is a recognized leader. Eli knew that since Ella had spoken that she would be recognized as the leader. Eli looked over at Ella and tried to communicate their need, but Ella was already working on it.

“Sir, is there anything we need to know before we begin our patrol?”

The wolf dressed like the agent looked at her as he rubbed his temples with his paws.

“No, not really. Stay on the main walkway and report anything that seems out of the ordinary. Stay alert, Lucre sent word that Polytheist believes the defender will try to strike here first.”

“The defender?” asked Ella innocently, “The defender would be foolish to attempt to strike here when we have so many security measures and such an experienced leader.”

Eli thought the flattery was a bit much but it seemed to work wonders on the mood of the lead wolf.

“Exactly what I said! Now, get out there and prove me right.”

“Yes sir! Come on boys, we have some patrolling to do.”

Eli and Aiden grunted and followed Ella as she walked out of the security room and into the main floor of the wolves’ den. Before the door shut behind Eli, he could hear the main wolf state how much he liked Ella and her crew and how nice it was to meet wolves who could recognize his expertise.

As the three walked into the main floor of the wolves’ den, Eli walked close to Ella so they could talk without being overheard. Knowing that the wolves had security cameras everywhere, Eli knew they had to act naturally and blend in as best as they could, but it was difficult for him not to stand and gawk at the luxury around him.

The wolves' den looked like a shopping mall inside of a palace. Looking up from the main floor, Eli could see six different floors, all connected by a large ramp that wound all the way up the tower. The floor and the walls of the wolves' den were covered in beautiful golden tiles with shiny mirror surfaces. Standing in the center of the den and reaching from the main floor all the way up to the sixth floor, was a gigantic cubed jumbo-tron-like-television that constantly aired promotions and advertisements. The cubed television was not the only screen in the den; every section of every level had their own large screens with advertisements and promotions.

The entrance of the wolves' den was on the trio's left as they walked out of the security room and so they turned right to walk towards the center of the den. On their right side was a large bank-like area concealed behind tall glass walls. Eli could see several awakened lost sitting on large red couches facing a wall of cubicles in which wolves in fancy suits sat typing away on computers. A large sign hung on the wall that read, "Happiness is found in the size of your house. What you need is a bigger house". Mounted on the wall just under the large sign was a television screen showing unnaturally happy people standing in front of different beautiful homes.

In the other half of the bank area was a line with several awakened lost standing in line waiting to talk to wolves dressed as bank tellers. Above the tellers was another sign that read, "Happiness is found in piles of money. Nothing will meet your need like money". Directly under the sign was another large screen television that showed incredibly happy people spending lots of money on all sorts of things.

On the left side of the main floor, extending from the entrance to the ascending ramp, was a large showroom full of cars, trucks, and boats. Walking around the showroom were wolves dressed in flamboyant clothes wearing sunglasses. On the top of the wall stretching the entire width of the room was a sign that read, "Happiness is found in the things you possess. Our vehicles will meet your need". Spread throughout the large showroom were many different televisions showing different ways each of these things could bring a person happiness.

As the trio walked past the open door to the showroom, Eli could hear an awakened lost speaking to one of the sales wolves.

"I get it, I do, but I am looking for something more. I just don't think that these things are what I am looking for. Is there anything else?"

"Why of course there is more." answered a very cheery sales wolf, "Keep walking up the golden ramp and you will find several floors dedicated to more. On the second floor, you will find the entire floor dedicated to improving your image! From workout equipment to the latest fashions, you will find happiness in having the best image. And then, if that is not enough, the third floor has all the latest gaming and entertainment options available. I mean seriously, what could possibly be happier than relaxing while experiencing the greatest entertainment technology out there?"

"I don't know, that sounds great and all, but I just feel like there has to be something more. I just don't think that is what I *need*."

"Yes you said that." replied the wolf in an agitated tone, "Well then you will have to continue to the fourth floor, where you will see how happiness can be found in relationships. And if you are still not satisfied, the fifth floor is dedicated to helping you find happiness in a high paying job. Now, go on and see for yourself."

The sales wolf then ushered the awakened lost out of the doors and toward the ramp. Seeing the trio of what the sales wolf thought were security wolves, it approached Eli, Ella, and Aiden.

"Listen. That awakened lost may need to be detained. Follow him around and keep a close eye on that one. I think he has been too awakened to be caught up in our little world."

Stunned by the wolf's words, all Eli could do was nod his head and look suspiciously toward the awakened lost now walking slowly up the ramp.

"Thanks and have a great day."

The sales wolf looked at the trio and rolled his eyes as he walked back into the show-room.

Out of earshot, Eli leaned in close to Ella, "I don't get it. Why are the wolves so caught up in the material goods of the physical realm? Why would they build a mega-mall as a trap to catch the awakened lost?"

"The wolves' strategy is to get the wandering lost, as well as, those who have found the life of the King to focus on the material things of the physical realm. Think about it. This den is built to counter the tower of conviction. The gospel light convicts the wandering lost by showing the lost their need for the life of the King and it convicts the saved to be more like the King. When the lost feel this need awake inside of them, the wolves attempt to distract the conviction of the light by filling that need with things that do not satisfy."

Eli wanted to respond, but at that moment, every screen in the den, including the giant cubed television in the center of the den, flashed with the same picture. The picture was of a man that Eli thought looked identical to the televangelist who had just purchased a sports stadium for a church because his congregation was so large. This man had pale white skin that looked like it was stretched a little, black greasy hair cemented in place, beady brown eyes, and a creepy looking smile.

"Welcome, welcome, welcome. Welcome all to the Pursuit of Happiness, our latest project designed with you in mind. I'm F. Lucre and here at the Pursuit of Happiness we have done our best to make sure your every need will be met. We have gone to great lengths to secure the best of the best this world has to offer and we are making it available to you through unbelievable deals. Take your time, look around at all our inventory, and then make your dreams come true by taking whatever you want. You might wonder why we would do this for you, but we do this because you deserve to be happy. You are here because you have a need, and we want to fill that need with the very best this world can provide. I'm F. Lucre and I am here to make your dreams come true. Remember, happiness is found in the very best of everything. Enjoy your time here at the Pursuit of Happiness."

The screens all returned to their normal advertisements and promotions.

"We need to find Mr. F. Lucre and introduce ourselves." whispered Aiden.

"I agree." said Eli, "But first, we need to do what we are called to do."

Eli then took the lead and walked briskly to the ramp in pursuit of the awakened lost who was questioning the sales wolf about wanting more.

Ella and Aiden looked at each other for a brief moment.

"I know that look." said Ella under her breath, "That is the same look dad gets when he is about to do something mom isn't going to like."

"Yeah I know. I can't wait to see what trouble we are about to get into."

Aiden winked at his sister and then ran to catch up with Eli.

chapter 20

a risky rescue

When Ella and Aiden caught up to Eli, he was walking up to the awakened lost who was talking with two more wolves. By the looks of things, Ella could tell that trouble was already brewing. There were two wolves, dressed as a male and female fitness instructors, attempting to convince the awakened lost that his need would be met through image. The wolf dressed as the male fitness instructor was just getting off of "The Home Gym of Happiness", apparently giving a demonstration as to how this equipment could meet the need of the lost when the group walked up.

"So you see." said the wolf in the workout costume breathing heavily, "As you invest in this machine, this machine invests in you. The more you work, the more you are rewarded. No wonder they call this machine the Home Gym of Happiness, I'm feeling happier already! I'll promise you this, you pick up one of these machines and soon that need you're looking to meet will be history. You will find happiness in a sweet looking body."

"Yes!" said the female instructor "And it is a happiness that keeps on giving. You see, when your body looks amazing, then you will want to show everyone how amazing it looks by picking up the latest fashions. You will be the talk of the town. And what brings happiness more than being the person everyone else wants to be like?"

The wolves stopped and looked at the awakened lost with the most ridiculous looking smiles Eli had ever seen. But the smiles quickly faded away as it was clear the awakened lost was not impressed with the wolves' presentation.

"Yeah, you know, I'm just not feeling it. I think I'm just going to keep looking."

The wolves' eyes narrowed and Eli could see that the awakened lost was in serious danger. That's when he moved in.

"Hey everyone. It looks like we have a hard customer to please."

"Yes we do." said the wolf in the stylish clothes, "And we are glad you're here. I'm afraid this young man might need a little convincing if you know what I mean?"

"I sure do. It appears that he gave the good folks downstairs some trouble too. I've been told to escort him around to make sure we find exactly what he is looking for."

The wolves gave a nod like they understood Eli's meaning. "Well, with as picky as this one is, I wonder if you will not have to take him all the way up."

"All the way up?" asked Eli, "Like to the top?"

"Of course." replied the wolf in the workout costume, "You know, to see Mr. Lucre himself. I'm sure he would be able to help this young man get exactly what he is looking for."

"Oh, yes of course, I'm sure Mr. Lucre would be happy to help."

The wolves smiled one more time at the awakened lost and then turned away in disgust and walked in the direction of other awakened lost wandering the second floor.

"Come on son." said Eli loudly so to be heard by all the wolves around, "I think it's time that you and I get to the bottom of your stubbornness."

Eli took the awakened lost and gently grabbed him under the arm and lead him toward the dressing room area.

"Hey." objected the awakened lost, "What are you doing? I didn't do anything."

"I know." whispered Eli, "Trust me, I understand your problem. Come with me and I will show you where you will really find what you are looking for. And believe me, it is not here in the Pursuit of Happiness."

"Really? Okay then, I'll play along."

Eli walked over to the dressing room area and looked around.

"Alright boy." Eli called loudly, "Let's get to the bottom of this."

Moving in close to the awakened lost, Eli dropped his voice down to a whisper.

"Listen to me. You are in great danger. You were brought here because you know you have a need, but this is not the place to meet your need. This is a trap that was built to keep you from finding the truth that will satisfy your need."

"I knew it!" whispered the awakened lost, "I knew there had to be something more."

"There is. There is so much more than all of these things. What you are looking for is life and the life that you are looking for is only found in the King. It is the King's light that helped you understand your need and it is only the King's light that will satisfy your need."

"Yes! Yes, that's it, that's what I am looking for. Where can I get this light?"

"Well, you can't get it in here, you are going to have to leave the Pursuit of Happiness, go outside, and look up to the sky. When you look up, you will see the light of the King and it will lead you to the City on a Hill. You will find what you are looking for inside that city."

"That sounds great, but there is one problem. The people here won't let me leave. I have tried twice already. I'm afraid that if I try to leave they will arrest me or something."

"Of course they won't let you leave." said Eli as he looked around for another exit.

"We could always break him out by destroying a few of the wolves." suggested Aiden excitedly.

"Sure we can little bro. And all the work we have put into infiltrating the den and taking out Lucre will be destroyed as well."

"Oh yeah, I didn't think about that."

"Who are you guys?" asked the awakened lost with a confused look on his face.

Eli looked around and then looked at Ella, "You said that these disguises will allow me to make the people I come in contact with see what I want them to see, right?"

"Yes." Ella answered cautiously.

Eli turned to the awakened lost, "I want you to see me for who I really am."

Eli could feel the air around his face shimmer and the awakened lost's eyes grew large.

"How did you do that? You are the, oh what did the security guards call you, the defender."

"Yes I am. And I am here to help you find the life that is in the King. Listen to me, you are going to walk over to the clothes and pick out a hooded jacket in medium size and some medium sized wind-pants. When you do so, you are going to talk about how these clothes are going to make you so happy. Then, you and I are going to go into the dressing room. You are going to take my disguise. This disguise is specially made to transform you into whatever you imagine yourself to be. You are going to imagine yourself to be one of the security guards. You will then walk out the front doors and down to the street. When you reach the street, look up and find the light of the King. It will lead you all the way to the gates of the City on a Hill. There you will find the life that satisfies your need."

"What about you? What will happen to you?"

"That is a good question, Eli." added Ella, "What do you think will happen to you?"

"The clothes he picks out ought to give us enough of a start to get up to the top floor. I suspect that is where Lucre is hiding based upon the wolf's suggestion to take him up to the top floor. Once we get there our disguises won't help us anyway. If we don't get that far, then we follow Aiden's advice and start destroying some wolves."

"Righteous!" said Aiden excitedly.

"I'm not so sure." said Ella, "But I can't think of anything else, so, why not, let's do it."

The awakened lost walked over to the clothes section talking loudly about how happy the perfect hoodie will make him. The wolf in the clothes section looked over to Eli and gave a head-nod of approval. Once the awakened lost returned, he and Eli went into the dressing room. Soon, the awakened lost stepped out dressed like a security guard.

"The boy said he needs a few minutes and that I should start on my way before he comes out just to make sure." announced the awakened lost in the deepest voice he could muster.

"Sounds good." replied Ella, "Good luck and don't forget to look up."

"Will do, and thank you!"

Ella and Aiden watched the security guard walk out of the store and down the ramp. Fearful that they might hear an alarm, they stood ready to move in case the awakened lost was discovered. After a few minutes, they assumed that the ploy had worked and that there was one more soul on the path the City on a Hill. Eli too must have been waiting until he thought the lost could leave the building because about that time, Eli stepped out of the dressing room wearing the clothes from the store with the hoody as his only concealment.

"Let's move." whispered Eli, "And don't forget to tell me how happy I look now that I have stopped being so hard to please."

The trio walked through the store up to the ramp as Ella and Aiden spoke loudly about how happy Eli now looked as Eli nodded his head vigorously. The group had walked out of the store and past the third and fourth floor when the alarms rang.

The lights in the Pursuit of Happiness flashed several times and then glowed red as a siren rang through the building. A female computerized voice repeated the phrase, "Red alert, red alert, intruders discovered."

At that point all the screens zoomed in on the target that set off the wolves' alarm and a large group of wolves came sprinting down the ramp right at Eli.

"You, there!" shouted the wolf in the head of the oncoming group, "Don't move!"

chapter 21
mr. f. lucre

Eli figured they would have to fight at some point, but he had hoped it would not be in this type of a situation: hopelessly outnumbered and in an open space in which they could easily be surrounded. Aiden drew his light spear, which looked like an ordinary night-stick thanks to his disguise, but thankfully, he did not strike. At that moment, the screens all focused on the intruder that caused the alarm: a black and gold ninja-looking shepherd standing on the golden ramp by the main entrance.

This took Eli off guard because he was sure their picture would be plastered all over the live-feed cameras. At that moment, the large group of officers approached.

"You two, what are you doing out in the open? Can't you see that we have an intruder alarm? Would you please follow protocol and take our honored guest out of danger's way?"

"Why, of course, sir." sputtered Ella, and Eli was thankful she was so quick on her feet, "We were actually on our way up to make sure that our guest is as far from the front entrance as possible."

"Then why are you standing around talking to me? Get moving soldiers! The rest of you, follow me, we have an under-shepherd to deal with!"

The group of wolves followed their leader down the ramp toward the front entrance.

"What's wrong with dad? Is he crazy?" asked Aiden.

"No, he's brilliant!" replied Eli. "I bet they knew we would need a distraction and not only has your dad kept the cameras off of us, he has also succeeded in pulling Lucre's personal guards away from him. He has given us the opportunity we need to shut down the Pursuit of Happiness and re-claim the reflector of Conviction! Come on, let's move!"

Ella and Aiden walked up next to Eli, placed their hands on his back, and acted like they were escorting him up the ramp. The group ran past the 5th floor and came to the top of the ramp on the 6th floor. The moment they reached the 6th floor Eli could tell that they were close to their goal. The floor was completely empty save for a gigantic doorway with two ornately designed gold doors. The roof of the Pursuit of Happiness was gold tinted glass and Eli could see the golden spire stretching into the sky intercepting the light of the gospel.

"Be on your guard." Eli said as the group ran up to the golden double doors. "Once we get in there, I need you two to find a way to bar the doors. I don't know how long your dad can give us and we don't want an army of wolves interrupting our meeting with Lucre."

"Got it." the Thomas kids said in unison.

Looking around once more to make sure there were no traps or unseen guards, Eli swung the doors inward and raced into the room.

Lucre's lair was extravagant. The room was the size of a basketball gym and it was covered from floor to ceiling with all sorts of precious treasures. The treasures lined the walls on both sides of the room with little paths cut through the horde. A large walkway was cleared from the doorway to a large desk that looked to be made out of pure gold. Standing behind the desk with his back to the doorway looking out the window was the man Eli had seen on the television screen. As soon as the group entered the room, Ella and Aiden slammed the doors closed and grabbed several long golden spears from several life-sized suits of armor standing near the doors and ran them through the door handles.

"There." said Aiden, "That ought to keep the baddies out long enough for us to take care of business."

Cautiously, Eli threw off the hoodie and break-away wind pants, drew his sword, and approached the large desk. About half-way between the door and the desk, Lucre, with his back still to the intruders started clapping his hands loudly.

"Clever! Very clever I must say! Ingenious really. First you find a way to sneak into the fabulous Pursuit of Happiness and then you send the under-shepherd to cause a diversion and barge into my lair."

Still clapping, Lucre turned around and faced Eli. Lucre looked like the epitome of old Chicago gangster. He wore a double-breasted black suit with white pinstripes, a shiny white shirt with a solid red tie, a large gold chain with a large gold and diamond dollar symbol on it, a large gold Rolex on his left wrist, and several precious stone-studded gold rings on his fingers.

"I am impressed. But I wonder, did you ever think about what would happen once you found me? Do you think that I am going to simply surrender? Oh no, young defender, I am afraid that when you barred the doors, you did not prevent others from coming in, you have successfully cut off your only way of escape."

Lucre chuckled cruelly and Eli stopped walking long enough for Aiden and Ella to join him.

"So that's how you did it." said Lucre as he examined the disguises Ella and Aiden still wore, "Well then, I will make a note of that. You won't be needing them anymore, I am not a low-functioning creature; your disguises won't work on me."

Lucre waived his hand dismissively and the disguises evaporated off of Ella and Aiden.

"Ah, that's better." continued Lucre as he sat down at his desk. "Come now defender, you have a choice to make. Look around you, I can offer you more riches than your finite, mortal mind, can imagine. And I'm not only talking about here in the spirit realm, if you accept my offer and team up with me, I can make sure these riches fill up your coffers in the physical realm."

"Nice try, but he doesn't even drink coffee!" Aiden blurted.

"Not coffee, you fool; coffers, like treasuries. What do you say, Eli, look around you. I know there is something here that speaks to you."

Eli was not interested in Lucre's offer, but there was something about the large treasure horde that drew his attention. As Lucre spoke, Eli could feel energy radiating off of the treasure like heat radiating off of a fire. The energy radiating off of the treasure kept drawing Eli's attention to the magnificence of Lucre's wealth and Eli could feel a longing to own that treasure rising up inside of his chest.

"Yes." Lucre hissed as he noticed Eli's looking at the treasure horde, "Listen to the treasure. Let it speak to you. Tell it what you want and it will grant you your wish."

Eli tried to focus on Lucre, but his eyes kept scanning the horde. Eventually, Eli's eyes landed on a beautiful golden Rolex watch with a gigantic diamond on the face.

"Nice choice, Eli, I knew you had good taste."

Lucre snapped his fingers and the watch Eli was looking at flew into Lucre's hand.

"But you know what is so nice about this watch? It comes with a boat.

A loud commotion behind Eli drew his attention as a massive state-of-the-art fishing boat emerged from under a pile of gold coins.

"These things can all be yours, Eli. In fact, I will give them to you before you leave here. And what you see is just a small sampling of what I can offer you. Fame. Fortune. Happiness. Think about it: any clothes you want, any cars you want, any job you want, anything you could ever wish for, and of course, all the happiness you can fit into one lifetime. You are, as a matter of fact, inside the very Pursuit of Happiness!"

"No." said Eli, "I can't accept your bribe."

"This is not a bribe, this is a contract from two interested parties."

"It sure sounds like a bribe to me." Aiden interjected.

"Well it's a good thing I'm not speaking to you. I'm not interested in any low-level harvester. I'm speaking to the true talent, the defender."

"Not only will I not accept your bribe, I will not allow you to talk about my friends that way!"

"Don't act so righteous, boy, there is no need for it. This is not a bribe, this is an offer for partnership. You would not be the first defender who accepted my offer and I am sure you will not be the last. I can still remember a man, not that long ago, who came to challenge my rule, as you have done. This man saw all that he could have and he chose to accept my offer. Do you know what happened to him Eli? He lived a long and happy life full of riches and wealth. I overflowed his barns until he had to build more. He lived a happy life and so could you defender, if you accept my offer."

"So you are seriously offering me a life full of riches and wealth?"

"Eli!" exclaimed Ella, "you can't seriously be considering his offer!"

"Yes I am." Lucre continued completely ignoring Ella, "I'm offering you a life in the physical realm full of more money and wealth than you can imagine."

"And all I have to do to receive the wealth is what? Stop being a defender? Walk away from my calling? What?"

"It is easier than that! You can still be a defender, you can still fulfill your calling, but instead of working for the King, you will work for me. I still want you to share the King's Word, just not all of it. I want you to use the King's Word to show people that they have a right to be happy, healthy, and wealthy. That's it. That is all you have to do and when you serve me, I will fill your bank account and wallet by giving you favor and charisma in the eyes of your peers. People will flock to you, throw money at you, and worship you even, when you follow my instructions. But that is not even the best part, I will allow you to spend the money on flashy living to show everyone how happy F. Lucre has made you."

"That's it? I just work for you and you will do all that for me? I will live with great wealth and fame forever?"

"Yes, exactly. For as long as you live. So what do you say? Do we have a deal?"

Lucre extended his hand toward Eli and a pen appeared in his grasp. Simultaneously, a contract made of a single gold sheet appeared on the desk that said "contract" on the top and had a place for Eli to sign at the bottom. Lucre placed the Rolex watch on top of the contract and slid the contract closer to Eli.

Eli could feel the energy of the wealth tug at his heart, but there was one question that kept coming up in his mind.

"But what about after I die?"

Lucre's smile faded instantly.

"What do you mean? What kind of stupid question is that?"

"Well, you say that if I serve you that you will fill my life with riches and fame for as long as I live, but what about after my life in the physical realm is over? What can you do for me then?"

"Well." started Lucre obviously grasping for an answer.

"The reason I ask." continued Eli without waiting for Lucre's answer, "Is because I am familiar with the man you are speaking about."

"You are?"

"Yes I am. In fact, the man's story is found in the King's Word. The man's betrayal was so drastic that the King used it as an illustration when warning us about living for earthly wealth rather than living for the King. You know, the exact thing you're trying to get me to do. Anyway, you're right, you filled his barns to overflowing so much so that he had to build more barns. But you and I both know that he never got the opportunity to build those barns or spend all that earthly wealth because his time had come and his earthly life ended."

"And that is where things get complicated, Mr. Lucre. You see, that day, after all those years living for the wealth you offered him, he had to give an account of how he lived his life and what he lived his life for. Now, I'm not sure exactly how things went, but I can promise you they went poorly because the King shared his view concerning the life lived for riches. The King states to this man, 'Thou fool, this night thy soul shall be required of thee: then whose shall those things be, which thou hast provided'.

"Here is the problem, Mr. Filthy Lucre: you say it is better to live for the temporary pleasures and wealth of the world and you have convinced many a child of the King to forsake the service of the King for the reward of wealth. But the King's Word has two big problems with what you say."

"First, you think that earthly riches bring satisfaction and happiness, but the King's Word tells us the opposite. The King's Word tells us;

'He that loves silver; shall not be satisfied with silver, nor he that loves abundance with increase: this is also vanity'

'Wilt thou set thine eyes upon that which is not? For riches certainly make themselves wings; they fly away as an eagle toward heaven'

Lucre shifted uncomfortably in his chair as Eli quoted the King's Word.

"Second, you claim that I can still be a defender and still do what I am called to do while serving you, but you're either lying or just plain stupid! The King's Word makes it clear that no person can serve two masters. Either I can live for the King and the eternal treasures He offers, or I can live for you and the temporary treasures you offer."

"Knowing these truths, could you please tell me why I would even consider your deal?"

"That's simple," answered Lucre, "if you refuse my invitation, I will end your life as a defender and your friends' lives as harvesters, dip what is left of your confiscated armor in gold and hang it on the wall of my treasure trove."

"Those are tough words coming from a creature wearing a silk shirt!" mocked Aiden.

Lucre's facial reaction made it clear that he was not one who was ever laughed at.

"You think my choice of clothing is funny, do you? Well, perhaps I should change to something more comfortable."

Slamming both of his fists on the golden desk, Lucre growled loudly as his body bubbled. Suddenly, Lucre's body burst out of his suit like the Incredible Hulk would burst out of his clothes. In a few scary moments, Lucre had completely transformed from the televangelist gangster into a gigantic wolf fully clad in golden, Roman-gladiator armor.

"Back up, back up!" yelled Eli

Eli had expected Lucre to take wolf form, but he did not expect Lucre to be so much larger than the other wolves. Wolves are generally about seven feet tall, Lucre stood now at least ten to twelve feet tall. Eli expected Lucre to be different from the other wolves, but for whatever reason, Eli did not expect Lucre to be clad in armor. Most of the wolves Eli fought had only their claws and fangs, but Lucre had way more, and Eli was beginning to realize that he had foolishly underestimated one of the top Desolate City villains.

Lucre towered over his golden desk looking terrifying in solid gold armor. His armor looked like a solid gold body suit that covered every inch of his body from his waist to his feet, from his neck down his arms to his massive paws. On his head, Lucre wore a solid gold helmet that looked like it was made to fit his head giving him the appearance of having a golden head. Lucre's Rolex watch had turned into a large round diamond shield with a golden frame, and his rings had turned into an ornate golden scepter studded with precious jewels which he carried in a threatening position in his right paw.

"I'll give you one last chance, defender." snarled Lucre, "Join me, accept my generosity or be destroyed."

"Would you listen to that super-sized, bejeweled, Chihuahua? He thinks that just because he is all glamorous that we are just going to lay down our weapons," Aiden yelled, "Well Fido, you're barking up the wrong tree. Light Train of Pain, let's light him up!"

Aiden's spear exploded with light and Ella had a light arrow notched in her bow. Both Aiden and Ella attacked sending a light spear and several light arrows at Lucre. Lucre laughed and did not even make an attempt to move or dodge the assault. The light spear and arrows bounced harmlessly off of Lucre's golden body-suit.

"Please tell me that's not all you can do." laughed Lucre, "Otherwise this is going to be a rather short affair."

"Not even close!" quipped Ella as she unleashed another barrage of arrows aimed at all different parts of Lucre. The arrows all struck their targets or were effortlessly batted away by Lucre with his shield. Again, Lucre suffered no damage.

"That body armor." called Ella in disbelief, "It is impenetrable! Our weapons cannot get through it!"

"You are an intelligent one aren't you?" mocked Lucre

Frustrated by Lucre's mocking, Eli gripped his sword tightly.

"We will see just how impenetrable that armor really is."

Eli closed his eyes to connect with the King's Spirit.

"Oh no you don't defender! It's not that I think you can really do any damage with that little sword, but why risk it?"

Lucre's words broke Eli's concentration and it might just have saved Eli some serious pain. Lucre's scepter had a large ruby on the top of it and the ruby glowed with red light. Lucre lifted his scepter and as he did the golden desk rose off the ground into the air. With a swish of his scepter,

Lucre launched the large golden desk at Eli. Jumping to his left as fast as he could, Eli only just managed to not get smashed by the desk. The desk smacked the ground where Eli had been standing and then slid down the walkway, slamming into the doors.

"Not bad, young defender, not bad at all! But I am only just getting started!"

Lucre pointed his scepter at a mountain of precious stones just off to the side of where his desk once stood. The stones shook and then a large group of them rose into the air and over to where Lucre stood. Lucre smiled as he had the stones circle his head before sending them soaring at Eli.

Eli managed to bat several away with his sword and dodge a few others. When the last couple of stones were coming too fast for Eli to dodge or bat, he lowered his head and allowed the stones to bounce harmlessly off of his helmet of salvation.

"Hahaha, yes!" yelled Aiden, "Way to use your head Eli."

"Silence fool!" shouted Lucre as he waived his glowing scepter at a mountain of gold bars sending them cascading at Aiden. Aiden's eyes widened and he just had enough time to block his body with his spear as the avalanche of gold slammed into him sending him crashing into the far wall.

"Aiden!" cried Ella, "You'll pay for that Lucre!"

Once again Ella unleashed a massive amount of arrows, this time aimed directly at Lucre's face. Though the arrows did not penetrate Lucre's helmet, the bursting light of the King did temporarily blind Lucre and by the sound of his angry growled, hurt him.

Taking advantage of Lucre's temporary blindness, Eli charged and sliced his sword across Lucre's right thigh. But just like the light arrows and spears, Eli's sword harmlessly bounced off of Lucre's armor. Eli stood stunned as Lucre laughed. Swinging his golden scepter like a tennis racket, Lucre batted Eli into the air sending him crashing into a pile of treasure chests.

Lucre looked to capitalize on Eli's condition but as he approached Eli, a light spear smacked him on the side of his head. Lucre tried to ignore the attack but several other light spears followed. Finally a light spear landed in front of Lucre and stuck in the ground. Lucre stopped because this light spear was different from the other spears. Eli recognized the difference immediately as the same type of spear that landed on the tare before exploding. In an instant, this spear also exploded catching Lucre off guard and sending him crashing backwards.

Eli felt a pair of hands help him up from behind.

"Eli." Ella said, "You have to get somewhere and connect with the Illuminator or we are all going to die. Lucre is too powerful for our weapons and even for your sword if you do not have the power of the King's Spirit energizing it."

"Yeah, you're right. But what about you. What are you going to do?"

"Aiden and I will hold him off as long as we can. Don't worry about us. You have to be the one to take Lucre out. The sooner you connect with the Illuminator, the safer Aiden and I will be."

"Right. I'm on it."

Eli ran back toward the door and then cut to his right down one of the paths that cut through the treasure horde. After weaving around several turns, Eli felt he had gone far enough in that Lucre could not find him before connecting with the Illuminator. Eli closed his eyes trying to concentrate.

Lucre's rage-filled roar followed by Aiden's painful cry momentarily broke Eli's concentration.

No, I can't help them now. The only way I can protect them from Lucre is to wield the power of the King's Word. Concentrate Eli.

"Mighty King." Eli prayed, "All powerful Father, please show me the truth of your Word that I must have to vanquish Lucre."

Eli felt his sword hum with life and he could feel his body glow with the light of the Spirit. This time, it was Ella's cry of pain followed by a loud crash that threatened Eli's concentration.

"Can you hear this, defender?" yelled Lucre, "Your friends are dying, and you are hiding like a coward."

Another noise echoed through the chamber; it was the noise of wolves banging on the doors trying to get in. Eli could feel his concentration slipping when Zephyr's voice rang in his mind.

"Eli, don't lose your focus! You are almost there. You have connected with the Illuminator and now all you have to do is harness that power."

"But Zeph, what about Ella and Aiden, and the army of wolves? What am I supposed to do about that?"

"Eli, you can do nothing about any of those things unless you complete your connection and harness the power of the King's Word. Now focus while you can still save them!"

Eli doubled his efforts and felt the power of the Illuminator radiate through his body. Eli could tell that his body was glowing powerfully with the King's light.

Several things happened at once. Eli heard the doors to the chamber burst open followed by the howls of an unknown number of wolves and the entire horde of treasure Eli was hiding behind shook and slowly rose off the ground controlled by the glowing scepter of Lucre.

Lucre laughed in victory as the army of wolves surrounded Eli ready to pounce. But they were too late. Eli had connected with the King's Word through the power of the King's Spirit. A powerful verse, custom tailored for Lucre and his army burned in Eli's mind just waiting to be unleashed.

Eli opened his eyes, looked directly at Lucre and spoke with authority the words of the King.

"But godliness with contentment is great gain.
For we brought nothing into this world, and it is certain we can carry nothing out.
And having food and raiment let us be therewith content.

But they that will be rich fall into temptation and a snare, and into many foolish and hurtful lusts, which drown men in destruction and perdition.
For the love of money is the root of all evil: which while some coveted after, they have erred from the faith, and pierced themselves through with many sorrows."

The powerful blue light of Eli's sword engulfed the floating treasure. Lucre growled in frustration as he tried to regain control of the horde to no avail. The group of wolves looked around nervously not knowing if they should run or attack.

Suddenly, a coin from the floating horde shot away from the horde and struck a wolf in the chest. The coin went through the wolf leaving a hole filled with the blue light. The wolf howled and then disappeared in a burst of light. Without warning, countless coins, precious stones, and other forms of treasure, were shooting from the floating horde and striking the pack of wolves, and Lucre himself, piercing the wolves like bullets from a machine gun.

Soon all the wolves were destroyed and Lucre had his back to the wall of glass using his shield to defend against the piercing horde of treasure. Several pieces of treasure would get past the large shield, and though Lucre would call out in pain, the treasure could not pierce his golden armor.

"Give it up, boy. My armor is too thick for your little party tricks. You cannot defeat me so easily."

Eli lifted his hands and the rapid fire attack ceased. Lucre slowly stood up keeping his shield in place just in case the attack resumed.

"So, are you ready to accept my offer since it appears your little attack fell short?"

"I'm not finished. I have a message especially for you from the King's Word."

"Not if I can help it!" yelled Lucre as he charged Eli with his scepter in position to strike.

"Go to now, ye rich men," yelled Eli and the power of the King's Word threw Lucre back into the glass wall, cracking the glass. *"Weep and howl for your miseries that shall come upon you. Your riches are*

corrupted, and your garments are motheaten. Your gold and silver is cankered; and the rust of them shall be a witness against you, and shall eat your flesh as it were fire."

Eli could feel the power surge through him as light burst from Eli's sword and struck Lucre's armor. Lucre cried out in pain and threw his shield and scepter down. Falling to his knees, Lucre tried to peel off his armor, but it was too late. Smoke was pouring out from under his armor and the smell of burning hair filled the lair. The impenetrable golden armor that had saved his life, was now the instrument of his own destruction. The armor burst into flames and Lucre cried in agony.

"This is not over, defender! We will meet again!"

Then, in a burst of blue light, Lucre disappeared and his fiery armor fell to the ground. With Lucre and his army of wolves gone, Eli knew there was only one more thing for him to do. Eli willed the horde of treasure to form a gigantic wrecking ball. Eli sent the large wrecking ball tearing through the side of the Pursuit of Happiness. Then, starting at the bottom of the tower, Eli sent the wrecking ball of treasure tearing through the Pursuit of happiness over and over until the structure swayed as its foundations were destroyed. A loud crash gave warning that the structure was crumbling under its own weight. The building swayed heavily to the right, knocking the golden spire and orb off the top of the building and freeing the light of the gospel to reach the reflector tower of Conviction.

The light of the gospel flooded what was left of the Pursuit of Happiness instantly dissolving the structure into nothingness. With the Pursuit of Happiness completely gone, Eli, Ella, and Aiden hovered in midair as they now rested securely in the light beam of the gospel.

chapter 22

an enemy turned ally

With the enemies gone and the Pursuit of Happiness destroyed, Eli felt his power calm down and the glow around his body subsided. It was at this point as Eli hovered in the light beam with Ella and Aiden that Eli saw just how damaged both his friends were.

Though the light beam was rejuvenating and healing his friends, the marks from their previous battle were still evident. Aiden hung in air with a goofy smile on his face as several large cracks in his helmet were slowly mending themselves in the light. His leather vest looked as if it had been shot with an automatic weapon having several holes ripped into it.

"Dude that was amazing! You totally took Lucre's treasure from him and beat him with it."

"Yeah, I guess I did, but what happened to you?"

"Well, after I saw the impact of the exploding spear, I was determined to keep Lucre occupied by sending a few more his direction. But, he recovered faster than I expected. I was in motion to launch another one when he sent a large pile of pearls my direction. I did what I could to bat them aside with my spear but there were too many. They hit me like rapid fire paint-balls. Before I could recover, I saw a large golden chest soaring at me. I did not have time to react so I took a page out of your book and lowered my head to absorb the blow. Well, I absorbed the blow but it knocked me silly. I was dead in the water. Thankfully Ella jumped in and bought just enough time for you to do your thing."

"Yes, you owe me big time little bro."

Turning his attention to Ella, Eli could see the extent of her wounds which were also being mended in the light. Ella's right shoulder guard had been smashed to pieces and the right side of her body armor had several large cracks running from her underarm to her waist. Ella's bow was also damaged having been broken into two pieces.

"I don't even want to know what happened to you." said Eli jokingly.

"Well, I'm going to tell you anyway. Someone has to give me the credit I deserve for saving Aiden's life."

"I saw Lucre charge Aiden after Aiden decided to use his head to block the chest." Ella continued shaking her head at Aiden for his decision.

"What, it was all I could think of."

"It's my turn little bro, let me finish."

"Whatever, continue your majesty."

"I will, thank you."

Eli could not help laughing at the exchange between the two siblings.

"Anyway, where was I? Oh, yes, saving Aiden's life. Lucre was charging so I shot as many arrows as I could but they were not touching him, so I picked up a soft-ball sized diamond and chunked it at Lucre's face. I missed, but it actually turned out for the better. The diamond hit Lucre in the throat and staggered him. I saw an opening so I charged Lucre. I knew my arrows were not going to work, but I could also feel your power rising and I knew I did not have to stall for long. So, I did what any awesome big sister would do, I jumped at Lucre's head and slapped him in the face with my bow."

"You did what?" exclaimed Eli in disbelief.

"She totally did! She broke her bow across his face! You should of heard him yelp. It was amazing!"

"Yes it was." added Ella, "But unfortunately, it did not end the battle. Lucre hit me in the ribs with his scepter and then slammed me with his shield sending me crashing into the wall next to Aiden. I was done, and we were helpless. I thought Lucre would finish us off right then, but for some reason he stopped to taunt you about us dying."

"Yeah, and then the army of wolves burst through the door, which actually helped us because it distracted Lucre even more." Aiden continued, "With the wolves there, Lucre decided to come find you. When he did, and we saw you glowing in the power of the Spirit, we knew it was over."

In the time it took for the two siblings to relate their stories, the light of the gospel had successfully healed all the damage incurred in battle. At that point a hologram of Aquila appeared in the light.

"Greetings Eli, Ella, and Aiden. Congratulations on your victory over Lucre and the army of wolves. I am sure that the record of your deeds here will be sung throughout the realm for ages to come. I am contacting you to let you know that the Council of Light will be sending the King's Recovery Team to re-fortify the reflector tower of Conviction shortly. You do not need to stay until they arrive. You have successfully destroyed the army of wolves and sent Lucre back into the realm of his master. The tower is safe. Please return to the City on a Hill immediately so we can prepare you for your next mission. God speed to you all."

The hologram ended and Aiden was the first one to speak, "You heard the man, last one there is a rotten egg!"

Aiden turned toward the lighthouse in the City on a Hill and sped away.

"Come on." cried Ella as she turned to follow, "We can't let him win!"

Eli took one last look at the reflector tower of conviction which now flooded the Desolate City with the light of the gospel. Eli noticed a group of awakened lost standing on the road looking up into the light.

These must be the awakened lost who followed the light into the wolves' den.

"Hey, you down there. Follow the light and you will find something that will truly meet your need!"

When Eli finished speaking, a ray of light shot from the main beam of light and struck the ground by the awakened lost. That light then formed a path that would lead the awakened lost to the narrow way. Immediately, the group of awakened lost waived to Eli and took off down the path. Satisfied, Eli turned and sped back to the City on a Hill.

The light beam took the group back into the top of the lighthouse, through the crystal globe, and landed them safely on the walkway. There they were met by Aquila, Priscilla, Zephyr, and Pastor Thomas.

"Dad!" shrieked Ella as she and Aiden ran over and hugged their father. "We were worried about you!"

"You kids need not worry about me, it takes more than a few wolves to bring down your old man."

"Yeah, but how did you know when to show up? How did you know that we needed a diversion at that exact time?"

"We didn't, actually. Aquila was told by word from the King that my job would not be to go with you, but we were not told anything else. And so we waited and prayed for you all here in the tower. Suddenly Michael appears and tells me that the time for my mission has arrived. So I asked him what it is and he smiles at me and says, 'stay alive and make a scene'. Before I could ask what he was talking about, he transported me to the ramp of the wolves' den. When I did not see any sign of you, I figured this was some sort of diversion and so I did what I was told to do. I stayed alive and made quite a scene for the wolves. Then, as I was on the middle of battling the wolves, I was transported back here in time to see the wolves' den come crashing down. Tell me, what happened, how did you gain the victory?"

Eli, Ella, and Aiden all took turns telling the story of how they infiltrated the wolves' den and defeated Filthy Lucre.

"I'm so proud of you guys." said Pastor Thomas in admiration.

"Yes." added Zephyr, "I especially like the part about how Eli heard the voice of reason in his head listened to his guardian Angelos for once."

Everyone burst out in laughter. As things settled down, Aquila gathered everyone's attention.

"Praise the King the reflector tower of conviction has been liberated, but there are two reflectors left still in the hands of the Enemy. We must now turn our attention toward the second tower, the tower of acceptation."

Aquila pointed his hands at the crystal globe and the images of the reflector tower of application appeared as if the globe had turned into a giant computer screen.

"If you remember, this is the tower that communicates to the wandering lost that the salvation of the King is a free gift and not something to be earned. Though the watchers are made up of shared leadership, we have learned that to capture the reflector, Polytheist teamed up with the original watcher to unite the watchers and overtake the reflector. This watcher goes by the name of Taze and though he may not look intimidating, he commands the loyalty of all the watchers."

A picture of an older man with an old-time style of beard appeared on the screen along with pictures of a creepy looking dark stone tower with several large chains attached to the top of the tower.

"Taze has erected a tower of stone using the slave labor of the watchers that stands directly in front of the reflector tower cutting off the direct beam of the gospel. This tower has multiple support anchors spread around the tower in a large circular pattern. Manning each of these support anchors are several watchers who are on high alert for you. Surrounding the support anchors and forming a solid perimeter around their base is what they call the 'kingdom hall', it is a continuous barrack full of countless watchers on guard against any intruders. Your mission is to sever the tower from the anchors and bring the tower down."

"I see." said Eli contemplatively, "But how are we supposed to get through the kingdom hall barrack and into the area with the anchors without bringing the entire army of watchers upon us?"

"For that," answered Zephyr, "you will need our secret weapon."

"Secret weapon? Did the King send it while we were gone?"

"No Eli, you sent it before you ever left?"

"I don't understand, what do you mean?"

"I mean you sent this weapon to us before you ever left. Eli, let me introduce you to one of the newest citizens of the City on a Hill."

Zephyr flew over to the beam of light coming from the bottom of the tower, "Hey Jared, come on up here. There is someone I want to introduce you to."

In a few brief moments, a familiar looking dark haired man came soaring up the light beam and landed next to Zephyr. Eli knew that he had seen this man before but could not place where.

"Eli, I want to introduce you to Jared Guess."

"It's a pleasure to meet you again." said Jared.

"Again? I know you look familiar but I don't remember where I have seen you before."

"Well, I believe I was swinging a large iron ball on a chain at your head when the ball and chain crumbled and the light of the gospel opened my eyes to the power of the true King."

"You were the watcher?"

"Yes. When I was sent back into the Desolate City, I was not sent to the broad street but to the narrow street. Once there, I sought out the light that had awakened me and I followed the light all the way to the gates of this city where I was met by Philip. I have now placed my faith in the true King and have received the life He offers. I'm here because I was trained inside those barracks and I know a way to get you in."

"Right on brother." said Aiden as he walked over and shook Jerad's hand. "I for one am glad to have you on our squad. So tell me, what is your weapon of choice? You a sword guy, knife guy, archer, or are you one of the few of us trained to use the greatest weapon ever; the spear."

"Actually," cut in Zephyr, "Jerad has not yet been trained in spiritual combat, but we feel that he might just be the key to destroying the dark tower and recapturing the reflector of acceptation."

"Really," asked Ella, "How so?"

"Well," said Aquila, "Jared has only recently been converted from the ranks of the watchers. This means that Jared has a great knowledge of the workings of the watchers, as well as, the thinking of the watchers. One of the greatest weapons citizens of the City on a Hill have is the weapon of their personal testimony. You see, Jared knows what it was like to be in the bondage of the watchtower and he also knows what the King used to awaken his soul to the truth. With his knowledge and burden for other watchers, Jared might just be the deadliest enemy old Taze has in the Desolate City."

Eli stepped forward, "Well brother, welcome aboard the Light Train of Pain."

"The what?"

"It is the name Aiden gave to our group here in the Desolate City."

"That's right I did. And you are now an official member."

"Okay, then," said Eli, "We know our mission and we have a way inside. So what are we waiting for? Mr. Aquila, are we ready to go?"

"Yes, you four ought to leave as soon as possible."

"Four?" repeated Ella as she looked at her dad, "Dad, you're not coming on this one either?"

"Sorry, sweetheart, but the King has asked me to do some work in the Desolate City and to scout Polytheist's fortress. But I will pray for you and I know that you will honor the King in victory."

Ella ran over and hugged her dad, "Thanks dad, I love you."

"I love you too. Now go and reclaim that reflector tower for the King!"

"Yes sir!"

"Are we ready?" asked Eli.

Everyone nodded.

"Jared, travelling to the tower is simple, just jump into the light beam and use your body to speed up, slow down, stop, and exit the beam. Follow our lead and hang on for the ride of your life. Light Train of Pain, let's roll."

Eli jumped into the gospel light beam followed by Ella, Aiden, and Jared and soared through the crimson sky toward the dark tower of stone.

chapter 23

the kingdom hall barracks

Soaring through the light beam, Eli, Ella, and Aiden slowed down so that Jerad could catch up to them. Flying side-by-side, the group of four now soared over the Desolate City toward the tall dark tower of stone.

Slowing down as they approached the tower, Eli turned to Jerad, "Where is this way in you were talking about? Where should we exit the beam of light?"

Jerad took a moment to survey the kingdom hall barrack that formed the perimeter of the watcher's camp. After a few moments, Jerad pointed to an abandoned street that lead from the Desolate City into the watcher's camp.

"Right there. We should land over there and then find cover. Soon the next group of scouts will return from the Desolate City with awakened souls. The scouts will lead them through that side entrance to begin their conversion process. That's our way in."

"I don't understand." replied Eli, "Won't there be watchers inside the side entrance?"

"Not for long. When the watchers bring in awakened souls, they go to great lengths to deceive the souls into thinking the watchers are a loving family. There will only be two watchers in the side entrance and they will act as tour guides who will walk with the awakened souls through the barracks drawing the awakened lost deeper into the camp. When the group leaves, the scouts will close the entrance and return to the Desolate City. All we have to do is to take out the two scouts before they close the doors and we will be inside the kingdom hall barrack without detection."

"And there will be two less scouts in the Desolate City." Aiden added nodding his head and smiling.

"Exactly." answered Jerad.

"Sounds like a good plan to me!" said Eli, "Follow me."

Eli flew out of the beam of light down toward the abandoned street. Strewn all across the street were several large pieces of rubble that looked like the top half of the corner apartment complex next to the street.

"Over there," said Eli as he pointed to the rubble, "we can hide there and still be close enough to spring the attack on the scouts."

The group agreed and carefully they all ran to their hiding place.

"How long do you think?" Ella asked Jerad.

"I'm not sure. Usually there is a team returning."

Jerad did not finish his sentence because the group heard voices echoing off of the buildings down the street and the scouts rounded the corner close by the group.

"Oh of course!" came a grizzled voice, "We know exactly what you are looking for, and we know exactly where you will find it. Keep walking, we're almost there."

"Good." came a young woman's voice, "I am so happy I found someone who could help me meet this longing in my heart."

"Well, that is what we do." replied the scout as they walked past the group's hiding place leading a group of three awakened lost toward the kingdom hall barrack, "We think of it as our ministry. Here we are, come right in. I'd like to introduce you to two of my good friends who will show you around."

The group entered into the side entrance and their voices became too muffled to understand.

"Now's our chance." whispered Jerad, "We need to get close before the introductions are over."

"Go, go go!" whispered Eli as he ran to the side of the entrance doors and crept along the wall until he was standing right behind the open doors. Soon Eli had Jerad standing next to him and Ella and

Aiden standing on the other side of the open doors. From their positions, they could hear the interactions inside.

"Okay, are we ready to go then?" came a soft and perky voice from inside, "Thank you two so much for bringing our new friends. We will take it from here."

"It's our pleasure, you all have fun." replied the scout.

Eli heard the group walk down the barracks and the sound of muffled laughter grow closer.

"Every time," said the scout, "I love it every time."

The scout walked out and placed his hand on the door to close it when Eli jumped out and sliced down with his sword. The watcher immediately disappeared and his spirit was sent back to the broad street. The second watch opened his mouth but before any sound could come out, a light arrow dissolved his body and sent his spirit back to the broad street.

"Hurry now," whispered Jerad, "we must get inside and close the doors."

Aiden entered first and made sure the room was deserted. When he signaled, the rest of the group followed him inside and closed the doors behind them.

The inside of the barracks reminded Eli of a fancy hotel lobby. All the walls were painted white with deep red chair-rails. There was a red, ornate welcome desk with golden accents facing the door. A large gold-framed mirror hung on the wall behind the desk. The room, which was a fairly large room was filled with red plush old-fashioned looking furniture with gold trim, and the floor was covered with a very soft white carpet. On the two side walls of the room were sliding pocket-doors like the sliding doors that separated train-cars. These doors were gold with a square of glass about eye level.

"Okay," said Jerad, "to the left, where the guides took the awakened lost will be the auditorium, the cafeteria, the museum, prayer room, and rec room all designed to impress the awakened lost. I would not recommend going that way because the rooms are mainly open spaces with little to hide behind and there are watchers who are positioned all throughout these areas. Though you would have the element of surprise, I fear your presence will be discovered sooner than you might like."

"To the right is the metal shop in which the collars and blindfolds are made and fitted. There are a lot more watchers that way but the constant noise and the large warehouse-like spaces will give you more protection from discovery."

"Which way is the fastest way to get inside the barrack circle and sever the anchors to the tower?" asked Eli.

"That would be to the right, through the metal shop, warehouse, and chapel. There is only one door to the inner circle and it is located in the chapel."

"I think we should go through the metal shops." said Eli, "If we do, how soon will we find the door leading to the anchors?"

"The door from the shop leads to a warehouse in which all the collars and blindfolds are kept. On the other side of the warehouse is the ceremonial chapel in which the new converts are collared and blindfolded. In the front of the chapel is the door through which new converts are welcomed into the congregation. That door leads inside the inner ring."

"That sounds like the best option we have." said Eli.

"I agree." said Ella.

"Good. Because I want you to lead the way."

"Really?" asked Ella excitedly, "Why?"

"Because you are a great shot with the bow. If we walk into the warehouse and are discovered, you can take out the watchers from a distance before they can sound the alarm."

"Well, it's about time someone noticed the great value of a professional archer." said Ella as she looked at her brother teasingly. "I would be happy to lead the way."

"Whatever. He only wants you to go first because you are the most expendable."

"Maybe so."

"There is something seriously wrong with you two." joked Eli, "Now can we please focus on the mission?"

"Fine." said Ella.

"Kill-joy." replied Aiden.

Ella reached behind her and grabbed one of the light arrows in her quiver notching it into her bow. With a nod of her head, the group fell into formation with Ella and Eli leading the way, Jerad behind Eli, and Aiden bringing up the rear. The group bent down as low as they could and scuttled across the welcoming area to the sliding-door that led to the workshops. Huddled against the door, the group could hear the sound of hammers pounding on metal and what sounded like welding machines. Ella nodded at the group to make sure they were ready, and then slowly slid the door open wide enough for the group to enter single-file.

The workshop was a long curved room full of worktables, machines, and a large group of watchers who were busy crafting and checking blindfolds, collars, and the ball and chain weapons Eli encountered in the Desolate City. The walls of the workshop looked like a sheet metal quilt being completely covered in sheet metal with large bolts attaching each square to the wall. To the group's left as they entered the workshop were stacks of black iron blocks Eli assumed were used to make the different products. Ella led the group over to the blocks and ducked down behind them. With everyone there, Eli slowly lifted his head above the blocks to get an idea of their next move.

The pile of iron block took up the entire left corner and stretched outward to about the center of the room. In the center of the room were three long assembly lines with watchers lined along them. In the far end of the room were rolling baker's racks of blindfolds, collars, and weapons. In the middle of the far wall of racks was the sliding door to the warehouse.

As Eli looked around the room, three watchers, one from each assembly line, walked over and picked up an iron block apiece and took it back to their respective lines. The block of iron was placed on the slow moving conveyor belt. The block would first go through a large stamping machine that would spit out a collar, blindfold, or ball and chain. Then the assembly line of watchers would pound the product, sand the product, and shine the product. A watcher at the end of the line would then examined the product and place it on a rolling baker's rack. After each product was placed on the racks, the watchers would return and pick another block of iron.

Eli ducked back behind the blocks.

"Whatcha think?" asked Aiden. "What's the plan?"

Eli just shook his head, "Don't have one. There's nowhere for us to hide and no way to slip by the watchers. And I don't see how we would be able to defeat all the watchers before they could raise the alarm."

The group sat there looking at each other waiting for someone to come up with a plan. After a few moments, Jared spoke.

"I know a way you can get by without a fight or alarm."

"How? What is it?" asked Ella.

"Let me go back to the door and reveal myself. The watchers will sound the alarm and chase me. I will run through the barracks causing all sorts of disturbances. Remember, I know my way around this place, I know exactly how to cause the most trouble. Then, whatever watchers you have to take out you can do freely because the alarm will have already been sounded and they will think the alarm is because of me."

"No way!" said Eli flatly, "There's no way I'm going to let you do that!"

"Eli's right." interjected Ella, "What if they catch you? What then?"

"Oh, I am sure they will catch me eventually, but that is exactly what I want to happen."

"What do you mean?" asked Eli.

"Trust me on this one. I was a watcher not that long ago. I know what it is like to be enslaved and I know what it is like to be given the freedom by the King. Believe me, you don't need to worry about what they will do to me, they need to worry about what I am going to do to them."

Jerad smiled mischievously and Aiden nodded his head, "Right on brother!"

"Okay." said Eli hesitantly trying to convince himself that this was the best plan, "But if you get in trouble, just run out to the inner circle and find us."

"Will do. And thank you again. If it were not for you, I'd still be wearing one of those blindfolds."

"Thank the King, He is the one who freed you. God speed brother."

Jerad scuttled back to the door, opened it and then slammed it loudly. The watchers looked up and stood stunned seeing Jerad looking back at them.

"Hey ladies, nice necklaces! I was wondering, do you wear those blindfolds to look ugly, or because you don't want to see how ugly you look?"

Jerad waived at them, slid the door open, and took off running.

"Get him!" yelled one of the watchers.

"Sound the alarm!" yelled another watcher.

"It's not nice to call people ugly!" shouted a third watcher.

At once, all the watchers were in motion. One of the watchers who took the finished products and placed them on the racks ran to the back of the room and hit a large red button setting off blaring sirens.

"You two," yelled one of the watchers to the other two watchers who placed the finished products on the baker's racks, "go through the warehouse and chapel and let them know we have an intruder running through the barracks. The rest of you, come with me!"

The watchers did as they were told and soon the workshop was empty save for the watcher who set off the alarm.

"Now's our chance." said Eli, "We don't know how much time we have."

"On it." responded Ella, "I'll take care of the watcher."

In a flash of movement, Ella stood up and released a light arrow. In an instant the watcher had disappeared and his soul was sent back to the broad street.

Eli, Ella, and Aiden stood up and ran for the back door. Eli stopped in front of the door and looked through the square glass on the door. The warehouse was a large open space filled with organized baker's racks of blindfolds, collars, and weapons. Fortunately, it appeared that the warehouse only had two watchers in it: a watcher sitting behind a desk and a watcher standing next to the desk leaning on an empty baker's rack.

As Eli looked into the warehouse, the door on the other end of the warehouse opened up and the two watchers from the workshop made their way back to the workshop. One of the two stopped by the desk and said something to the watcher behind the desk. That watcher then turned to the watcher leaning on the baker's rack who then sped off through the warehouse collecting items as the two watchers made their way back to the door of the workshop.

Eli quickly moved to the right side of the door. Eli turned to Ella and Aiden.

"There are two watchers coming this way. Stand beside the door and let them enter. When they enter I will slide the door shut and you two take the watchers out. If we are lucky, the sirens will drown out the sound of the door slamming and any calls for help from the watchers."

"It's about time we had some action." Aiden said looking at his spear.

The two watchers opened the door and walked into the workshop.

"Hey where did Russel go?" asked one of the watchers looking for the watcher who set off the alarm.

Before the other watcher could answer, Eli slid the door shut and Ella sent an arrow through the head of one watcher as Aiden sent a light spear through the body of the other.

"That was perfect!" said Eli. "There are only two more in the warehouse. Ella, you go first and take out the watcher behind the desk. If you see the watcher pushing the baker's rack, take him out too. If not, Aiden and I will look for him."

"Understood."

Eli stepped to the side of the door as Ella stood in front of the door and notched another light arrow. Eli motioned to Ella and then slid the door open. Ella shot an arrow and took out the watcher behind the desk, notched another arrow and entered the warehouse scanning for the other watcher. As soon as Ella entered the warehouse, a baker's rack crashed into her side knocking her to the ground. A guttural cry coming from the right of the door, where the baker's rack came from, told Eli that the watcher was on the attack. Not waiting for the watcher to get closer to his friend, Eli stepped out of the door and right in front of the charging watcher who was clearly surprised to see him. The watcher was swinging a large iron ball but accidently let go of the ball when Eli appeared out of the doorway. The iron ball went crashing into the baker's racks and the watcher turned to run away. By this time Aiden had also come through the door and gave chase to the watcher.

"That's my sister you loser! Nobody hits my sister with a baker's rack unless it is me!"

Aiden launched a light spear at the watcher who was soon nothing more than a soul on its way back to the broad street. Eli walked over to Ella who was slowly getting up rubbing her side and the side of her leg.

"Are you alright?"

"Yes, but I think our cover's been blown."

Eli followed Ella's eyes over to the door to the chapel where a watcher was standing with his mouth gaping at the sight of the defender. Immediately the watcher yelled out, "Lord Taze, we've been deceived, the defender is in the warehouse!"

chapter 24
an army of one

"Jaze is in the chapel!" yelled Eli, "Hurry we need to get to him before he gets away!"

Eli, Aiden, and Ella sprinted toward the doorway. The watcher quickly closed the door and a loud clicking noise told Eli he had locked it as well.

"Aiden, I need one of your exploding spears to blast a hole in the wall!"

"My pleasure."

Aiden held his spear tightly as he ran and Eli could see the spear pulsing with light indicating it was powering up. When the group was about half-way across the room Aiden threw a pulsating light spear into the far wall. After about a second, the spear exploded blowing a large hole in the wall just in time for the group to run through the hole and into the chapel.

The explosion knocked several watchers to the floor and before they could get up they were dissolved by light arrows and spears. Eli surveyed the chapel, there were several rows of comfortable church-looking pews lining a center aisle, a platform on the far left side of the room, and several ceremonial candle-stick holders. Standing on the stage, just in front of the door to the inner circle was an old, fragile looking man with a white beard, black suit, white shirt, and black tie. The man was bent over with age and looked to be in poor health.

"Taze?" asked Eli.

"That's *Lord* Taze to you, defender."

Taze's voice was much younger and far more sinister than his appearance would insinuate.

"In your dreams, Tazer-boy!" yelled Aiden defiantly, "There is only one *Lord* and you are not him! You can either come quietly, or you can try to run away, but it doesn't look like you will get very far."

"Cut it out Aiden," snapped Ella, "Don't judge him by his appearance. Remember how quickly things changed with Lucre?"

"Your lady friend is right, boy, you should never judge according to appearances. However, you are in luck, I don't have the ability to change my appearance. If you want me I am right here. All you have to do is *come get me*."

The words, "come get me", echoed off the walls in an eerie tone. Taze smiled and held his hands together out in front of him. Feeling like this could be a trap, Eli hesitated, looked at Ella and Aiden for confirmation, and then stepped toward Taze. A deep rumbling, like and earthquake stopped him in his tracks. The rumbling grew louder until the door to the inner circle burst open and a mob of watchers rushed in, grabbed Taze, and rushed out while other watchers stormed into the chapel.

Eli sprang into action raising his sword and slashing down watchers as Ella and Aiden sent arrows and spears into their ranks.

"We can't let Taze get away." called Eli, "We have to get passed these watchers and get outside."

"I got ya," replied Aiden, "Cover me and I will open another door to the outside, man-style."

Eli made his way in front of Aiden to keep the watchers off of him while Ella stood on a chair and rained arrows down upon the ranks of watchers. After a few seconds Aiden released a large pulsating light spear that landed directly in front of the door on the platform. A second later, a powerful explosion of light eradicated the rest of the watchers in the chapel and blew off the entire front of the chapel.

"You rock, Aiden, let's go!"

Eli ran through the chapel and into the inner circle.

Eli came to an abrupt stop as soon as he ran outside. The loud rumbling sound Eli heard was the sound of countless watchers pouring out of the dark stone tower like angry ants pouring out of an ant-hill. The large wave of watchers had already reached the ground from the top of the dark tower but they were not charging Eli, they were surrounding Taze.

Taze was laughing insanely as the group of watchers completely overwhelmed him and buried him underneath their bodies. The watchers continued to pour out of the tower and form a gigantic blob of watcher in the place Taze had been buried.

"What are you waiting for?" called Ella as she shot arrow after arrow into the blob of enemies. Each arrow struck a watcher and the watcher's body dissolved and his soul returned to the broad street, but for every watcher Ella struck, several more took its place.

Soon the blob of watchers began to rise higher into the air as the watchers were now climbing on top of each other. As the monstrous blob rose into the air, it began to take a humanoid shape. After a few terrifying moments, a gigantic watcher, made up of hundreds of watchers, stood in front of Eli. Resting on top of the gigantic watcher's shoulders was Taze's head, giving the gigantic form an even more monstrous appearance.

The turn of events was so shocking that Ella had stopped firing arrows into the blob and just stood there in astonishment with Eli and Aiden. Seeing their reaction spurred a fresh laughter from Taze.

"Why are you all just standing there staring at me? Did you not come to face me? Here I am, come get me."

No one moved.

"Okay then. If you are not going to come get me, then I'm going to get you."

Taze turned his head and looked down at the right arm of the conglomerate of watchers. The watchers shifted giving the arm a very clay-like appearance. Soon, the right hand of the monster turned into a gigantic ball and chain made up of watchers.

The monstrous form swung the ball in the air and then brought it crashing down on top of Eli, Ella, and Aiden. The trio dove out of the way just before the ball of watchers would have crushed them. The ball struck the ground and exploded sending watchers flying every direction. The giant watcher shifted appearance again as more watchers poured out from the tower into the large form and soon another ball and chain had formed. As if the gigantic conglomerate of watchers was not enough to deal with, the watchers who previously made up the ball were also getting to their feet and charging the trio from the ground.

"Any ideas?" asked Ella as she and Aiden returned to Eli's side.

"Yeah, okay." said Eli as he assessed the situation. "We need to sever the chains that anchor the large tower down."

"Got that bro." answered Aiden, "But there is a giant blob of baddies that would probably not let that happen."

Ella shot several watchers who were charging them, "Then we need to split up. Taze can't attack all of us at once. If we split up, at least one of us should be able to cut the chains."

At that moment Taze swung his giant ball and chain at the trio again, this time hitting and smashing a segment of the kingdom hall barrack.

"Sounds as good as anything else." yelled Eli as he ran toward the closest anchor, "God speed!"

Ella and Aiden nodded and ran in different directions blasting the watchers on the ground with arrows and spears.

Taze growled in frustration as his targets scattered. Eli disregarded Taze's frustration and quickly sliced through three watchers as he approached the first anchor. The anchor was a solid black stone the size of a dining room table. Etched into the outside of the stone were the words, "What does the Bible really teach?" The large black stone had a gigantic iron ring on the top of it from which the chain supporting the dark tower attached.

Looking at the stone stirred a righteous anger inside of Eli. He felt the King's pain as these wicked servants of the Enemy manipulated His Word in order to deceive the wandering lost the King loves so much. This righteous anger erupted like a volcano inside of Eli and soon his entire being was glowing with the light of the Spirit. Eli raised his glowing sword and sliced the chain. Eli's sword cut through the chain as if the chain were a piece of thread. Once the chain was severed, the large stone was engulfed with light and disappeared. The severed chain snapped back toward the tower like a piece of elastic. The chain slammed into the side of the tower sending a whole stream of watchers back to the broad street and effectively garnering the attention of Taze who was frustratingly attempting to run down Aiden who seemed to be enjoying this game of cat and mouse with Taze who was much slower than he.

"You will pay for that!" yelled Taze who turned to pursue Eli.

Taze lifted his ball and chain and began swinging it in a large circle. As the ball of watchers increased in speed, a bright yellow spear flew into the watchers that made up the chain. A moment later, a light explosion severed the chain and the ball of watchers went flying into the tower sending the ball of watchers and a large amount of watchers flowing out of the tower back to the broad street.

Taze turned in rage toward Aiden, but stumbled as Ella shot about 20 light arrows rapid fire into the watchers that made up his right leg. More watchers poured into the blob from the tower and Taze regained his footing.

"Run, Eli, take out the anchors, we can deal with this guy. Together, Aiden!"

Ella and Aiden released a barrage of arrows and spears that cut large chunks out of Taze's body of watchers. Taze yelled in rage, but was unable to hinder Eli while Ella and Aiden assaulted him.

Eli turned and ran around the tower cutting anchor after anchor. As Eli rounded the tower to cut off the last three around the area Taze was battling Ella and Aiden, he was blindsided by a direct hit from Taze's ball of watchers. Eli flew back into the crumbling tower of dark stone as Taze laughed in triumph. The top side of the tower fell down onto Eli's head. Though Eli's helmet broke the stone, the large pieces of stone covered Eli's lower body trapping him and separating him from his sword.

"No!" shouted Eli as he looked to Ella and Aiden for aid. At some point during Eli's trek around the tower, Taze redirected the flow of watchers from the large body to a large human wall that shielded him from the attacks of Aiden and Ella. Ella and Aiden still launched arrows and spears into the wall and attempted to maneuver around the wall, but for every watcher they killed, more took its place. The flow of watchers was too great and the wall had effectively cut off Eli from all sources of help.

"It is a shame that I am not allowed to kill you." growled Taze, "I take it very personally when someone steals one of my slaves from me. But at least I will have the pleasure of delivering you to Polytheist. Bind him!"

Half of the watchers flowing out of the tower continued to form the wall between Eli and his allies while the other half now ran over to Eli. Completely surrounded by watchers and unable to reach his sword, Eli thought for sure he was about to be captured when a bright flash of light engulfed the entire inner circle. Looking up, Eli saw that the kingdom hall was engulfed in bright yellow light-flames. Watchers were running out of the barracks screaming as the flames seemed to chase them. One by one the flames caught the watchers and sent them back to the broad street.

"What is this? What is going on?" Taze demanded.

That is when Eli saw him, walking out of the barracks engulfed in the bright yellow light-flames.

"Jerad!"

Jerad smiled at Eli and walked right up to Ella and Aiden who had temporarily stopped their assault on the wall of watchers.

"Allow me." said Jerad calmly.

Jerad walked up to the wall of watchers, "My brothers, listen to me. I was once one of you. I was in bondage to the law of Taze thinking that I had to serve the watchtower in order to earn my life. I worked tirelessly hoping that all of my efforts would bring me the satisfaction my soul craved. I was blind to the truth and bound to the law of sin and death. But now I am come to share with you the truth of salvation."

"Don't listen to him!" yelled Taze desperately, "He is speaking lies! Nothing but lies! You are on the road to salvation, you must obey the watchtower!"

"There is no salvation in the watchtower." continued Jerad as his words rang through the air as if he were speaking into a microphone. The King's Word states, *'Neither is there salvation in any other: for there is none other name under heaven given among men, whereby we must be saved.'* The watchtower denies the Lord Jesus but claims to honor the Father. However the King's Word states, *'Who is a liar but he that denieth that Jesus is the Christ? He is antichrist, that denieth the Father and the Son. Whosoever denieth the Son, the same hath not the Father: (but) he that acknowledgeth the Son hath the Father also.'"*

Jerad's words were having an immediate effect on the watchers. Hundreds of bolts were flying out of hundreds of blindfolds as the watchers came out of their brainwashed stupor. Watchers began vaporizing by the bucket full. Soon the entire wall was down to only a few suborn watchers who were immediately consumed by the yellow light fire jumping off of Jerad's body.

With the wall gone, Jerad approached Taze's giant conglomerate of watchers followed closely by Ella and Aiden.

"Come brothers and sisters, it is time for you to know the truth and find your freedom in Jesus Christ."

"Freedom?" laughed Taze with cruel laughter, "They will never be free of me. They belong to me and to my master. Nothing can free them."

"Silence!" shouted Jerad as the yellow flames exploded off his body, "Your lies can never change the eternal Word of the King. To know the truth of the King is to be free, for His Word states, '*Ye shall know the truth and the truth shall set you free. If the Son therefore shall make you free, ye shall be free indeed.*'"

Instantly, the whole of Taze's blob of watchers dissipated in a rush of souls leaving the body and flying toward the narrow street. Taze, who now found himself suspended in the air, fell to the ground with a painful thud. Ella and Aiden ran over to Eli and freed him from his stone prison. The three of them now walked over to where Taze was sitting on the ground facing Jerad.

"You think you have won, but you have won nothing. The watchtower will survive, it is the creation of the Enemy himself. It will endure, as will I. You cannot kill me, I will continue to serve my master and ensnare as many wandering lost as possible."

Taze laughed defiantly and Jerad looked to Eli.

"Would you like the honor?"

"Yes I would. Thank you."

Eli closed his eyes and concentrated on the King's Word. Soon the Illuminator gave Eli the answer he needed as his mind returned to the white triangles of stone at the base of the light house from which the gospel light originated. Eli burst into blue flames and spoke.

"Your precious watchtower can only endure as long as the King permits. One day both you and the Enemy's vile creation will stand in judgment before the King. On that day, He will vanquish you, the watchtower, and the Enemy. Until that day, the King permits you to live. However, wherever your life will be, it will not be here, among our Desolate City. For I have been given the power to send you from this place."

"Impossible!" shouted Taze, "You have no such power!"

Eli spoke again, but this time, it was the King's Word he was quoting with authority.

"'But though we, or an angel from heaven, preach any other gospel unto you than that which we have preached unto you, let him be accursed. As we said before, so say I now again, If any man preach any other gospel unto you than that ye have received, let him be accursed.' By the power of the King's Word, I hereby accurse you, ban you from this city until the time of your appointed judgement."

The blue light shot from Eli's sword and encased Taze in a large bubble of light. Taze smashed his fists against the bubble but he could not free himself. After a few moments of Taze screaming curses at the top of his lungs, the bubble shot into the air like a spaceship launching from the ground and soared into the crimson sky until it was out of sight.

With Taze vanquished, there was only one thing left to do. Still radiating with the light of the Spirit, Eli turned and pointed his sword toward the last three anchors. Light shot from Eli's sword and severed the final three chains from the anchors evaporating the anchors.

With all the chains cut loose from their anchors, the tower of dark stone wobbled back and forth and came crashing down. The light of the gospel reflected off the reflector tower and filled the area dissolving what was left of the kingdom hall barrack.

"Two down, one to go." said Ella.

"Yes." replied Eli as he turned to Jerad, "We could not have gained the victory without you. You were amazing!"

"No brother, our King is amazing. I simply gave testimony as to what He has done for me and it was His power that gained the victory. But I will tell you all about it soon."

Jerad's words trailed off as he saw several watchers come out of the shadows looking terrified.

"What have you done, traitor? How could you turn on the master?" one hollered at Jerad.

"Listen brothers." Jerad began before he was abruptly cut off by the watchers.

"No! We want nothing to do with your treachery. You are the false prophet, you are the true enemy. All who follow your King will find they have been deceived!"

The watchers turned and ran into the darkness before Jerad could respond.

Ella walked over to Jerad, "I'm so sorry Jerad. Maybe they will come to the light when they come to themselves."

"I pray they will, but it is as the King's Word prophesied, '*He bringeth out those which are bound with chains, but the rebellious dwell in a dry land.*' There will always be those who choose to dwell here in the Desolate City, but that is their choice, it is no fault of the King. I will continue to pray for them and attempt to reach them, but their destiny is in their own hands.

"Speaking of which, let's hurry back to the City on a Hill. I'm excited about the potential crowd of former watchers who could be entering the gates soon!"

"Sounds good." said Eli, "Why don't you lead us back Jerad?"

"It would be my honor."

Jerad then jumped into the light beam followed by the others and sped back to the City on a Hill.

chapter 25

going solo

"So there I was," continued Jerad in relating the story behind his appearance in the battle, "running down the corridors setting off every alarm possible as I went. There must have been at least 20 watchers chasing me, but they could not catch me. I could hear them asking each other how I knew where to turn and all the different passages that allowed me to evade their grasp. As I ran, I could hear the commotion going on outside and I figured you all had engaged Taze in some sort of battle. Finally, I had run full circle and entered into what had once been the chapel but looked like a war zone. When I entered the chapel, the watchers who circled around to cut me off stood before me while the watchers chasing me finally caught up to me."

"What did you do?" asked Aiden excitedly.

"Well, they demanded to know who I was, what I was doing, and how I had such knowledge of the kingdom hall barracks. So, I told them. 'I am Jerad Guess, former follower of the watchtower and current child of the King. I am here because I love you and want to see you freed from your bondage to the false teachings of the watchtower.' As I spoke I could feel the King's power radiate from inside of me and the watchers backed away slowly. The King's Spirit took over and I began quoting the King's Word I quoted when I was outside with you. I told them that I was once blinded as they are now but now I have received my sight thanks to the truth of Jesus Christ which has set me free. When I quoted the King's Word telling them that if Jesus has set them free, they would be free indeed, my body erupted into the bright yellow flames."

"When the flames erupted on my body, the entire kingdom barracks exploded as if the barracks were filled with explosive gas just waiting to be ignited. With the side of the barracks gone, I could see the predicament you all were in. Prodded by the power of the Spirit, I walked out to battle. You all know the rest."

"It was truly a remarkable feat." said Aquila as he perceived Jerad was finished speaking, "And the most incredible thing about it all is the large amount of those watchers who have come and found salvation through the gates of this city."

"Indeed," added Priscilla, "and with Taze now banished from this Desolate City, there is great hope that the watchtower's presence will diminish greatly."

"Two big baddies down and one more to go!" said Aiden, "Hey Jerad, do you want to come with us as we go crash Polytheist's party?"

Before Jerad could respond, Aquila spoke up, "Sadly, Jerad's time here in the spirit realm is ending.

The King desires Jerad to return to the physical realm and minister to the watchers. But I would not be surprised if this is not the last time we all gather here in the City on a Hill."

"Goodbye, my friends." said Jerad as his body glowed with light, "I will find you back home."

The light consumed Jerad's body and in a flash he was gone as the others said their goodbyes.

"Now," said Aiden rubbing his hands together like he was warming them up, "let's get down to business. It is time that Polytheist gets a visit from the Light Train of Pain."

"Right on." said Eli and gave Aiden a high-five.

"Yes!" said Ella.

"Well, not exactly." said Zephyr.

"What do you mean Zeph?"

"After Polytheist received word that you had teamed up with two other harvesters, he set up a barrier that will prevent anyone other than a defender from entering his sanctuary. Ella and Aiden will not be able to travel through the barrier into the fortress. The task of defeating Polytheist and tearing down his fortress belongs to you, Eli, the defender of the realms. You must be the one who takes the truths of the King's Word and frees the reflector tower of direction. Come, we have important things to discuss and not a lot of time to discuss them."

Zephyr flew over to the edge of the crystal globe as Eli turned to look at Ella and Aiden.

"I'm really going to miss you guys out there. I can't tell you how much you have helped me get this far. I couldn't have done it without you."

Ella smiled at Eli and gave him a hug.

"I know you are going to do great. Go out there and show Polytheist the power of the Living God!"

"Thanks Ella."

"Yeah man, just don't forget everything I taught you. Now go on and show the spirit realm there is only one God, and that ugly, shapeshifting, smelly, giant aint he!"

"Will do buddy. Make sure you two hold down the fort while I am gone."

"Oh they will." Priscilla added, "By the looks of it, we will need them to help with the large amounts of wandering lost who are already making their way to the gates of the city. God be with you, defender, and never lose sight of the truths of the King."

"Thank you."

Eli watched Priscilla, Ella, and Aiden walk over to the light beam and jump into it flying back to the floor of the light tower. Aquila walked over to Eli.

"Listen, Eli. Polytheist has an army of tares waiting for you. He has a fortress that he has prepared specifically to defeat you. He has thousands of years' experience in destroying the faith, and he has defeated many who would challenge him in the name of the King. But you have the truth of the King's Word! If you will grasp that fact and claim the power found in an unapologetic faith in the King's Word, then you will find that Polytheist's power is nothing more than an illusion."

Aquila winked at Eli and then walked over to the light beam and disappeared down to the tower floor below. Eli walked over to where Zephyr was hovering.

"What did he mean by that? What did he mean that if I had an unapologetic faith in the King's Word that Polytheist's power would be nothing more than an illusion?"

"He meant exactly what he said. You have known from the beginning that this mission is meant to be a claiming for you. Stop and think about how you have found success and victory thus far. First you ran into Lucre's Pursuit of Happiness that is designed to show the world that the need they have for the King is something that can be satisfied with silver and gold. When you squared off against Lucre, you were confronted with an agreement in which you would serve Lucre in exchange for riches and pleasures. When you rejected the great temptation of earthly pleasure and wealth you were able to use

Lucre's own greed to defeat him and bring down the Pursuit of Happiness."

"Then you faced off against Taze who enslaves millions through his teaching that the salvation of the King is something that has to be earned by following him and his commands. Though Jerad's testimony destroyed Taze's power, it was not until you claimed his gospel to be false that Taze faced banishment."

"And now you must go to the very heart of the Enemy's scheme to dim the light of the King's gospel and square off against one of the oldest and most powerful generals in the Enemy's service. Eli you cannot gain the victory on your own. Polytheist is wiser than you, stronger than you, and has been battling the servants of the King for thousands of years. The only way you will walk out of that fortress in victory is by claiming the truths of the King's Word in some very difficult areas."

"But I don't understand, haven't I already done that? I mean, I made it through the cemetery and all the rooms of testing and I have already taken down two of the Enemy's servants. Have I not already claimed I believe in the King's Word?"

"You have already won several great victories, Eli, but the trial ahead of you is different. It is one thing to believe in the King's Word and to gain victories through the power of the King's Word and another thing to truly claim the King's Word to be what the King's Word claims to be. For you to claim the King's belt of truth from Polytheist will require you to answer difficult questions of faith you have yet to deal with. But do not despair, I know that you will be victorious and that you will defeat Polytheist. Now come, let me show you what information we have on Polytheist's fortress."

Zephyr waived his hands and the crystal globe filled up with one large picture: Polytheist's fortress. The fortress was a large two-tiered building with the first tier being a rectangular building with large white pillars wrapping around and the second tier being a large dome. Leading up to the fortress was a very familiar looking courtyard. The courtyard was a large round courtyard with a broad walk way leading into the courtyard from the Desolate City and then from the courtyard to the steps of Polytheist's fortress. Bordering this courtyard was a tall stone wall held up by countless stone pillars.

Eli looked at the picture with a nagging sense that he had seen this fortress and courtyard somewhere before.

"That looks so familiar. I'm telling you, I've seen Polytheist's fortress somewhere before."

"That is very likely, because Polytheist's fortress is one of only a few buildings that are found in both the physical realm and the spirit realm."

"So I have seen it before, somewhere in the physical realm? But where?"

"Most likely you have seen it on television or in history books, because as far as I know, you have never been to Rome."

"Rome? Yes, that's it! Polytheist's fortress looks identical to the Vatican! But how could that be? I mean, why would Polytheist use the Vatican as his fortress?"

"We do not have time to explain everything right now, but know Eli, that some of the greatest enemies you will face, and have faced for that matter, are enemies who wear the guise of servants of the King. The difference between these enemies and you is the difference between your potential failure and success on this mission."

"Now let's take a moment and evaluate where you will be going. Unfortunately, because of Polytheist's barrier, we do not have any pictures or reports of what awaits you in the courtyard or inside the pillared fortress. But we do know that the light beam of the gospel ends where the walkway to the courtyard begins. You will not have the ability to hide or sneak up on your enemies. They will see you from the time your feet hit the ground. Be sure that you are ready to fight before you ever enter the light beam because it is assured that your enemies will be ready for a fight."

"What kind of enemies am I going to find in there?"

"We are not for sure everything, but we do know that Polytheist has been actively growing an army of tares far greater in number than anything we have seen in the Desolate City to this point. Because of the great number of tares, I'm guessing the only place that can fit them all is the courtyard. Although we don't know much more than what I have told you, we do know that the King's belt of truth is waiting for the King's defender to claim it as his own."

"Okay then, well, it is time for this King's defender to go and claim that belt. Thank you for everything, I mean it, for everything you have helped me with in training and for always being there to encourage me."

"You don't need to thank me. I have enjoyed it tremendously! I really do believe in you and I will pray to the King that He will give you great success."

"Thanks man, but could you do one more favor for me?"

"Anything, just name it."

"Keep your ears open in case I get in a situation in which I need a good guardian Angelos. Okay?"

"You bet. If you need me, call for me. If the King allows, I will be there in an instant."

"I know you will, but we both know that the best thing you can do for me now is to pray."

Eli followed the beam of light into the darkness in the direction of Polytheist's Vatican fortress. Taking a moment to steady himself, Eli leapt into the beam and his showdown with Polytheist.

chapter 26

a gift from the enemy

Eli shot through the sky of the Desolate City directly above the buildings of downtown. Eli could see the thousands of wandering lost walking down the broad street like zombies and he could also see several wandering lost walking down the narrow road toward the City on a Hill. This evidence of success gave Eli a boost of confidence that he could gain the victory and that the victory was worth fighting for.

Looking ahead of him, Eli could see the large barrier of darkness approaching. Preparing himself for a fight, Eli drew his sword and steadied his resolve.

For the King! Thought Eli as he lowered his head and shot through the barrier of darkness.

On the other side of the barrier of darkness, Eli caught sight of Polytheist's fortress. The fortress looked just like the Vatican and courtyard with one dreadful exception: the courtyard was covered in creepy looking wooden stakes on which vines that looked like humans grew. In the middle of the courtyard, where a large pillar stands in the physical realm, stood a giant tree with several large hanging fruit that also looked like humans.

So that's how tares are grown, that might just be the creepiest thing I have ever seen.

The tares growing on the stakes in the courtyard numbered in the hundreds if not the thousands and Eli knew that he would somehow have to fight his way through them to make it into the fortress. However, Eli noticed that the tares looked as if they were still growing, and not yet ready for battle. Further, Eli noticed the hanging tares, which were considerably larger than the ones growing on the ground were also still maturing.

A spark of excitement grew up in Eli's mind as he realized that though there were several tares walking around the rows of stakes and the large tree, the majority of Polytheist's army of tares looked like they were not ready for battle.

Well, well, well, it looks like they are not as ready for me as Zephyr thought. Ha, well, ready or not, here I come!

Eli had reached the end of the beam of the gospel light and jumped out of the beam onto the center of the walkway that fed into the large courtyard of tares. As soon as his feet hit the ground, something weird happened. Time stood still. The tares that were walking around the rows of stakes and the tree stopped in mid turn as they were sounding the alarm. Also, all of the color drained from the surroundings leaving Eli staring at a frozen picture of a black and white colored courtyard. Though Eli's clothes protected him from the chill, Eli could feel the temperature drop dramatically all around him. Before Eli could figure out what was going on, he heard a voice that seemed to penetrate his armor with ice water.

"It's such a beautiful sight, is it not?"

The voice was smooth, welcoming, and familiar to Eli. It was the same voice he heard speak to him in the cemetery, it was the voice of the Enemy.

Eli turned toward the voice as fast as he could with his sword drawn ready for battle. The Enemy stood, just a few feet from him with his back to Eli. With his perfect and powerful physic wrapped in his all-black form-fitting body armor, Eli was reminded of how shockingly similar the Enemy looked to Michael.

"What do you want?" growled Eli.

The Enemy did not turn around but simply lifted his hand in the air to quiet Eli.

"I'm just here to admire the beauty of the Desolate City. Just look at them all; wandering souls so caught up in the physical world around them that they have no idea a spirit realm even exists or that they are walking to their own eternal destruction."

"Do you see them Eli? Thousands upon thousands of souls willingly walking to their eternal death. Even with all the annoying work you and your little groupies have been doing, there are still thousands of souls dying to spend eternity in my presence instead of the King's."

"I do see them, but I also see the others who are walking toward eternal life as we speak."

The Enemy burst into mocking laughter, "Yes, I do see the *few* walking down the narrow way, but seriously, are you comforted by such a small percentage of souls when so many still belong to me? And this is just your Desolate City, I literally have *billions* of souls walking headlong down the broad street!"

The Enemy turned and smiled at Eli revealing a wicked glow from his all black eyes, "I'm sorry, I was bragging. Go on, tell me about how happy you are so few have responded when you have risked your very life to bring them the light of the gospel."

"Your plan is not going to work on me. I know the great value of one soul."

"Oh really, then by all means, enlighten me."

"My grandfather was just one soul, one soul who had walked for many years down the broad street. But my grandfather won many great victories for the King, brought many more souls to the King, and defeated you and your minions in both realms."

"So you think, but it does not matter because your grandfather is dead!"

Eli could tell that the Enemy was attempting to hurt him by the way he said, "dead", but Eli was not phased.

"You're wrong again, my grandfather is not dead. He is more alive now than you will ever be and he will be living in the presence of the King long after you are suffering the eternal death that awaits you. But you're wasting my time. Tell me, why have you decided to show up? Are you here to fight me or are you here to try and get me to turn around like you did in the cemetery?"

"Neither, you arrogant little brat! The King has given command that I am not to touch you. Though I care not for His command, I do not want to push the issue. I'm sure that if I were to teach you the lesson you need to be taught that Michael would show up. Don't get me wrong, I would love a chance to repay Michael for all of his insults and grievances toward me, but right now the King protects His puppet and won't allow direct contact between us."

Eli started laughing and the Enemy paused being caught off guard by Eli's reaction.

"What's so funny? Why are you laughing?"

"I find it funny that you would want to fight Michael. That's all. But I would not worry about it if I were you, I have a feeling that one day you will get your wish, but I don't think it will end the way you think it will."

The Enemy paused giving Eli a quizzical look that made Eli wonder if the King had somehow blocked the Enemy from access to the book of the Revelation. After a brief moment, the Enemy continued.

"It does not matter what you think, mortal, because soon you will be dead. You asked if I were here to get you to turn around like I tried to do in the cemetery, well the answer is no. Your opportunity to save your life has passed. I don't want you to turn around, I am looking forward to watching you walk to your death."

The Enemy smiled and walked around Eli, no longer facing the Desolate City, but now facing the frozen courtyard full of tare vines and the tare tree.

"I'm here to give you a special gift. You see, even though Polytheist knew you were coming, and even though he had plenty of warning as you tore down the Pursuit of Happiness and banished Taze from this Desolate City, the big lug just could not get his army of tares ready for battle. Not that he is going to need them, he is more than capable to rip you limb from limb, or pummel you into dust, or set you on fire, or whatever he chooses to do in whatever form he defeats you in."

"But that death is not so uncommon. Polytheist has been a special servant of mine who has slain countless defenders, harvesters, and other pesky slaves of the King. Death in one-on-one combat is not all that honorable. Definitely not what such a fine young man like you deserves. No, you deserve an honorable death. You deserve to be remembered as falling surrounded by countless enemies. Fighting until your last ounce of life is ripped from your body. You deserve a truly inspiring death, a death at the hands of countless tares."

"This is the death that we had planned for you, however, our army of tares is not yet ready. Seeing our dilemma, I went and I asked a petition from your King, who you think loves you, and believe it or not, He granted me my petition. I guess your so-called King agrees with me that your death ought to be much more memorable, and painful, than a death at the hands of the great Polytheist."

"So I am here to give you a wonderful gift that has been approved by the King. That gift is an honorable and memorable death. You see, when our little conversation here is over, I will leave. Before I go, however, I will bring every single tare vine and tare fruit to maturity. When I leave, you will not be looking at a courtyard unprepared for battle, you will be facing a vast host of seasoned and mature tares."

"The thought of you being torn apart by my army makes me so happy I want to end this conversation and just get it done! But then again, I can't gloat when you're dead. So I am here to gloat. You see Eli, when they are done with you, no one will ever dare volunteer to be a defender again. I am not going to have them kill you, I am going to have them destroy you in such a terrible way that your memory will serve as a warning to any fool who desires to test my power. Is that exciting or what?"

Eli tried to respond but he could not find any words. All he could do was look at the Enemy with a face of disbelief for what he had just heard.

"Speechless I see. Don't worry, you can thank me later. Oh wait, no you probably won't be able to!"

The Enemy lifted his hands in the air as if to form the letter "Y" with his body. A cloud of pure black energy rose up from the ground of the courtyard like fog covering all of the vines and the tree. Hundreds of bolts of lightning flashed through the fog giving the appearance of a dreadful lightning storm. When the lightning stopped, the fog dissipated giving Eli a clear picture of the battle before him.

Where row upon row of wooden stakes used to stand stood hundreds of tare warriors. These warriors looked like humans and were uniformly dressed in clothes that resembled Eli's clothes he received from the castle. The difference was that the clothes the tares wore were black, had a white backward collar around the neck, and instead of a symbol of a cross on the left breast like Eli's, they had a symbol of a woman with her head covered holding a baby. These warriors also carried a sword that looked like Eli's sword but where Eli's sword blade proceeded out of the lion's mouth, the tare's sword proceeded out of a man's mouth.

Interspersed among the ranks of smaller tare warriors were giant tare warriors. These warriors came from the tare tree and were vastly different than their smaller allies. These tare warriors were several feet taller and broader than their smaller counterparts. These tare giants looked like old men with white hair and they all wore small red caps that covered the crown of their heads. These tares wore elaborately decorated white and red robes with golden thread interwoven. In one hand these giant tares carried large wooden stakes and in the other hand they held a fire torch.

"There you are my beauties."

The Enemy turned to face Eli as his dark energy swirled around him.

"Now go, and die with honor!"

In a flash of dark energy, the Enemy was gone. With the Enemy gone, time resumed and color flooded back into the courtyard now full of Polytheist's battle-ready tare army.

chapter 27

a fundamental difference

Eli lifted his sword and stood ready for the attack, but the attack did not come. Instead of rushing at Eli and overwhelming him with numbers, the tares kept their distance and slowly encircled him. The tares surrounded Eli in rings, like the rings of a tree, with the first two rings the smaller tares, the third ring made of the giant tares, and several other rings of smaller tares behind them.

The tares were talking amongst themselves, but their voices were so low and quiet that Eli could not make out any words. Eli noticed that all of the tare's mouths were moving but there were only two variety of voices: an airy hushed voice, and a grumbling harsh voice. Finally the chattering stopped, and a single voice spoke out in an airy and hushed tone.

"Who are you?" the voice whispered, "What are you doing here?"

Before Eli could respond, the same voice seemed to continue asking questions, but not directly to Eli.

"Why is he dressed like that?"

"Why does his sword look so strange?"

"Who does he think he is coming here wearing such strange clothes?"

Eli stood there confused and a little weirded out at the strange voice asking questions from all around the ring of tares. Eli's silence seemed to perturb the grumbly harsh voice because it soon spoke out.

"He has no answer!" the harsh voice spoke and Eli looked up to see that the grumbly harsh voice was coming from the giant tares, "He is obviously a blasphemer! We ought to tie him to the stake and burn him as we have the others!"

"Yes." agreed the same harsh voice coming from another section of the tares.

"Agreed!"

"Nothing but a blasphemer! Set him ablaze!"

"I don't think so!" called out Eli who had heard enough. "You ask who I am, well I'll tell you. My name is Elijah Storm and I am a Defender of the King! I am here to deal with your master and free this reflector tower. You can either get out of my way or face destruction!"

Eli burst into blue flames and the voices gasped in unison.

"Flames." echoed the hushed voice, "He has flames like us."

"No, not like us. His are blue, his are weak. Deceived this one has been."

"Ah, you see," cried the grumbly harsh voice, "he wants to be set on fire. Let's tie him to a stake!"

"Silence!" shouted the hushed voice and all the chattering stopped.

"What do you mean I have flames like you?" asked Eli.

The hushed voice laughed, "Let us show you."

The smaller tares in unison lifted their swords to the exact position Eli had lifted his and they too burst out in flames, only their flames were black flames that matched their clothes.

"You think you're the King's only representative, but you're wrong. As you can see, we too have been given the same armor and sword you have. We too have been given the same power to represent the King."

"And the heavenly Mother." echoed the hushed voice from behind in the crowd.

"Yes," answered the grumbly harsh voice, "and don't forget the earthly Father as well. You must not neglect the papacy!"

"The heavenly Mother? The earthly Father? What are you talking about?"

"He doesn't know about the heavenly Mother!" cried the hushed voice.

"Nor about the earthly Father!" replied the grumbly harsh voice.

"I told you he had been deceived." continued the hushed voice, "Come brother, let us show you the *whole* gospel truth."

All of the smaller tares lifted their swords in unison shooting their black flames into the air. The flames created a large round ball of flame in the sky that soon turned into what looked like a giant round mirror.

"Let us introduce you to the heavenly Mother." said the hushed voice as an image of a young lady appeared on the mirror.

This young lady looked to be in her early to middle teenage years. The appearance of the lady created a frenzy among the tares.

"There she is! Hail Mary! Hail Mary!"

Many of the smaller tares fell to their knees.

"Yes. Hail the heavenly Mother! This, Elijah Storm, is the heavenly Mother. She was chosen by the King to be the mother of Jesus because of her great righteousness."

"And because she was without sin." echoed the hushed voice.

"Yes, she was perfect like God!"

"Yes, she was perfectly righteous and without any taint of sin and so the King chose her to be the mother of Jesus."

"The Bible never says that Mary was sinless." interjected Eli.

"Silence, let us continue. We will speak of your King's Word shortly."

The picture on the mirror turned from the young Mary to Jesus as He was hanging on the cross.

"Tragic!" called out the hushed voice in echoes.

"Yes, tragic." answered the main hushed voice, "This is the day the King died."

"A heroic death!"

"Indeed heroic! He died to pay the penalty for our sin. But died He did. No longer living. With the King dead, one had to take His place."

"Yes, take His place the heavenly Mother did!" echoed the hushed voice as the picture of Jesus on the cross changed to a larger than life Mary holding the dead body of Jesus.

"Yes, Mary became deity to take the place of the King. Now she reigns as our heavenly Mother. We pray to Mary and seek her power and forgiveness in life."

"Don't forget about the saints." echoed the hushed voice.

"Nor the papacy!" interjected the grumbly harsh voice, "For that is the presence of the King on the earth!"

"Yes, yes," continued the main hushed voice, "we honor the saints, pray to the saints, and worship the earthly Father as well. For in Mary, the saints, and the earthly Father, we have the ability to live a life deserving of eternal bliss. This Eli is the whole gospel truth."

The words of the tares felt to Eli like they were invading his mind and heart making it difficult to think. Eli felt like a sponge in water, soaking up the words of the tares and becoming heavy and bloated with confusion.

"No!" shouted Eli as he tried to clear his mind, "None of what you said is found in the King's Word! I don't know where you heard those things, but they are not the truth of the gospel!"

"The King's Word?" asked the grumbly harsh voice of the giant tares, "The so-called *King's* Word is out-dated, useless, incomplete, and inferior to the tradition of the Church! The tradition that came to us from the earthly Fathers: the Papacy. I knew you were a blasphemer from the time I saw your heretical sword!"

"Yes." chimed in the hushed voice, "Look at his sword! The blade comes from the mouth of a lion, not the mouth of our earthly Fathers."

"And his chest," echoed the hushed voice, "he carries the emblem of the King's death instead of the emblem of our heavenly Mother's life!"

"He must be destroyed!" called out the grumbly harsh voice as the giant tares began moving toward Eli.

"Wait!" called out the hushed voice, "We must first give him a chance to convert to the truth!"

"He must recant!" demanded the grumbly harsh voice as the giant tares stirred once again.

"He will." assured the hushed voice, "Now that he has seen the truth, of course he will recant and place his trust in the tradition of the papacy and the life of the heavenly Mother."

"And if he doesn't?" asked the grumbly harsh voice, "Then we will burn him at the stake!"

"Of course we will. It is the only fitting way to deal with those who deny the faith."

In unison, all of the tares, both large and small turned their attention directly to Eli. With every fiery sword and large wooden stake now fixed upon him, Eli knew that the battle was about to begin. Concentrating on the King's Word, Eli's mind began to clear.

"So what will it be, Elijah Storm, defender of the King? Will you recant your blasphemous beliefs in light of the truth of the tradition, or will you chose to remain a heretic and die at the stake?" asked the hushed voice as the entire army of tares began to slowly close in on Eli.

Before Eli could respond, he felt the Illuminator connect with his spirit in a way unlike anything Eli had ever felt before. Passage after passage from the King's Word filled his mind giving him a power unlike anything he had ever felt before. When Eli felt as if he were going to explode with power, he focused on the eyes of the tares and spoke with authority.

"Recant? You want me to recant the truth found in the King's Word for the man-made tradition of sinners? I will die first!"

Eli's flames rose higher in the air and reached out farther from his body. Although the growth of his flames unsettled the tares, the giant tares responded, "So be it!"

Eli paid no attention to the giant tares or to the steady enclosing of the tare ring.

"You say that Mary is the heavenly Mother, and any who would deny that is blaspheming, but you are blaspheming! You say that Mary was without sin and perfect like God, but you deny the truth of the King's Word. The King's Word states, *'For all have sinned and come short of the glory of God'*. This was written after your so-called heavenly mother was born and therefore declares that Mary was as sinful and wicked as the rest of humanity!"

Streams of flames erupted off of Eli's body and went flying into the ring of tares like missiles burning up the tares they landed on. Fear and uncertainty echoed through the army of tares but Eli continued.

"You say that the King is dead and that He died on the cross no more to live, but you deny the stated truth of the King's Word! The King's Word states that not only did Jesus rise again, but that He was seen by many witnesses, '*For I delivered unto you first of all that which I also received, how that Christ died for our sins according to the scriptures; And that he was buried, and that he rose again the third day according to the scriptures: And that he was seen of Cephas, then of the twelve: After that, he was seen of above five hundred brethren at once; of whom the greater part remain unto this present, but some are fallen asleep. After that, he was seen of James; then of all the apostles. And last of all he was seen of me also, as of one born out of due time.*'"

More flames leapt from Eli's body consuming the entire front ring of tares that surrounded Eli causing the rest of the tares to halt their march toward him.

"Further, you claim to pray to the saints and to worship them along with Mary, but that very act is something the apostles refused to receive during their time on the earth. The King's Word states that when Paul, one of your most beloved saints, was worshipped by the people of Lystra that he responded thus, '*Sirs, why do ye these things? We also are men of like passions with you, and preach unto you that ye should turn from these vanities unto the living God, which made heaven, and earth, and the sea, and all things that are therein.*' So you see, not only does Paul refuse the worship you give him, he also claims that the King is still alive!"

"But why stop there? The King's Word states that when Cornelius fell down at Peter's feet, the same Peter for whom you built this great basilica and from whom you claim the papacy originated and receives its deity, Peter responded as such, '*Stand up; for I myself am also a man*'. Instead of allowing them to worship him, Peter shared the truth of the *whole* gospel with him:

'The word which God sent unto the children of Israel, preaching peace by Jesus Christ: (he is Lord of all:)
That word, I say, ye know, which was published throughout all Judaea, and began from Galilee, after the baptism which John preached;
How God anointed Jesus of Nazareth with the Holy Ghost and with power: who went about doing good, and healing all that were oppressed of the devil; for God was with him.
And we are witnesses of all things which he did both in the land of the Jews, and in Jerusalem; whom they slew and hanged on a tree:
Him God raised up the third day, and shewed him openly;

Not to all the people, but unto witnesses chosen before of God, even to us, who did eat and drink with him after he rose from the dead.
And he commanded us to preach unto the people, and to testify that it is he which was ordained of God to be the Judge of quick and dead.
To him give all the prophets witness, that through his name whosoever believeth in him shall receive remission of sins.'"

"So you give worship and send prayers to people who refused to receive such on the earth while you deny the King the people you worship preached about."

This time large missiles erupted out of the flames with the other smaller missiles and struck down several of the giant tares while even more of the smaller tares were consumed.

"Silence!" shouted the grumbly harsh voice in desperation, "We shall hear no more of his blasphemies! Destroy him!"

At once the remaining army of tares and giant tares rushed toward Eli. The first tares to approach lifted their swords still burning with black flames and brought them down upon Eli. But Eli did not move. Eli could feel the great power of the King's Spirit and knew that he was not in danger. As the swords with their black fire made contact with the flames around Eli, the swords, fire, and the tares wielding the swords exploded with blue light. This new development brought the remaining tares to a halt, except for one of the giant tares who lifted his wooden stake high and brought it down to skewer Eli. As soon as the large spike touched the flames, an explosion of blue flames leapt from Eli and bound the giant tare like ropes. The giant tare yelled in pain as more flames picked him up and threw him over against the large tare tree in the center of the courtyard. Now bound to the tree, the giant tare and the tare tree were both consumed by blue fire.

Panic broke out among the tare ranks as some took off running but others stood their ground.

"You claim to follow the faith, but your faith is not founded upon the truth of God, it is founded upon human tradition. Your faith does not require a genuine relationship with the King and is therefore not a faith, it is a folly."

"No!" cried out the hushed voice, "That cannot be. Just look at all of our good works we do in the name of the heavenly Mother on behalf of the King! We preach to the people, we fight against the darkness, and we do so many wonderful works! Our faith is the faith and we will one day be rewarded greatly for our work!"

"All together now!" echoed the hushed voice.

"Destroy this infidel!" joined in the grumbly harsh voice.

All together the small tares pointed their swords at Eli sending a gigantic stream of black flames in his direction while the giant tares lit their large wooden stakes on fire and sent them flying at Eli like giant spears.

Moved by the King's Spirit, Eli held out his left hand and yelled, "Stop!"

All the spears froze in mid-air while the stream of black flames extinguished immediately.

"I have one more message from the King for you. Then it will all be over. This word comes from the very King you claim to be dead. This is what the King says will be your end.

'Not every one that saith unto me, Lord, Lord, shall enter into the kingdom of heaven; but he that doeth the will of my Father which is in heaven.
Many will say to me in that day, Lord, Lord, have we not prophesied in thy name? And in thy name have cast out devils? And in thy name done many wonderful works?
And then will I profess unto them, I never knew you: depart from me, ye that work iniquity.
Therefore whosoever heareth these sayings of mine, and doeth them, I will liken him unto a wise man, which built his house upon a rock:
And the rain descended, and the floods came, and the winds blew, and beat upon that house; and it fell not: for it was founded upon a rock.
And every one that heareth these sayings of mine, and doeth them not, shall be likened unto a foolish man, which built his house upon the sand:
And the rain descended, and the floods came, and the

winds blew, and beat upon that house; and it fell: and great was the fall of it.'

Eli felt as if he were a volcano that was about to erupt. Returning his outstretched left hand to his sword, Eli lifted his sword into the air. A massive burst of fire erupted from Eli and shot into the sky forming large blue clouds. Crystal clear rain began to pour from the clouds falling upon the tares and filling the courtyard with water.

"What is this?" cried the tares, "There is no water in the Desolate City. What is going on?"

"It is the test to see which faith is the true faith: your tradition or the King's Word. If your house is built upon the truth, you have nothing to worry about, if not, then I suggest you find higher ground."

The tares dropped their swords and frantically ran away from Eli, but it was already too late. The rain had filled the courtyard like a giant pool and the tares could not wade through the water. A bright streak of lightning erupted from the sky striking the center of the courtyard destroying the burnt remains of the tare tree and creating a bottomless pit in the center of the courtyard. As if someone had taken the plug out of a giant bathtub, all of the water rushed toward the pit dragging all of the tares with it. The tares screamed and fought against the water to no avail. Soon all of the tares had been sucked into the dark pit.

The destruction did not end with the tares. More bolts of lightning struck the large pillared walls surrounding the courtyard blasting them to pieces. What remained of the large pillared walls that bordered the courtyard cracked, toppled over, and broke apart. The pieces of stone fell into the water and were also sucked into the large hole.

With the courtyard cleansed of all tares and structures, the rain stopped, the clouds dissipated, and Eli's flames slowly died out leaving him standing looking at the Vatican fortress of Polytheist with nothing between him and the showdown with the Enemy's great general.

chapter 28

the fortress of the gods

Eli walked across the ruined courtyard and up to the steps of Polytheist's Vatican fortress. The fortress looked identical to the Vatican in the physical realm with one exception: everything was giant-sized. Even if Eli did not already know that Polytheist was a giant, he was pretty sure he could have figured it out by looking at the entrance to the fortress.

The steps leading to the entrance of the fortress were each about four feet in height made out of white stone. The entrance to the fortress was a giant-sized rectangular doorway nestled in between two giant pillars of stone. Eli slowly crawled up the stairs, careful to not put his sword away in case of a surprise attack. But no attack came. Finally, Eli reached the top of the stairs and crossed the stone porch and stood in front of the giant doorway. Looking into the fortress, Eli could see that the fortress was little more than a long dark hallway with a ray of light at the end. There were no torches on the wall or any source of light save for a giant bowl-shaped torch with a large fire of green flames suspended in the air at the end of the hallway. Eli stood there waiting for his eyes to adjust to the darkness when a wheezy laugh echoed through the hallway followed by a gust of frigid air.

Eli raised his sword in a battle-ready position and slowly stepped inside the fortress. Slowly, Eli's eyes adjusted to the darkness inside the fortress. The inside of the fortress was a gigantic hallway lined with large rectangular pillars. The floors and walls were decorated with extravagant paintings of people worshipping different idols throughout history. Some of the idols looked familiar to Eli such as a picture of Buddha, an Indian god with a body of a man, four-arms, and the head of an elephant, and pictures that included the Olympian gods; while other paintings pictured bizarre looking creatures that Eli had not seen before.

Eli had just walked past the first set of columns when the appearance of light to his right side made him jump to his left. There, standing about 20 feet tall was a statue of a primitive-looking god. The god had a square head with an over-sized smile and a long beard carved into the stone. The god stood upright with his two hands cupped in front of him as if he were waiting for a sacrifice. The god wore only a leather girdle around his waist with ancient looking sandals on his feet. In the middle of the god's torso was a giant hole from which green flames had ignited when Eli walked by.

Eli froze in place anticipating an attack from the giant statue, but the statue did not move so Eli continued down the hallway to a faint echo of that wheezy laughter and another gust of icy wind. A few steps further and a light exploded in the darkness to his left. Again, Eli jumped and prepared for battle only to find a stationary giant idol looking back at him. This time Eli recognized the statue. The statue was one Eli had read about in school when his class covered Egyptian history. This statue was of Anubis, an Egyptian god with the body of a man and the head of a dog. The statue of Anubis carried a large staff that was now engulfed in green fire. Once again, Eli prepared for an attack, but no attack came. The faint echo of laughter reached Eli and spurred Eli to continue down the hallway.

One by one, Eli passed different gods from all ages and all regions of the world. Some Eli knew, some Eli did not, but all bore the same green flames Eli had seen in Polytheist's eyes. After crossing through the hallway, Eli walked into a gigantic round room with the large dome for a ceiling.

Carved into the walls of the room from the floor to the ceiling were hundreds of cubbies in which smaller statues of gods stood. In the center of the room were four gigantic wooden pillars that looked like giant twisted branches reaching all the way to the dome ceiling. In the center of the four pillars sat a giant throne and sitting on the throne was Polytheist. Above the throne, suspended in mid-air, was the large bowl of green fire.

Polytheist was not in one of his forms that Eli recognized, but looked like a giant man, an old man, wearing bright white robes with golden trim. On his head, Polytheist wore a tall white hat and had large golden chains around his neck.

"Welcome, Elijah Storm, defender of the King." bellowed Polytheist in a wheezy voice that echoed through the chamber, "Did you enjoy looking at my collection?"

Polytheist laughed the same wheezy laugh Eli had heard several times since he stood on the doorstep of the fortress. Eli was surprised by this greeting and not knowing how to respond, he stood there in his battle stance looking intently into the green-flame eyes of Polytheist.

"Oh don't be so serious! We don't have to be enemies, you know, we could become very good friends you and I. I have been watching you, and I see the potential for greatness in you. If you would allow me to work with you, I am sure that I could make a modern god out of you!"

"Not likely. I don't think I would look good in statue form."

Polytheist pounded the armrest of his throne, causing the ground to shake, as he belly-laughed.

"A statue, that's a good one, but you are thinking too ancient times. The gods you people worship in modern times are not statues, they are perceptions, ideals, and they are the gods created in the mind. And you, defender, have all the elements needed to create a top-of-the-line modern god."

Eli opened his mouth to respond when Polytheist stood up and cut him off.

"No, no, no, hear me out. Think about it. If we were to work together, I could make you the star at your high school. I could make sure that you are the one the girls love and the one the boys would love to be. I can guarantee you getting into the best college, earning the best degree, and together, we can make you a modern-day star!"

"Oh really? And why would you do that for me?"

"Because, contrary to what you have been told, I am not your enemy. You and I are allies."

"Allies? You and I are not allies; we are enemies."

"You are only saying that because you were told we were enemies."

"No. We are enemies because I stand for truth and your entire existence is based upon lies. Your lies pave the broad street leading to eternal death. For that reason, I'm here to destroy you and free this reflector tower!"

"Listen to you, 'your whole existence is based upon lies' how would you know that, son? You are what, 14 years old? I have been around since Cain's children walked the earth. I have lived for thousands of years, I have seen things that you can only read about. I have witnessed events that you have never heard of. You think that you know me because of a small amount of information you received from those who would have you try and destroy me, but you don't know me. If you truly knew me, you would know that you *need* me."

As Polytheist finished speaking, he transformed into a handsome warrior wearing ancient Greek armor with a large sword hanging from his waist. The transformation startled Eli, but soon he collected his thoughts.

"What do you mean I need you?"

"You need me because of the narrow-mindedness of your beliefs. You need me because you have never stopped to reckon the eternal devastation that you would be condemning billions of souls to if what you believe is true!"

Eli looked puzzled.

"I see that you, like so many others, have never stopped to think about what I am telling you. That's so typical of you gung-ho defenders who think that you are on the only road to eternal life and who think you are serving a loving and caring God. But I am here to enlighten you on the truth about your beliefs."

Polytheist drew his sword and pointed it down the hallway and the first statue that Eli passed came to life and walked down the hallway toward Eli.

"Let me introduce you to Molech. Molech was the god the Ammonites worshiped, the same Ammonites you read about in the King's Word. Thousands upon thousands upon hundreds of thousands of men, women, and children worshipped Molech for generations. The people of Israel and

Judah also worshipped Molech and built a large statue not unlike this one in order to worship Molech. Thousands of people sacrificed their own children in the fires of Molech's chest. Are you prepared to condemn each and every one of those souls, many of whom never had the opportunity to read or even know about the King's Word, to an eternity of torment?"

Polytheist began pacing back and forth through the large chamber as he pointed his sword down the hallway again summoning another statue to life. This time the statue was of a large muscular man with a curly white beard.

"Aw Zeus, also known as Jupiter, was the main god for millions of Greeks and Romans for hundreds of years. Countless generations were born under this belief, lived under this belief, and died trusting in Zeus! Are you willing to stand where you are, look me in the eyes, and tell me that they are all doomed for eternity?"

"Why stop there?" asked Polytheist as he once again pointed his sword down the hallway. This time the rest of the statues came to life and walked to join the other statues who were standing where the hallway met the large room.

Eli tensed up as he could tell that Polytheist was becoming more agitated as he spoke. Further, Eli did not like the fact that now he had the giant in front of him and several giant statues standing behind him.

"Just think about all of the Egyptians who lived and died praying to Ra! Where are they now Eli? Or what about Buddha, yes you are familiar with Buddha, I am talking about hundreds of millions of souls, defender. Can you even grasp that number? Or one of the more popular gods in your modern time, Allah. I am not talking about millions of souls here, I am talking about billions of souls. Men, women, and children who were forced on threat of their lives to worship Allah. Does that sound fair? Does that sound like they had a choice? Yet, if what you believe is true, that child who never had a chance to choose what he would believe is suffering for all eternity the wrath of your King."

Polytheist transformed again, and this time, Eli could see the correlation between Polytheist's mood and his shape. Polytheist transformed into the giant orc-looking warrior with the giant club that Eli saw in the briefing. The giant stopped pacing and walked rapidly until he was standing directly in front of Eli. Up close, Eli was only as tall as the giant's knees, yet, Eli could see the green flames in Polytheist's eyes blazing with intensity. Polytheist squeezed the giant club with his hand and Eli could hear the wood contract under the giant's strength.

"And what about all of those undiscovered tribes and unreached peoples who have never heard the name of your King before? Are you so grossly arrogant that you will look right at me and tell me they are in the lake of fire? Give me a break. That doesn't sound like a loving and caring King to me. That doesn't even make sense."

"Do you understand now why you need me? Can you see how we are not enemies but allies? If what you believe is true, then your King has condemned billions of souls to a doomed eternity who never had a chance to receive salvation. I think you would agree with me that this description does not sound like the King you think you are serving. What I do is offer another way to eternal life for all of those who do not believe the way you do. I have opened up countless paths to eternal life through countless deities of all shapes and sizes. What I do helps people like you sleep at night for I give a reality that does not include human suffering. I am not a villain, your King is the villain! I give the message of life, your King gives the message of death."

"You have come here, to the fortress of the gods, bringing your narrow-minded, condemning, hate-speech of death into the very shrine that represents the many personalities of life. You have come into my house that I built in order to give hope and a future to billions of souls and you come carrying a sword that tells me all of those souls I love are doomed for eternity. You insult me greatly. You have not approached me as an ally but an enemy."

All the statues rumbled angrily behind Eli.

"See, you have angered the gods and they desire me to destroy you and do to you what you have come here to do to me. But I am not like your King. I will not destroy you without giving you a chance to receive life. I am better than that. My whole existence is to give life, not take it. So I am going to give you one chance defender. Only one chance to refute your narrow-minded beliefs that I have just proven to be false and to join me as together we make you into the new hope for your generation and offer life to the world through whatever way they feel comfortable finding that life."

A deep growl rumbled through the large pack of stone giants standing behind Eli. Polytheist stood up as tall as he could make himself and placed his giant club on his shoulder.

"What will it be defender? Will you join me or will I have to destroy you and cleanse your hate-speech from this fortress of life?"

chapter 29

the truth about gods

Surrounded by giants and bombarded by a powerful verbal assault, Eli felt as though he should be more afraid than he was. Standing there listening to reasoning that had destroyed any type of belief Eli had in the King prior to his salvation, all Eli could think about was the incredible feeling the new life brought to him when he decided to put his trust in the King. Eli was not bothered by the reasoning of Polytheist because Eli's faith was not based upon reasoning, it was based upon his experience with the King and the King's Spirit. As Polytheist spoke, Eli remembered every victory he had gained through the power of the King's Word, both in the Cemetery of the Old Man and the Desolate City. With each victory Eli relived, Eli's loyalty to the King grew. The more Eli's loyalty to the King grew, the greater connection Eli felt with the Illuminator and the King's Word. By the time Polytheist stopped speaking and presented the ultimatum to Eli, Eli was fully prepared for battle.

"Wow, I have never thought about it that way before. You're absolutely right. You have been around for thousands of years and have seen things that I could never dream of. Your long life has given you incredible insight that has allowed you to come to the conclusions that you have presented to me just now. I admit, you have completely blown my mind!"

"Wonderful! I knew you were more intelligent than"

"But not in the way you might think." said Eli in a forceful manner cutting off Polytheist's response.

Polytheist's eyes blazed as he lowered his giant club from off of his shoulder and into an easier position to attack Eli.

"What do you mean? If I were you, I would think very carefully about my next words."

"Well, I just thought that with all of your vast experience from your existence that you could come up with a more compelling argument than there has to be more than one way to be saved because of all the people who reject the King's way."

"Fool." Polytheist shouted, "The eternal existence of souls is the most compelling argument!"

Polytheist swung his giant club at Eli like a baseball bat. Eli's sword instantly burst into flames and Eli met Polytheist's giant club with his sword. Eli's sword produced a gigantic lights-wave that sliced through Polytheist's giant club sending the top half of the club cascading into the group of giant statues behind him. The top of the club bounced off of the ground and smashed the top half of the statue of the god with the elephant head leaving only the legs and torso. The statue's legs ran around frantically until it slammed into the wall knocking itself over.

Polytheist took a step back in surprise while he glared at Eli.

"You're right," continued Eli with vigor, "the eternal existence of souls is the most compelling argument, especially in the sight of the King. The King's Word states, *'The Lord...is not willing that any should perish, but that all should come to repentance.'"*

Flames leapt from off of Eli's sword hitting Polytheist, burning him and causing him to step backward.

"No one loves the souls of man more than the King! No one wants to see the souls of man saved more than the King! That is why your existence is so abominable to the King and to your own professed love for souls."

"By your own admission, your life began with the children of Cain. Cain, the man who first rejected the way of the King when there was no other way offered. You were created by the line of him who rejected the Creator. Your life began when the people who received life from the Source of Life, rejected the Life, and chose to use their lives to bring upon them eternal death."

"All that you have done since your life began, all the gods you have fashioned for man, all the ways you claim to bring eternal life to the souls of men, have done nothing but made death more readily available and acceptable. It is not the King who has brought condemnation upon men, it's you!"

"Enough of your lies!" growled Polytheist as he transformed once again.

This time Polytheist took on the form of Kali, an ancient Indian goddess that Eli had seen in his history class. Kali, known as the goddess of time and change, had ten arms, blue skin, and was described as, "the lord of death," and "the black one," in Eli's text book. This description was fitting for Polytheist who now towered in Kali's form with ten arms, ten hands, and a gigantic deadly weapon in each hand.

"How fitting," Eli continued, "You have taken the form of a god who brings the death of men. This is your nature! You are lying to yourself to think anything else. Tell me, Polytheist, how many of your creations have taken upon them the sin of their followers? How many of your creations deal with the sin that condemns man to eternal doom? Tell me, what have you done to cleanse men from their sin in the eyes of the King?"

"The answer is nothing! You have done nothing to save men from their own sins. You have done nothing to reconcile the sin-debt that all mankind is plunged into because of their sin. All you have done is create ways to distract and deceive men from accepting the sin-payment the King has provided through His own sacrifice. You see, the King did what you nor any of your creations were able or willing to do: the King took our sin upon Himself. As the Word of the King states, *'Who his own self bare our sins in his own body on the tree, that we being dead to sins, should live unto righteousness: by whose stripes ye were healed.' And further, 'And he hath made him to be sin for us, who knew no sin; that we might be made the righteousness of God in him'.*"

Flames shot from Eli's body, which was now consumed with fire, like lightning bolts destroying many of the statues of gods which stood in the carved out holes in the walls. Pieces of stone rained down upon the giant statues and on Polytheist, but all the pieces of stone avoided Eli. The stone hit the statues chipping pieces off of them and also knocked a few of Polytheist's weapons out of his hands.

"You are such a hypocrite, Polytheist. For you claim that the King destroys any who reject Him, yet you are the one who calls for the death of any one who refuses to follow your idols and creations. Even now, you have taken on the form of death to destroy me simply because I reject your idols and serve the Living God. So tell me, who offers life and who offers death?"

Furious, Polytheist picked up the weapons that had been knocked out of his hands and yelled, "Kill him!"

Immediately the eyes of all the statues blazed with green fire as they drew their weapons or raised their fists to attack Eli.

"Your creations cannot harm me, the King's Word has declared, '*Their idols are silver and gold, the work of men's hands. They have mouths, but they speak not*'".

Fire shot from Eli's sword striking every statue's mouth leaving a hole where their mouths used to be.

"'*Eyes have they, but they see not*'".

Fire shot from Eli's sword striking every statue's eyes leaving a hole where their eyes used to be.

"'*They have ears, but they hear not; noses have they, but they smell not:*'"

Fire shot from Eli's sword striking every statues ears and nose leaving a hole where their ears and nose used to be.

"'*They have hands, but they handle not: feet have they, but they walk not: neither speak they through their throat.*'"

Fire shot out from Eli's sword exploding the statues' hands, feet, and throats. All headless, handless, and footless, Polytheist's army of giant statues all fell over and smashed to pieces on the floor.

His army in pieces, his temple in ruins, Polytheist's face contorted with rage.

"You insolent little fool! You will pay for your actions! I will crush you!"

Polytheist rushed Eli attacking him with all ten of his weapons. Eli just looked at Polytheist with grim confidence. First Polytheist tried to slice Eli in half with a curved sword, but the sword passed right through Eli without harming him. Then Polytheist tried to skewer Eli with a large triton, but the triton also passed through Eli. Getting more frustrated by the moment, the giant attempted to crush Eli with one of his giant hands, step on Eli with one of his feet, stab Eli with a giant knife, and clobber Eli with a large club. But all of Polytheist's attacks simply passed through Eli without harm as if Polytheist was nothing more than a ghost.

Shaking his head at Polytheist's attempt to destroy him, Eli took his sword and plunged it deep into the giant's right foot. The giant howled in pain and fell to one knee as darkness poured from the wound like blood. Eli ran underneath the giant and sliced across the giant's left hamstring on the back of his leg. Another howl of pain followed as more darkness poured from Polytheist's other leg. Polytheist fell to his knees and ten hands and tried once more to kill Eli with one of his weapons. But the spear passed right through Eli's body as Eli walked around to face the giant.

"I don't understand. Why can't I kill you? Why can't I even touch you?"

"You have no power against me in the same way a lie has no power against the truth. A lie can only harm those who will put their trust in the lie. A lie can never destroy the truth. Your entire existence is a lie fabricated by men who chose to not believe the truth. The power you have over people and nations is a power that you can only have because they allow you to have it. If a person were to put their faith in the truth, that person would then strip you of all your power, as I have done. I understand what Michael told me to remember when I faced you, that your greatest power was the ability to shape-shift in order to become the god that men desire to have, but that this was also your greatest weakness."

"Michael knows nothing! How can my greatest power be my greatest weakness?"

"It can't, unless you run into a child of the King who knows the truth about you."

"Oh really, and what truth is that?" growled Polytheist as he painfully rose to his feet.

"That you are nothing more than an idea, a dream created by the wicked minds of those who hate the truth. To those of us who know the truth, you have no power against because we know the truth about you from the Word of Truth: *'We know that an idol is nothing in the world, and that there is none other God but one. For though there be that are called gods, whether in heaven or in earth (as there be gods many, and lords many). But to us there is but one God, the Father, of whom are all things, and we in him; and one Lord Jesus Christ, by whom are all things, and we by him'.*"

When Eli finished quoting the King's Word, fire shot from his sword and struck Polytheist's feet. As soon as the fire hit Polytheist's feet, his feet slowly turned to stone. Once his feet were stone, the stream of fire from Eli's sword slowly started climbing up Polytheist's body turning his body into stone. Polytheist struggled to free his legs from their stone prison to no avail. Crying out in pain as more of his body was being turned to stone, Polytheist morphed into different shapes trying to break free. First Polytheist morphed into the Minotaur and tried to free his lower body with the incredible upper-body strength. When that failed, Polytheist morphed into a dragon and attempted to break free by flying into the air. Finding no success, and seeing more of his body turned into stone, Polytheist changed one last time into a very gentle and kind looking old man. As Polytheist's chest and arms succumbed to the stone transformation, he spoke one last time.

"But Eli, what about all those souls? Who will reach them with life if I don't?

"The King has proven that He, '*will have all men to be saved, and to come unto the knowledge of the truth*'"

"But what about those who never hear? How will they be saved?"

Eli felt a deep sensation in the pit of his heart as if a tidal wave of power had just been released. The King's Word filled his heart and soul with such tremendous force that blue flames shot from his mouth as he quoted the King's answer to Polytheist's question.

"For the grace of God that bringeth salvation hath appeared to all men. Because that which may be known of God is manifest in them; for God hath shewed it unto them. For the invisible things of him from the creation of the world are clearly seen being understood by the things that are made, even his eternal power and Godhead: so that they are without excuse.'"

"The King is communicating to them the great truth that brings salvation. You have battled for the hearts of the awakened souls for far too long. The sooner I tear down your fortress of gods, the sooner the gospel light can shine throughout the Desolate City without interference. Now, be gone!"

"No, no noooo!" cried Polytheist as his neck and head turned to stone, "Master help me!"

Polytheist's voice echoed off of the walls of the fortress of the gods, by the time the echo had subsided, Polytheist was nothing more than a stone statue. Polytheist had been defeated, but the gigantic Vatican fortress of the gods still prevented a majority of the gospel light from reaching the tower. Eli knew he had to destroy the gigantic fortress, but he did not know how he was going to do that. Eli knelt on his knees.

"Your Majesty," prayed Eli, "Father, thank you for the victory. Thank you for revealing your truth to me and allowing your truth to vanquish the lie that is Polytheist. Now I need your help once more. I need to know how to bring down this fortress of darkness once and for all."

Light engulfed Eli's mind. When the light dimmed, Eli looked up in shock. He was no longer in the fortress of the gods, but in a large room in an ancient looking house. Inside the room was a large eating area with 13 couch-like seats occupied by 12 men. The empty seat was located near the man speaking to the others. When Eli saw this man, his heart overflowed with the most incredible joy he had ever felt. Eli knew exactly who the Man was, and Eli quickly figured out where in time he had landed. Walking closer to the group, Eli could hear the words of the King.

"Let not your heart be troubled: ye believe in God, believe also in me. In my Father's house are many mansions: if it were not so, I would have told you. I go to prepare a place for you. And if I go and prepare a place for you, I will come again, and receive you unto myself; that where I am, there ye may be also. And whither I go ye know, and the way ye know."

One of the King's disciples interrupted Him, *"Lord, we know not whither thou goest; and how can we know the way?"*

The King faced the man, *"I am the way, the truth, and the life: no man cometh unto the Father, but by me."*

When the King had finished that sentence, time froze and the King made direct eye-contact with Eli.

"I am the way, the truth, and the life, Eli, no man comes to the Father but by me. Do you understand?"

All Eli could do was nod his head and attempt to stay on his feet as the sensation to fall face down on the ground nearly overwhelmed him.

"Good, now go my beloved child and free the light of the gospel."

Once again Eli was engulfed in a bright light. When the light cleared, he was back in the fortress of the gods kneeling in prayer. Remaining on his knees, Eli grasped his sword with both hands, pointed it toward the floor, and plunged it into the ground as he quoted, *"Jesus saith unto him, 'I am the way, the truth, and the life, no man comes to the Father but by me'."*

Eli's sword vibrated with intense power. The entire fortress began to quake as if a giant earth quake was rocking its foundation. A wall of blue flame erupted from the ground in a whirlwind of fire. Every piece of the fortress of the gods lifted off of the ground and disintegrated in the whirlwind of flame. With the fortress gone, the powerful beam of gospel light connected with the reflector tower and the gospel light burst out into the streets of the Desolate City.

Eli looked up to relish in the glow of the gospel light when he saw a shining silver belt floating down from the light beam of the gospel. The belt was silver with a radiant blue cross buckle and radiant blue sheath for his sword. The belt floated all the way down and hovered directly in front of Eli's face. Eli was about to reach out and take it when a voice that Eli had never expected to hear again called out from behind him.

"Well what are you waiting for, Bub, take that belt! You've earned it!"

With lightning speed, Eli turned around ignoring the belt of truth. There, standing just a few feet from him was the man who Eli thought he had lost before this great adventure had ever begun: his grandfather.

chapter 30

the passing of the torch

Eli ran to his grandfather who was standing with his arms spread, and hugged him tightly. Eli's grandfather looked much younger than when Eli last saw him, but the sparkle in his eyes had not changed at all. Eli and his grandfather embraced for several moments before Eli could speak.

"I'm so sorry for all those times I ignored you when you tried to tell me about Jesus! I'm so sorry I did not team up with you and work for the King together when I had the chance! I love you and I miss you so much!"

"Don't be sorry, Eli, I could not be more proud of you than I am right now. Angelos have not ceased telling me about all of your great accomplishments since the time you entered the spirit realm. It is hard for me to believe that the great hero I am hearing about is the same grandson I knew in the physical realm. I admit, I laughed with pride when I heard the way you went toe-to-toe with the Enemy and how you called him a coward in the cemetery! That's my boy! And then I received updates on how your training was progressing way ahead of schedule. Would you believe that I spent twice as much time in that training room as you? Well I did, and I still was as shaky as a new-born giraffe when I went on my claiming mission. But you, Eli, you were solid. You faced off against a powerful trio of enemies who focused their attack on the gospel light that I strove to defend during my time as a defender. Honestly, son, I cannot tell you how absolutely proud of you I am."

Eli looked up at his grandfather with tears rolling down his cheeks.

"Thanks grandpa. That means the world to me. But I could not be where I am today if it were not for you. I still can't believe that the man I knew as Cowpa back in the physical realm was the hero of legend who served the King with such fervency that the Enemy and all of his minions rejoiced to see the day of his promotion. And if it were not for you, and the message you left behind for me at your funeral, I might still be wandering the broad street heading toward destruction. I'm glad for you, grandpa, I really am, but I have to say that the physical realm is not going to be the same without you."

"No it's not, it is going to be even better. I know the great potential you have for the King. The King has not only called you to be a defender, He has also given you two companions your own age who share your love and desire for Him."

"You mean Ella and Aiden don't you?"

"Yes, you, Ella, Aiden, and Pastor Thomas make a team that will make any minion of the Enemy cower in fear. The King has great plans for our home in the physical realm and I believe He is putting you all in place to usher in a time of revival the likes of which that little town has not seen in years!"

"You know what, grandpa, I think you're right! Come on, let's get back to the City on a Hill and tell them. I know they will be happy to see you!"

"No Eli, we're not going back to the City on a Hill right now. You're going to go back to the Atrium and then you will return to the physical realm for your next mission."

"But what about Ella and Aiden? What about the Council of Light and Zephyr?"

"The Council of Light is busy welcoming new citizens thanks to your victory over Polytheist. Ella and Aiden have already been summoned back to the physical realm and will be awaiting your return to my old house. As for Zephyr, I know he will see you off before you leave. Now, take that belt of truth. As soon as you put it on, a portal will open sending you back to the atrium."

Eli turned and looked at the glowing belt he had come to claim and then he turned back to his grandfather.

"But I don't want to go yet, I want to stay and talk with you. I miss you so much, I don't know how I am going to handle going back to the physical realm knowing that I will not see you there and may never see you again until my own promotion. I love you."

"I love you too Eli, but do me a favor and don't miss me too much. Eternal life is far superior to the temporal life on earth. One day we will have all of eternity to be together worshipping the King. One day we will be together never to have to part again, but that day is not today. The King will promote you when your mission is completed. Right now, the King has a mission for you that requires you to return to the physical realm and let the world know the King is alive and reigning today."

"Eli you have accepted the King's calling on your life and have seen the great power that is found in the King's Word when you claim the truths in your life. Now it is time for you to return to the physical realm and challenge the Enemy and his philosophies that are running amuck ruining lives. It is your turn to take up the torch of the defender of the realms and stand for the King."

"I must go now, but don't be sad. One day we will sit together in the presence of the King and rejoice over the great victories you have yet to claim. I will not say goodbye, because I don't know what the King has in store for us in the future, I will simply say that I will see you again. I love you Eli and I am so proud of you. Please give my love to your mother."

A blinding light engulfed Eli's grandfather and soon disappeared taking Eli's grandfather with it. Standing alone, with tears in his eyes, Eli turned and looked at the belt of truth. There in front of him was his prize he had come to claim. Eli had survived his claiming, defeated an ancient foe, and freed the light of the gospel to reach the citizens of the Desolate City. Along the way, Eli had discovered a powerful trio of allies who would be waiting for him in the physical realm. Understanding now why the King had asked Eli to fulfill this mission before sending him back to the physical realm, Eli felt grateful for the King's plan and knew that he was now ready to go back and face the Enemy in his former realm. Eli knew that whatever traps and minions the Enemy had waiting for him back in the physical realm, he could overcome them for he had learned the truth that the belt of truth represented: there is only one God and that God is the King Eli serves. More confident now than he had ever been in his life, he reached out and touched the belt of truth. Instantly, the belt disappeared and reappeared around his waist. Before Eli could appreciate its beauty, light engulfed his body and he was sucked into a portal.

chapter 31

back to the physical realm

Soaring through the portal, Eli was in a state of bliss. Not only had he just completed a seemingly impossible mission for the King and acquired the belt of truth, Eli had just spent time with his grandfather, something he never thought he would be able to do again. Not even the incredible sensation of flying through the portal could distract Eli from reminiscing the conversation, the feel of his grandfather's arms, and the incredible love Eli felt for him.

Soon Eli felt his feet hit a solid surface and watched as the bright light vanished from his body leaving him standing in the white stone gazebo back in the atrium. Eli's success in the Desolate City had already brightened up more of the atrium bring brilliant color and life back to the once majestic room. With two gazebos conquered, the entire left half of the room was now restored to its former grandeur. Eli could smell the incredible scents of the plants that bloomed in full color. The streams of water were now flowing freely throughout the room with crystal fish of brilliant colors swimming under the two bridges of the gazebos Eli had conquered. Waiting for him, just across the bridge was Michael and Zephyr. Eli walked out of the gazebo and over the bridge.

"You know," said Zephyr to Michael, "I think my favorite part was when Polytheist tried to knock Eli with the giant club only for Eli to slice it in half and continue speaking as if Polytheist's attempt to kill him was as threatening to Eli as a fly."

Michael laughed, "Yes that indeed was funny, especially when the severed piece of club smashed one of Polytheist's abominations. Personally, I enjoyed watching the shock on Polytheist's face when Eli confronted him with the difference between the truth of the King's Word and Polytheist's lies."

"Oh yes," laughed Zephyr, "That giant looked real pathetic attempting to stab and slice Eli with weapons that could not even touch him."

"Yes," continued Michael who was laughing so hard that he had to pause before continuing, "and the look on his face as he kept trying to kill Eli as if the only reason his weapons were not harming Eli was the fact that he was not trying hard enough!"

Michael laughed so hard he had to bend down and put his hands on his knees to hold him up as Zephyr nearly fell out of the air laughing.

"I'm glad you all were amused by those things, but my favorite part was when Polytheist actually tried to convince me that by offering up his idols to mankind that he was the one trying to lead men to eternal life and the King was the one bringing eternal doom."

"You know guys," said Eli as the laughter died down, "I'm really going to miss you when I go back to the physical realm. I've really loved being here with you and to be honest, part of me doesn't ever want to go back."

"For what it is worth, Eli," replied Zephyr, "I feel the same way. To see you come to Christ and then to have you transported into the spirit realm has been a greater joy than I can say. And then to see you take up the role of defender and serve the King with such success has been one of the greatest delights I have ever experienced. Though I will miss the type of relationship we have had here, I will not be far from you at any time. It is like your grandfather said, one day we will have all eternity to worship the King and celebrate the victories you have yet to win. Besides, as a defender, you will be summoned back to the spirit realm more than you or I know. I will see you again, Elijah Storm, and we will serve the King together!"

Zephyr flew over and hugged Eli tightly.

"I too have greatly enjoyed getting to know you and watch you progress." Michael added, "I look forward to seeing you honor the King in the physical realm to the same degree you have honored the King here in the spirit realm. I wish you nothing but the best!"

"Thanks guys. So what is this mission in the physical realm?"

"I'm glad you asked." replied Michael, "First, your mission will be to team up with the Thomas' and continue the work of a defender that your grandfather did before you. With the combined power of the Thomas family, you ought to gain many victories for the King. The Enemy anticipates this and it enrages him. The Enemy thinks he owns the physical realm. He employs his minions in brazen confidence that no human will oppose him. Now that you have accepted your calling and have accomplished your claiming, the King is sending you back into the physical realm to challenge the Enemy's claim on the physical realm. The King desires you to go back and show the physical realm how powerful the truths of His Word are and how life-changing they can be. You have freed the gospel light here in the spirit realm, now you must go and awaken the lost with the gospel light."

"In anticipation of your return and your teaming up with the Thomas family, the Enemy is attempting to fortify his claim in your town by constructing a vile dungeon of death and sending one of his most vile servants to take up residence in your town."

"Who?"

"I do not have permission to reveal that to you at this time, but this servant volunteered to fight you after your victory over Polytheist. In human thinking, Polytheist and this other servant are like siblings. Think of Polytheist as the older more dignified brother and this new threat as a much younger, and much viler younger brother."

"The Enemy knows that you have shown yourself powerful in the spirit realm, and now he seeks to test you in the physical realm. But the Enemy has learned that to defeat you will take more than he once anticipated. We do not know when the Enemy's servant will attack, but we do know that they are preparing for war as we speak."

"A battle is coming, Eli, a battle that will be fought in your realm. Your task is to go home and prepare for the battle through teaming up with the Thomas' and recruiting as many souls as you can through reaching them with the gospel light. I do not know the time nor the place in which the Enemy will choose to attack, but be assured that when it comes, you had better be ready."

Eli drew his sword from its brilliant blue sheath on his new belt of truth and looked at his reflection in the blade.

"I wear the helmet of salvation, the belt of truth, and I wield the Sword of the Sprit; I will be ready!"

"I believe that to be true, master defender, and I believe that you will collect yet another piece of armor through your success."

Michael pointed to the large gazebo in the center and a pair of shoes appeared above the gazebo in the bright yellow light.

"Your mission, Defender Storm, is to return to the physical realm and challenge the Enemy's claim on the domain of creation. You accepted your calling and you have claimed the powerful truths of the King's Word as your own. You wear the helmet of salvation, the belt of truth, and you wield the greatest weapon in all creation; the Sword of the Spirit. You have the support and love of all the King's army and the King Himself. Go now and fulfill your destiny as the Defender of the Realms! And may the King's face always shine upon you!"

Eli stood straight up in attention and saluted Michael, "Yes sir."

With confidence, Eli walked over into the large gazebo and turned to face Zephyr and Michael.

"Hey Zeph, hold down the fort while I'm gone!"

Zephyr smiled and replied back to Eli, but Eli never heard his words. The light from the atrium had already swirled through the gazebo walling him in. When the light reached the top of the columns, it shot in beams to the center of the gazebo and formed a giant ball of light. Eli could see the picture of the shoes glow above and saw that his ring now included the same symbol of shoes. The ball of light in the center of the gazebo grew large and then shot a beam down that hit Eli and engulfed his entire body. In an instant, Eli was soaring through a portal.

The feeling of being tossed to and fro at incredible speeds ended abruptly as it felt like Eli hit a wall. Opening his eyes and inhaling deeply, Eli awoke to find himself sitting against the trunk of the large oak tree in the physical realm. Standing up excitedly, Eli checked his body to find that he was wearing the same clothes he wore to his grandfather's funeral. Everything was the same as it was before he ventured into the spirit realm: the sun was in the same place, the wrapping paper from his grandfather's gift was still on the ground, and Eli's body had not been chewed on by any wild animal.

Thanks for that, thought Eli as he checked his body for bite marks.

"I told you that we return you to the physical realm the instant you left."

Eli looked up in shock to see Zephyr sitting on one of the branches in the oak tree.

"Zeph! What are you doing here?"

"Well Eli, I know you well enough to know that you were about to ask if it had all been a dream. Not wanting you to wonder, the King gave me permission to appear and remind you of your new commission as a defender. So go and get to work, I have a feeling there are a few guests at your grandfather's reception who will be eagerly waiting for you to make an appearance."

Zephyr vanished and Eli stood there for a moment thinking of who he was talking about.

"Ella, Aiden, Pastor Thomas, of course!"

Eli collected his gifts from his grandfather and the wrapping paper from off the ground.

As he was doing so, Eli noticed his grandfather's ring on his finger. Sure enough, the black center that was blank when he received the ring now contained emblems of a helmet, sword, and belt.

As if I would think it was a dream. Ha!

With all of his belongings collected, Eli ran to his grandfather's house as quickly as he could. Topping the hill before the house, Eli could see two kids standing by the back door waiting for his arrival. Eli ran all the way to where Ella and Aiden Thomas were standing cheering on Eli as he approached.

"You have to tell us what happened!" squealed Ella as she gave Eli a big hug.

"Yeah man, it was like everyone could see what was going on except for us. Then all of a sudden, the fortress crumbles, the light is freed, and we get sent back to the party without getting any details! It was totally not cool."

"I can't wait to tell you all what happened, but first, we have work to do. The Enemy is bringing the battle to our home turf, and we need to be ready!"

"Is he really?" said Ella as she placed her hands dramatically on her hips, "I guess some beings just can't admit when they are out-classed."

"Three words." added Aiden, "BRING-IT-ON! If he thought we were tough before, wait until he sees us protecting our own home. We will protect this house!"

"Yes we will." said Eli as he placed one of his hands on each of his friends' shoulders, "and we will do it together! Come on, there is no time to waste, we have work to do!"

Also By Nathan D. Thomas

Be Confident in Your Creation

If you've ever asked why God allowed your friend or family member to experience loss, injury, or tragedy or why He created you with a physical challenge or placed you in a difficult family, Be Confident in Your Creation is for you. Nate Thomas describes his personal struggle with disability, tracing his spiritual journey from bitterness to trust. He explores several Bible characters, showing how each one responded to God-ordained difficulties. Through the grace of God, you can learn to be confident that God created you exactly the way He wanted you with His special purpose in mind.

Be Confident in Your Calling

In Be Confident in Your Calling, Nathan Thomas focuses on the spiritual doldrums, a place of doubt, discouragement, and apathy in the Christian's walk with God. Using the book of Hebrews, he explores the factors that can lead you into these dangerous waters and shows how you can sail back into the trade winds of a close relationship with your Savior, renewing the passion and vigor you once had for God. This is a companion book to Nathan's book Be Confident in Your Creation also available from JourneyForth.

What's Stopping You?

What's Stopping You?, written by Nathan Thomas, is a Christian living book for teens. Sin, fear, and discouragement often prevent Christian youth from moving forward for God. They stumble over the same obstacles again and again; and though they ask for forgiveness every time, they become discouraged, afraid to move forward lest they fall.

The Calling: Book One Defenders of the Realms

Fourteen-year-old Elijah Storm is a typical teenage boy who thirsts for adventure and puts up with his family's Christianity. It is not that Elijah doesn't want to be a Christian; it is that he loves adventures and sees the Christian life as boring. Through the sudden death of his grandfather, Elijah learns that the Christian life is the greatest adventure in all creation as he discovers an amazing new realm and embarks on a life-long quest to take his grandfather's place as a defender of the realms.

Nathan D. Thomas has a passion for making the Scriptures come alive in a relevant and inspiring way for all ages. Residing in South Florida as lead pastor of Temple Baptist Church in North Fort Myers, Nathan has dedicated his life to sharing his passion through teaching, preaching, and writing. A multiple published author through Journeyforth publishers in Greenville, SC, Nathan has been burdened by a lack of quality Christian literature for children and teenagers. As a result, Nathan has authored the *Defenders of the Realms* series designed to engage the imaginations of his readers while teaching doctrinally sound biblical truth.

Nathan's ministry has taken him all around the world. He has travelled the mountains of Guatemala ministering in several orphanages, he has witnessed God perform the "impossible" as he has led souls to Christ on the streets of post-Christian London, and Nathan has used his gifts of teaching and preaching in missions work throughout the islands of the Philippines. Though burdened for the peoples of the world, Nathan's passion is to see American children and American teenagers come to Christ and answer the call to serve the Lord with their lives.

Nathan D. Thomas is also a popular event speaker who enjoys speaking at graduations, closing ceremonies, youth rallies, camp settings, revivals, and conferences for both teenagers and adults. You can follow Nathan's future projects and contact him by following his blog at www.defendersoftherealms.blogspot.com

Made in the USA
San Bernardino, CA
28 January 2019